1069386I

A BEACH BUM BOOKS ROMANCE

Published by Beach Bum Books. First edition, 2025.

Beach Bum Books is an imprint of Gordon Publishing Collective and a proud supporter of Save the Manatee Club, an award-winning national nonprofit and membership-based organization established in 1981 by the late renowned singer-songwriter, author, and entrepreneur Jimmy Buffett and former U.S. Senator Bob Graham when we was governor of Florida. Save the Manatee Club's mission is to protect manatees and their aquatic habitat. A portion of proceeds from all Beach Bum Books sales are donated to the organization.

www.BeachBumBooks.com
www.GordonPublishingCo.com
info@GordonPublishingCo.com

ISBN: 979-8-9913656-2-8

Fins and Flames

*For everyone who wants to quit their job,
move to Key West, and fall in love*

PROLOGUE

Casey sat at her desk in the high-rise law office, the hum of fluorescent lights overhead pressing on her already pounding headache. The air smelled faintly of stale coffee, and the stacks of paperwork surrounding her were as daunting as they were endless. Her once pristine desk, now a chaotic mess of files, sticky notes, and empty coffee cups, felt like a physical manifestation of her life—disorganized, cluttered, and running on fumes.

Her computer screen pinged, the alert pulling her eyes away from the legal brief she was struggling to finish. She clicked on the email, her stomach sinking as she saw the subject line: **URGENT: Need This by Monday.** The sender was her boss, a man she rarely saw but who had a knack for swooping in to derail her plans at the worst possible times. Her weekend had been mapped out meticulously: a short hike at the state park, a day to catch up on reading, and maybe even finally trying that painting class her friend had recommended. But now, those plans crumbled under the weight of her boss's demands. Casey clenched her jaw, her fingers hovering over the keyboard as she considered typing out a sarcastic response. Instead, she sighed and pushed the email into a mental pile with the rest of her grievances. Another weekend gone. Another piece of herself lost.

That morning, she'd sat through yet another meeting about the Anders case, the kind of long-term litigation that never seemed to end. The plaintiff—a grieving mother—had been battling the system for years, and Casey had become the reluctant middlewoman between corporate denial and human heartbreak. With every deposition, every legal loophole, she felt her sense of purpose being chipped away. The work was heavy. The injustice was heavier. And yet, no one else in the office seemed to notice. Or care.

Her gaze drifted to the corner of her desk, where a small corkboard hung. Its contents were sparse and utilitarian—case deadlines, a few receipts, and one bright, out-of-place artifact: a postcard. She'd kept it from a client's vacation portfolio as a kind of cruel joke—a photo of Key West, with its dazzling turquoise water and vibrant streets lined with palms and colorfully painted buildings. The words *Welcome to Paradise* were scrawled across the top in cheerful, looping font.

Casey stared at the postcard, feeling its pull like a rip current. When she'd pinned it there six months ago, it had been a lifeline—a reminder that somewhere out there, life was happening. People were sipping piña coladas under the sun and diving into the ocean without a care. But now it felt like a mockery, a window into a world she'd never get to touch. She ran her thumb along the edge of the postcard, her throat tightening with a familiar ache she refused to name.

She used to dream of places like that. As a child, Casey would trace maps with her fingers, imagining herself as a fearless explorer charting unknown territories. She'd planned to see the world—to live boldly and freely, untethered to anyone's expectations. But somewhere along the way, the dreams had faded, replaced by ambition and responsibility. She'd chased success, thinking it would bring fulfillment, only to find herself here, trapped in a box of her own making.

Her therapist had called it "functional depression," and Casey had brushed it off, insisting that everyone felt overwhelmed sometimes. But the truth of it clung to her like humidity: she wasn't just tired—she was hollowing out.

Her computer pinged again, dragging her back to the present. Casey closed her eyes, swallowing the lump in her throat. For a moment, she thought about tearing the postcard down and throwing it away. But she didn't. Instead, she left it there, a tiny beacon of light in the shadow of her reality. A reminder that paradise might still be waiting, if only she could find a way to reach it.

Casey stared blankly at her monitor, as her mind numbly processed the words on the page without absorbing them. She typed mechanically, her fingers moving faster than her thoughts, as though her body had become a machine that didn't require her soul to function. The office was eerily quiet, save for the distant hum of the HVAC system and the occasional footsteps of her colleagues. It was a stillness that only made the weight pressing on her chest feel heavier.

"Still here?" a voice sliced through the silence. Casey turned her head to see Melanie, her perpetually chipper coworker, leaning against the wall of her cubicle.

"Guess some of us don't have lives outside this place," Melanie added with a smile that didn't reach her eyes, her tone as sharp as a paper cut.

Casey froze, the words hitting her like a slap. Melanie was already walking away, her designer heels clicking against the polished floor as she neared the exit, but the sting of her comment lingered.

"No life outside this place," Casey whispered to herself, her stomach twisting. The truth of it was like a mirror held too close. When was the last time she'd done something just for herself? When was the last time she'd felt alive, not just functioning?

She remembered the trip she almost booked last month. After consuming an entire bottle of wine in her living room on a Friday night working late on whatever was being demanded of her that week, her email pinged. She booked so many flights for the partners at her firm that she constantly got emails from airlines. It was kind of like a taunt—all the places she wouldn't get to go. This email was yet another last-minute fare drop, but to New York or L.A.

or Dubai or London. It was marketed as a tropical getaway for the hardworking businessperson—a "treat yourself for all the hard travel you do," clearly targeting her boss. She'd normally hit delete, but the destination made her pause: St. John's, Antigua. Impulsively, she clicked "Buy Now," and added a ticket to her cart. She filled out her passport information and paused. Switching apps, she searched for an AirBnB listing in Antigua near St. John's. She put in the dates corresponding with the airline offer for a round-trip ticket, and inspected multiple listings before hitting "Reserve." She paused again. Switched back to her browser with the checkout screen for the flight. Her finger hovered over the "Pay Now" button. Her chest tightened, she groaned, and threw her phone on the couch. She went to sleep without bothering to remove her makeup and got mascara on her pillow.

All of those feelings bubbled up in Casey right then and there. Her hands trembled as she pushed herself away from her desk and stood. She grabbed her coat, her movements brisk and final, and ignored the concerned looks from a few colleagues as she walked past. Her heart pounded in her chest as she hit the elevator button, the adrenaline coursing through her making her hands clammy.

By the time she reached the street, Casey's resolve had hardened. She had built this whole life and career, but the thought of going back to her desk nauseated her. Something had to change, and it had to change now.

Her feet carried her without direction, her mind racing. She turned a corner and saw it: the grand facade of the downtown train station. Its arched windows gleamed in the afternoon sun, and the faint sound of announcements echoed through the open doors. She stopped in her tracks, feeling as though it had appeared out of nowhere just for her.

Before she could overthink it, Casey walked inside. At the ticket counter, she blurted out the first destination that came to mind. "Miami. One-way."

The clerk gave her a bemused look but tapped at his keyboard. Casey didn't care about the raised eyebrow. She handed over her credit card and took the ticket without a second thought.

Back at her apartment, Casey moved quickly, fueled by a sense of urgency she hadn't felt in years. She stuffed a duffel bag with essentials: a few pairs of shorts, some t-shirts, and a hoodie. She peeled off her suit, feeling like she was shedding her corporate skin, and pulled on a pair of leggings and a tee shirt with her worn-but-comfy sneaks. She tucked her sketchbook into her backpack, along with a pair of flip flops and a bathing suit.

"Ready for an adventure, Marley?" she asked her golden mutt, who wagged his tail as though he understood. Casey clipped on his leash and slung her bags over her shoulder.

As she locked the door behind her, she didn't look back. The life she was leaving wasn't worth a second glance. She was finally heading toward something new— something hers.

CHAPTER 1
SHE CAME DOWN FROM CINCINNATI

The train hummed steadily beneath Casey as she leaned her head against the window, watching the scenery blur past. Gray skies and skeletal trees gave way to open fields and patches of sunlight breaking through the clouds. With each mile, the Midwest faded into the distance, and Casey felt the cold, suffocating weight of her old life begin to lift, even if only slightly.

She glanced at her phone out of habit—no notifications, no unread messages. It buzzed once in her palm, a calendar reminder from her old life: "Anders deposition draft due." She powered it off without a second thought.

In her sketchbook, she idly drew the balance scale—only this time, it was tipping, cracking open to reveal a palm tree growing out of the break. The gavel she added next was split down the middle. A release. A beginning.

Marley dozed beside her, his head resting on her lap as the rhythm of the train lulled him into a peaceful sleep.

Casey ran her fingers absently through his fur, grateful for his silent companionship. Her duffel bag sat tucked under her seat, carrying what little she'd brought along.

On the second day, a man in his seventies took the seat across from her. He had a sun-weathered face and a straw hat that seemed out of place against the gray backdrop outside. He introduced himself as Carlos and offered her a piece of taffy from a bag he pulled from his pocket.

"Headed south?" he asked with a smile.

"Yeah," Casey replied, managing a small smile. "Key West."

"Ah, the end of the road," Carlos said, nodding knowingly. "Good choice. I used to go there every winter with my wife. It's a place where you can breathe again, where you can," he paused, considering, "find the sun." His eyes sparkled as he spoke, his voice tinged with nostalgia.

They spent the afternoon chatting, Carlos telling her stories of sunset sails, conch fritters, and endless stretches of turquoise water. "You'll love it," he said. "But don't just visit—live it. Let it teach you how to slow down, how to feel alive again."

His words stuck with her long after he fell asleep. 'Find the sun.' She scribbled the phrase in the margins of her journal, circling it twice. That night, as the train pulled into a station for a brief stop, Casey stepped onto the platform to stretch her legs and give Marley some much-needed outdoor time. The air was warmer now, carrying hints of salt and earth. She took a deep breath, feeling something stir in her—a glimmer of hope she hadn't felt in years.

Back in her seat, she pulled out her sketchbook and began to draw. She started with the train's windows, framing the shifting landscape: the steel-gray skies giving way to the soft pastels. She added the faces she'd seen along the way—Carlos's kind, weathered features among them. The lines flowed easily, and for the first time in a long while, Casey felt like herself. She flipped back to the pages where she'd once drawn courthouses and skyline silhouettes and began overlaying them with seashells, hammocks, and abstract waves. She wasn't just escaping—she was undoing. Layer by layer.

On the final day, Casey opened her journal and wrote: *This isn't just an escape. It's a beginning. A chance to find myself again—not the person I've become but the one I used to dream of being. I must remember that.*

She underlined the word "beginning" twice, then leaned back in her seat, staring out at the palm trees that had begun to line the tracks. The train slowed, announcing its arrival at her destination. Casey smiled faintly, resting her hand on Marley's head.

The sun was waiting. All she had to do was step off the train and into it.

The train slowed as it approached the station, the metallic screech of the brakes interrupting Casey's reverie. She straightened in her seat, her heart pounding with a mix of nerves and anticipation. Marley stirred at her feet, lifting his head as though sensing the significance of the moment.

The doors opened, and Casey stepped onto the platform, clutching Marley's leash in one hand and her duffel bag slung over her shoulder. She blinked against the dazzling sunlight, brighter and warmer than she had imagined during those gray days back in Cincinnati.

The air was alive here. The faint scent of salt and seaweed hung in the breeze, mingling with the earthy heat of the pavement. Palms swayed lazily in the distance, their fronds whispering promises of freedom. Around her, the station buzzed with life—travelers milling about, laughter echoing from a group of tourists, and vendors selling fresh fruit and cold drinks.

Casey inhaled deeply, filling her lungs with the air of a new beginning. Her lips curved into a smile, tentative but real. She felt the weight of her old life begin to lift.

Marley barked softly, as if urging her forward. She reached down and rubbed his head. "We're almost there," she murmured, though she wasn't entirely sure where *there* would take her.

Departing the train's loading area, Casey noticed a colorful bus idling nearby, its destination sign flashing: *Key West.* Casey tightened her grip on Marley's leash and stepped toward it, each footfall feeling lighter than the last.

As she reached the door of the bus, she paused and looked back at the station, at the train that had brought her this far. She reminded herself: *This wasn't the end of the journey—it was only the beginning.*

"Welcome to paradise," she whispered, her voice carried away in the humid breeze.

The bus rumbled to a stop, jolting Casey awake. She blinked as sunlight poured through the window, flooding the bus with golden warmth. The driver called out, "Key West, last stop!" Casey rubbed her eyes, her body aching from the long journey, but her heart fluttered with excitement. She nudged Marley, who wagged his tail enthusiastically, clearly sensing the change in the air.

As Casey stepped off the bus, the sheer vibrancy of Key West hit her like a wave. The streets were alive with energy: pastel-colored houses with weathered shutters, swaying palm trees, and bicycles weaving through the crowded sidewalks. The salty air mingled with the scent of Cuban coffee and fresh conch fritters from a nearby food stand. The island seemed to hum with life, each detail more vivid than anything she had imagined during her grueling days in Cincinnati.

Marley tugged toward a small patch of grass—and bolted after a rooster. The bird darted across the sidewalk, squawking indignantly. A man selling fruit nearby chuckled.

"You're not from around here, huh?" he called to her. "Careful with the chickens. It's illegal to mess with 'em—protected by island law."

Casey pulled Marley back, apologizing through laughter. "Noted."

The man winked. "Welcome to Key West."

She hadn't even realized she was smiling.

Casey wandered down Duval Street, clutching Marley's leash in one hand and her duffel bag in the other. The streets were lined with quirky shops and open-air bars, their music spilling out onto the sidewalks. She passed a small, colorful sign that read *Conch Cove Inn — Vacancy*. The building was a charming, sun-worn bungalow with a wraparound porch and flower boxes overflowing with tropical blooms.

She stepped inside, greeted by the blast of cool air and the smell of coconut-scented candles. A friendly-looking woman, who appeared to be in her sixties, stood behind the counter. Her name tag read "Betty."

"Need a room, sweetheart?" Betty asked, her voice warm and welcoming.

"Just something small for me and my dog," Casey replied, glancing at Marley.

"Well, you're in luck. We've got a cozy little cottage in the back. Pets welcome," Betty said with a wink. "It's nothing fancy, but it's got a bed, a kitchenette, its own little porch, and a hammock out front."

Casey exhaled in relief. "That sounds perfect."

"It ain't cheap, though," Betty grinned. "But if I like ya, we can work out a deal."

"Money isn't a problem; the job I'm leaving behind paid quite well, but it cost me in other ways," Casey sighed.

Betty handed her the key with a smile. "You look like you've been through the wringer, honey. Take a load off. Key West has a way of making things right." Casey took the key and Casey glanced at the walls on her way back out—faded photos of boats, dogs, musicians. She noticed a candid shot of a young woman sitting barefoot on a dock, paintbrush in hand, canvas propped on knees. Something about it sparked. Maybe she'd ask Betty about it later.

After unpacking her few belongings, Casey decided to explore. She slipped into a pair of sandals, leashed Marley, and set off. As they wandered away from bustling Duval Street, she found herself strolling through quiet side streets lined with quaint little houses. The cottages were painted in cheerful hues of turquoise, coral, and lemon yellow—their shutters wide open to catch the breeze. Porches were adorned with rocking chairs, strings of fairy lights, and potted palms, each home exuding its own charm. The textures around her were intoxicating: the uneven crack of sidewalk tiles, the rustle of hibiscus leaves, the way the light filtered through the palms like a moving painting. She'd never noticed this much color before. Maybe she hadn't been looking. She spotted a lazy tabby cat lounging on a sun-warmed railing, blinking at her and Marley as if to say, *This is the life.*

She turned a corner and came across a tiny diner, its sign hand-painted with the words *Maggie's Kitchen*. The smell of frying seafood wafted from its open windows, mingling with the faint scent of coconut. A chalkboard on the sidewalk advertised the day's specials: *Key Lime Pie Milkshakes* and *Shrimp Po'boys*. Casey made a mental note to come back another day, already feeling the allure of this tucked-away spot.

Further along, she passed a bookshop called *The Salty Spine*. The display in the window showcased old maritime maps, novels with frayed covers, and a handwritten sign that read, *Trade your stories for ours*. Casey's fingers itched to go inside, but she resisted for now. This was her night to take it all in.

Marley led the way, sniffing the ground with determined curiosity. Casey let him guide her, and soon they reached a park with children playing tag and couples lounging on blankets. She paused to sketch a tree in the park—just quickly, something about the curl of the trunk and the way the branches held the sun. Marley sniffed beside her, content, and Casey felt her heart settle just a little more. Palm fronds rustled gently overhead, and a faint breeze carried the sound of a distant steel drum.

She felt herself exhale a deep breath she hadn't realized she'd been holding.

The rhythm of the island was infectious. Laughter bubbled up from crowded patios where diners sipped mojitos, and a reggae band played at a corner café. The music's steady beat had Casey's body swaying slightly as she walked past, her feet moving in time with the carefree pulse of the evening.

Eventually, her wanderings led her toward the water. A flow of tourists and locals alike seemed to converge on a single point, and Casey followed the current. She soon found herself at Mallory Square, the legendary gathering place for the island's famous sunset celebration. The scene was alive with performers and artists, each adding their own flair to the vibrant atmosphere. A man on stilts juggled flaming torches while a woman danced with a live parrot perched on her arm. Vendors sold handmade jewelry and shell-covered trinkets, their tables lit by the warm glow of hanging lanterns. An elderly man played a soulful tune on his saxophone, his notes mingling with the sound of the waves lapping against the dock.

Casey paused at the edge of the square, Marley sitting obediently at her side. The horizon was ablaze with color—fiery reds and oranges fading into soft purples and blues. People cheered as the sun dipped lower, as though its departure was a triumphant finale rather than the end of just another day.

She closed her eyes for a moment, letting the applause and laughter wash over her. The salty breeze tugged at her hair, and for the first time in what seemed like forever, she felt truly free.

"Beautiful, isn't it?" a voice said beside her. Casey turned to see a man with a leathery face and kind eyes, holding a carved wooden trinket. He handed it to her with a smile. "Welcome to paradise."

Casey glanced down at the carving—a simple sunburst with waves curling beneath it. She ran her fingers over the smooth wood, her lips curving into a smile.

"Thank you," she said softly, clutching it to her chest. She turned back to the horizon, watching as the last sliver of sun sank below the water, leaving behind a kaleidoscope of colors that reflected her growing sense of hope.

The weight of her old life seemed to dissolve into the ocean breeze. Tomorrow would come with its uncertainties, but for now, she let herself revel in the magic of the moment. *This place*, she thought, *was exactly where she was meant to be.*

Nighttime did not mean bedtime in Key West like it did in Cincinnati. After all, it's not like she had a job to be accountable to. That reminded her: she really ought to send a resignation letter. She wondered what the folks at the office may think after she didn't show up today, but shook off the thought. It didn't really matter anymore, did it?

Her wanderings eventually brought her to a faded wooden sign reading Captain Tony's Saloon. The yellow building sported a giant fish with a gaping mouth—it reminded her of the weird singing mounted fish from her grandfather's basement. There was a line of people waiting for their turn to toss a coin backwards into the fish's mouth. Casey watched as one, two, three different women took their chance, all missing. She peered inside the door to the saloon, it was dark—almost cave-like—and it looked like the kind of place where stories were told and secrets were spilled. Something about it called to her.

Inside, the saloon was dimly lit and packed with a mix of locals and tourists—somehow it seemed obvious who was who. The air was thick with the smell of spilled beer and decades-old wood. Dollar bills covered the walls and ceiling, scrawled with names and messages from those who had passed through. Casey found a seat at the bar—a stool that read "Bob Dylan" in yellow, hand-painted letters. Marley settled at her feet. "Rum punch," she said to the bartender, a gruff-looking man with a long ponytail. As the drink arrived, the lights dimmed, and a voice crackled over the microphone. "Ladies and gentlemen, give it up for Jake!"

A man with sun-bleached hair and a guitar slung over his shoulder stepped onto the tiny stage. His white linen shirt was unbuttoned halfway, and his easy smile lit up the room. He strummed a chord, and the bar fell silent, captivated. The tone of Jake's voice was rich and warm, and had just enough Southern twang, like honey dripping over gravel. He sang a song about the ocean and freedom, and Casey found herself leaning in, mesmerized. Her mind wasn't racing with worries or plans. It didn't matter if her inbox was dinging nonstop because, well, it wasn't her inbox anymore. The emotional weight of her cases, the looming expectations of her boss. None of that was relevant anymore. She was just... there, soaking in the moment—and the view was pretty damn good.

After the set, Jake hopped off the stage, weaving through the crowd with the ease of someone who belonged here. He stopped at the bar and glanced at Casey with a curious smile.

"New face," he said, leaning on the counter. "First time on the island?"

"Is it that obvious?" Casey asked, smiling back.

"Just a little," he said with a chuckle. "You've still got that 'fresh off the bus' look. I'm Jake."

"Casey," she said, extending her hand. His grip was warm and firm, and his calloused fingers were evidence of his life playing guitar. He actually seemed to radiate warmth all around, the way skin does when it has been in the sun for hours on end.

"So, Casey," Jake began, tilting his head slightly, "what brings you to Key West? Running to something or running from something?"

"What…is that how everyone ends up here?" she said with a smile.

"Well, mostly everyone," he laughed.

"In that case, a little of both," she replied, her honesty surprising herself. "I needed a change."

Jake nodded. "This island's good for that. It's where people come to lose and find themselves—sometimes both."

Before she could respond, the bartender leaned over, wiping the counter with a damp rag. "You two done flirting?" he asked Jake with a smirk, then turned to Casey. "I overheard you're new. If you're looking for a job, you won't find one here—we don't do servers. But I know Des at the Moon-Dog Cafe is hiring. You got the kind of energy they'd like."

Casey blinked, caught off guard. "I... I guess I could use a job…I wasn't sure how long I was going to stay," she admitted, not sure she wanted to jump into employment after just walking out on her last job.

"You'll end up here longer than you think. Besides, Moondog is a good spot to get to know some of the locals. I can show you the way."

She hesitated. "Are you sure? I don't want to interrupt your night."

"Trust me, it's better than hanging around here. Plus," he added with a playful smirk, "I owe it to the island to make sure the new arrivals don't get lost on their first night."

As they stepped out of Captain Tony's into the balmy evening, Jake nodded toward the street. "You like sandwiches?"

"Love them," Casey said as Marley trotted happily at her side.

"Perfect. MoonDog has the best around," Jake said.

They walked a few blocks, passing dimly lit bars and quiet residential streets. As they neared the cafe, Marley paused, sniffing around the base of a palm tree. Another rooster strutted nearby, this one utterly unbothered by their presence.

"Island royalty," Jake joked. "They own the place. We just rent it."

Moondog Café glowed warmly under string lights, its laid-back charm spilling onto the sidewalk. Jake pushed the door open, and the smell of fresh bread and herbs washed over them. Casey was astonished to see such a large dessert display right near the entrance. So many tantalizing treats caught her eye—tarts and cakes and cookies galore. The entire restaurant was a vibrant burst of colors with mismatched chairs, a striking black-and-white pattern on the bar, and the eclectic nature of your hippy aunt's house.

Jake and Casey sat at a high top, and a server handed Casey a menu.

"Thanks, Marco," Jake nodded to the server; they looked like they could be surfer bros. "Everything here is great, but the Spicy Key West Club sandwich will change your life."

"I'll take your word for it," Casey said, ordering two Spicy Key West Clubs and a side of the truffle french fries. Jake nodded in approval. "Oh, and is Des around?" Jake asked before Marco could turn away.

"Just missed her. Why, what's up?"

"I found her the extra pair of hands she's always claiming to need."

Marco raised an eyebrow and looked at Casey, who awkwardly raised her hands in a spirit fingers gesture.

"Riiiiiight," he said skeptically. "She'll be in tomorrow morning if you want to swing by!" He added in a much more peppy tone.

"Will do! Thanks!" Casey replied.

When their food arrived, Marco placed the plates down with a flourish, the rich aroma of fresh bread filling the air. The club sandwiches were pressed to golden perfection, and had Swiss cheese oozing slightly from the edges. The fries were crunchy, and Jake wasted no time dipping one into the tangy sauce dripping off his sandwich.

Casey took her first bite, and her eyes widened. "Oh my god, you weren't kidding," she said, her words muffled through a mouthful of food. "This is amazing."

Jake grinned, leaning back in his chair as he finished a bite of his own sandwich. "Told you. MoonDog's is the kind of place that'll ruin other sandwiches for you forever. My go-to snack from this place is a cold brew coffee and slice of banana bread."

"Banana bread? Really? Not key lime pie?"

"Oh, if you want key lime pie, you go to Blue Heaven, but Moondog's banana bread is highly underrated, plus they do rum-spiced cold brew. What's not to love?"

Casey chuckled before returning to her sandwich. Casey studied him from across the table. He was attractive, sure, but it was the way he seemed to belong to the moment that caught her. She didn't want to want anyone—not yet—but something about him invited curiosity instead of defense. That was new.

They ate in comfortable silence for a while, the noise of the café creating a pleasant backdrop. "So," Jake said, wiping his hands on a napkin, "you think you're ready for the Green Parrot? It's a little less... quaint than this place."

Casey laughed, brushing crumbs from her lap. "I'm not exactly here for quaint. Lead the way."

The walk to the Green Parrot was short, but Casey could already hear the music and chatter spilling out into the street. Casey noticed how effortlessly Jake seemed to fit into the scene, his relaxed demeanor as much a part of the island as the swaying palm trees outside. She envied it, the way he carried himself like someone who had nowhere else to be.

The bar was lively, its neon sign glowing in the warm night air. Inside, the place was packed, the crowd a mix of locals and tourists, all moving to the beat of a bluesy guitar riff from the live band.

Jake held the door open for her. "Welcome to the Parrot," he said, motioning toward the bar. "This is where locals come alive."

Casey followed him to the edge of the bar. A bartender

appeared almost instantly. "What'll it be?" she asked, glancing between them.

"I'll take whatever beer is cheapest tonight," Jake said, then looked at Casey. "What about you?"

Casey scanned the menu on the chalkboard above the bar. "A mojito sounds perfect."

The bartender nodded. Casey took in the room, her eyes lingering on faded photographs covering the walls. Much like Captain Tony's, this place just felt like it oozed stories. The air was thick with the scent of lime and salt, the hum of conversation blending with the music.

Jake leaned back in his chair, a small smile playing on his lips. "What do you think?"

"I think I could get used to this," Casey admitted, the warmth of the place wrapping around her like an old friend.

Their drinks arrived, and as Jake raised his beer, he said, "Here's to new beginnings. And to the best sandwiches on the planet."

Casey clinked her glass against his, smiling. "I'll drink to that."

They stayed for hours, the drinks flowing easily and the music casting a spell over the night. Casey found herself laughing more than she had in years, her worries slowly dissolving into the rhythm of the island. By the time they left, her heart felt lighter.

CHAPTER 2
JUMPING IN THE DEEP END

Casey woke to the sound of seagulls calling in the distance, their cries mingling with the rustling of palm fronds outside her bungalow window. Sunlight filtered through the gauzy curtains, casting warm golden streaks across the small but cozy room. For a moment, she just lay there, staring at the ceiling, Marley curled up beside her, his rhythmic breathing a comforting presence.

Did I really do this?

The past seventy-two hours felt like a fever dream. One minute, she'd been drowning in legal briefs and empty coffee cups in Cincinnati, and the next, she was here—waking up in Key West, where the air smelled like salt and hibiscus, and people actually seemed happy. More than that, she couldn't believe how easily things were falling into place. She had a bungalow, a job lead, and last night, she'd already started making connections—Jake with his easy charm, the buzzing energy of the Green Parrot, and the feeling that, somehow, she was exactly where she needed to be.

Stretching, she rolled out of bed, scratching Marley behind the ears before getting up. "Come on, bud," she murmured. "Let's go make this official."

She tossed on a loose linen dress and sandals, tied her hair up into a messy bun, and headed out. The moment she stepped out the door, the warm ocean breeze kissed her skin, a stark contrast to the bitter Midwest cold she'd left behind.

As she walked down the quieter side streets toward MoonDog Café, she took it all in—the pastel-colored homes with sun-faded shutters, the smell of coffee wafting from open windows, a rooster strutting down the sidewalk. It was nothing like her life before.

It seemed she arrived at the cafe just as the breakfast rush was ending. Behind the counter, a tall woman with a shock of curly dark hair tied up in a bandana was expertly juggling orders while chatting with customers. Her name tag read *Des,* and her energy radiated a calm efficiency that instantly put Casey at ease.

"Hi, Des?" Casey said, stepping up to the counter with Marley at her side.

Des turned, a warm smile breaking across her face. "You must be Casey. Jake said you'd be by."

"Yeah, that's me," Casey replied. "I heard you might need some help."

Des wiped her hands on her apron and nodded toward a quieter corner of the café. "Come on, let's talk."

They sat at a small table, Marley curling up at Casey's feet. Des asked a few questions about Casey's experience—not just in serving but in handling chaos and staying on her toes. Casey answered honestly, admitting she wasn't a seasoned server but was eager to learn and not afraid of hard work.

Des seemed to consider this for a moment. "You'll do fine. Key West isn't about experience—it's about attitude. Can you start tomorrow at ten?"

Casey felt a wave of relief wash over her. "Absolutely. Thank you so much!"

Des shrugged good-naturedly. "Don't thank me yet. Brunch shifts can be brutal. But if you survive that, you'll survive anything."

With her first day of work settled, Casey decided to spend the rest of her day exploring. She wandered down Duval Street, which looked entirely different under the bright sunlight. Without the chaos of the nightlife, the vibrant buildings and quirky storefronts took center stage.

She passed art galleries showcasing vivid seascapes and wild sculptures, small boutiques overflowing with sundresses and souvenirs, and a café blasting reggae music where a few locals sipped rum cocktails before noon.

Stopping at a cart, she bought a fresh coconut, sipping the cool water as Marley investigated a nearby bush. Casey kept a close eye on him, praying he wouldn't get her kicked off the island for trying to "play" with a rooster. But Casey liked that she had time to even imagine that crazy scenario. The pace of life here was intoxicating, as if the island itself were a living thing, pulling her into its rhythm.

Casey noticed a bold sign above a shop window: *Southernmost Tattoo.* Intrigued, she stopped and peered in. The window displayed vibrant designs, everything from intricate floral patterns to bold nautical pieces.

Casey lingered in front of the tattoo shop, her eyes tracing the intricate designs displayed in the window. The bold lines of a compass merged seamlessly into swirling ocean waves, while a delicate conch shell was inked in soft, watercolor-like strokes. Each design told a story, and she found herself wondering about the people who carried them on their skin. Just as she was about to step away, a voice with a subtle French accent drifted over her shoulder.

"Admiring the art, or considering adding to it?"

She turned to find a man watching her, holding a paper bag in one hand and a to-go coffee cup in the other. He had an easy confidence about him, his dark hair slightly tousled, sleeves rolled up to reveal forearms covered in ink. His features were sharp and he wore a black nose ring, but his face was softened by amusement as he waited for her response.

Casey let out a small laugh. "Maybe both. Not sure I'm brave enough for the second part yet."

The man had the kind of knowing smile that suggested he'd heard that before. "Ah, but bravery..." He made a small *pfft* sound and shrugged. "Bravery is just hesitation waiting to be ignored."

She tilted her head. "So, you're saying I should make a rash decision and get a tattoo right now?"

He chuckled. "I am saying that the best tattoos are never about bravery. They are about knowing what you want." He took a sip of his coffee, then nodded toward the window. "And, sometimes, finding the right artist."

She extended her hand. "Casey."

He shifted the paper bag to his other hand before shaking hers. "Phillip."

At their feet, Marley wagged his tail furiously, sniffing curiously at Phillip's shoes.

"And who is this?"

"This is Marley," Casey said, scratching the dog's head. "He's my partner in crime."

Phillip crouched slightly, offering his hand for Marley to inspect before giving him a quick scratch behind the ears. "A good crime partner should be loyal. And food-motivated," he added with a smirk.

Casey laughed. "Well, he's definitely both."

Phillip stood, adjusting the coffee cup in his grip. "So, Casey-who-is-not-yet-brave, if you ever decide you are ready, come back. I promise, it will not be so scary."

She glanced at the designs in the window one more time before meeting his gaze. "I'll think about it."

Phillip gave a side smile. "Thinking is a good start." Then, with a nod, he pushed open the door to the shop, disappearing inside.

Casey walked away, her mind buzzing with energy

from the encounter. There was something about Phillip's effortless charm, the way he spoke about tattoos as if they were poetry instead of just ink. Maybe she wasn't ready now, but she was surprised the idea of permanently marking her skin didn't seem so intimidating like it always had.

She and Marley wandered toward the Southernmost Point buoy where a handful of tourists posed for photos against the backdrop of the endless ocean. "Ninety miles to Cuba from here," someone's dad said while snapping a picture. Casey lingered for a moment, staring at the horizon. The sky stretched wide, full of possibilities.

By the time she made it back to her bungalow, the sun had begun its descent, painting the sky in streaks of tangerine and lavender. She sank into the hammock outside, Marley settling beside her, his warm weight grounding her as she flipped open her sketchbook.

Her pencil moved across the page, lines forming instinctively—waves, a compass, something small and personal. Something she might, someday, be brave enough to carry on her own skin.

It had taken a massive change, but now Casey felt like she wasn't just drifting through her life. She was moving toward something.

Tomorrow, a new job awaited.

But today, she had taken a plunge into the unknown.

And maybe the deep end wasn't so scary after all.

CHAPTER 3
MOONDOG IN THE MORNING

The morning light filtered through the bungalow's slatted blinds, painting golden stripes across the walls. Casey groaned softly, rolling onto her side and burying her face in the pillow. For a few seconds, she was suspended between sleep and wakefulness, her body still heavy with exhaustion. But then it hit her—today was her first day at MoonDog Café.

Her eyes snapped open.

She sat up, rubbing her face, her heart already thrumming with a mix of anticipation and nerves. *I can't believe this is real*, she thought. Less than a week ago, she had been drowning in paperwork in a gray Cincinnati office, counting down the hours until she could go home and do it all over again the next day. Now, she was waking up in Key West, palm trees swaying outside her window, about to start a job at an island café.

She threw off the covers, stretching as Marley wagged his tail from the foot of the bed. "Morning, bud," she murmured, scratching behind his ears. His tail thumped happily against the mattress.

She padded across the tiny bungalow to the kitchenette, scooped some food into Marley's bowl, and made herself a cup of the cheap coffee she had picked up at the grocery store the night before. It wasn't anything special, but she took it outside onto the small porch anyway, sinking into a rickety chair as she let the warmth of the sun soak into her skin.

Everything about the morning felt different from the ones she used to have—no blaring alarms, no cold commutes, no sinking feeling in her chest as she braced for another day of monotony. Instead, the air was thick with salt and hibiscus, a developing familiarity, and the breeze carried the distant sound of roosters crowing. The rhythm of the island was already starting to seep into her bones. But as much as she wanted to revel in the slow sweetness of the morning, she had work to get to.

She glanced at her phone. 8:15 a.m. Enough time for a quick shower and to walk to the café.

Casey finished her coffee, showered, and dressed. Grabbing her bag, she turned to Marley. "Be good while I'm gone, okay?"

He blinked at her, unimpressed.

"I mean it."

Marley huffed, then flopped dramatically onto his bed, stretching out with a contented sigh. She laughed, giving him a final scratch behind the ears before stepping outside.

The moment she hit the street, the island greeted her like an old friend. The sun was already warming the pavement, and the scent of fresh bread and brewing coffee from nearby cafés drifted through the air. A cyclist breezed past her, balancing a surfboard under one arm while a woman walked by with a parrot perched on her shoulder as if it were the most normal thing in the world.

It was the kind of town where nothing surprised you—and oddly enough, Casey felt like she was fitting in somehow. Squaring her shoulders, she took a deep breath and set off toward MoonDog Café, ready to take on whatever the day had in store.

When she arrived, the morning rush was already in full swing. The place was alive with movement—servers weaving between tables with trays of steaming coffee, the steady hum of conversation, and the occasional burst of laughter from the outdoor patio. The scent of espresso, fresh pastries, and something warm and buttery filled the air, instantly making her stomach growl.

She hesitated just outside the entrance, adjusting the strap of her bag. *This is it. First real day in Key West. First real step toward... whatever this new life is supposed to be.*

With a deep breath, she pushed open the door.

Inside, MoonDog was even more charming than she had noticed the first time. A huge mural served as the background to the interior wall, featuring a woman in a headdress with flowers and fruit surrounding her, and a Frenchie? Casey made a mental note to ask about that later. The café was a perfect blend of laid-back and bustling, the kind of place where locals and tourists mixed effortlessly.

Behind the counter, Des was moving with practiced ease, flipping an order ticket onto the rack while calling out to the kitchen. She looked up just as Casey stepped in.

"Good. You showed up."

Casey laughed. "That would've been a pretty short career if I didn't."

Des nodded in approval and motioned for her to step behind the counter. "Come on, let's get you in the mix. I don't have time for long-winded orientations, so you're learning by doing."

"Sounds good to me," Casey said, tying the apron Des handed her around her waist.

"This here's Tia," Des continued, gesturing to the petite, energetic barista who was currently pulling an espresso shot with one hand while shaking cinnamon over a latte with the other. "She'll help you not completely screw up your first day."

Tia nodded. "I'll do my best. You ever worked in a café before?"

Casey winced. "Not exactly."

Des raised an eyebrow. "You at least know how to carry a tray without dropping it?"

Casey straightened. "That I can do."

"Good," Des said. "You're on drinks and food running for now. Orders come in through here—" she tapped the tablet screen near the register, "—and when they're up, you take them where they need to go. Keep the tables clear, refill coffee when needed, and try not to piss off Luca in the kitchen."

"Noted," Casey said. "Who's Luca?"

Before Des could answer, a voice from the back barked, "If you're talking about me, at least make sure I can't hear you."

Casey turned toward the kitchen window and found Luca, a broad-shouldered man with an unlit cigarette tucked behind his ear, flipping pancakes with a practiced flick of his wrist. He had the look of someone who pretended to hate people but secretly enjoyed watching them scramble.

"She's new," Des called back. "Try not to make her cry."

"No promises," Luca grumbled, but there was the faintest hint of amusement in his voice.

Tia nudged Casey. "He's all bark, but don't push your luck."

"Got it."

Des clapped her hands together. "Alright, first real test—table seven's waiting on their key lime croissant and café con leche. Go." She gestured to table seven, and then quickly fell back into the methodical fluidity Casey had seen her in when Casey arrived moments ago.

Casey grabbed the plate and coffee, balancing them carefully as she stepped out from behind the counter. The café was packed, but she spotted table seven easily—a middle-aged woman wearing oversized sunglasses, chatting animatedly with her husband.

"Here you go," Casey said smoothly, setting the plate and coffee in front of them without spilling a drop.

The woman peered up at her. "Are you new?"

Casey nodded. "First day. That obvious?"

The woman smiled. "I just know everyone who works here. And I don't know you."

"I'm Casey."

"Well, Casey, welcome to MoonDog. This place is the best—you'll love it here." She sipped her drink.

"I love it already. All of the island, really."

"Oh! So you're a total newbie here," the woman exclaimed. "How exciting! You know, I hate to be nosy, but you hear it on the Coconut Telegraph sooner or later anyway—where'd ya come from? And did you come alone?"

Casey laughed a little nervously.

"Oh uh, Cincinnati. And I came with my dog, Marley."

"Ah so no man—or lady, I don't judge—in the picture," she said coyly.

Casey chuckled. "No ma'am."

"I give it a week," she winked.

"I should get back to work," Casey laughed. As she turned back toward the counter, she caught Des watching her with a raised eyebrow.

"Not bad," Des admitted. "Let's see if you can keep that up during the lunch rush. You can't tell every customer your life story then." Des winked.

Challenge accepted.

Casey adjusted her apron and headed back to the counter, feeling like she just might be able to keep up with the pace of this new life.

The rush never quite slowed down—it built, like a rolling wave that never quite crested. Casey barely had time to catch her breath as orders poured in, customers filled every available seat, and the kitchen churned out plate after plate of steaming food.

By mid-morning, she had already made a few critical mistakes:

1. She accidentally gave an iced latte to a guy who had ordered a hot one.

2. She almost walked out with the wrong plate before Luca barked at her from the kitchen.

3. She completely forgot to refill a table's coffee until Tia nudged her with a "Hey, rookie, table five's about to start a mutiny."

Still, she was getting faster. Each trip across the café felt more natural, and she was quickly learning that the key to keeping up wasn't speed—it was rhythm.

"Good, you're picking it up," Tia said as she frothed milk for a cappuccino. "Some people never figure out how to move with the flow."

"Are you saying I don't look like I'm drowning anymore?" Casey joked, grabbing two plates from the pick-up window.

"More like treading water. But hey, that's progress."

Casey's next big challenge came when Des called out, "Alright, newbie—your turn to learn the espresso machine."

Tia stepped aside, waving her in like a game show host. "Come on down, contestant number one."

Casey squared her shoulders. *How hard can it be?*

Des pointed to the machine. "Double shot, oat milk, medium foam, dash of cinnamon. Go."

The pieces in front of her might as well have been dentistry tools. A scoop-looking thing that she'd seen baristas at Starbucks stick into the machine. She noticed the little wand on the machine. *I'm almost certain that's for steaming milk.*

Des interrupted her inspection of the machine.

"Pick up the portafilter."

Casey gave her a quizzical look. Des pointed. *Ah, yes, the scoop.*

Casey grabbed a portafilter, awkwardly twisting it into place in the electric grinder; she hit the grind button. The grounds spilled out like a waterfall—too much, too fast.

"Too much," Des said, not unkindly.

Casey dumped the grounds and tried again, this time managing the right amount. Removing the now-filled portafiler, she looked at Des for next steps. Des pointed at a small, weirdly shaped muddler. Well, she thought it was a muddler. Admittedly, she had made more cocktails than espresso drinks for herself.

She picked it up and tamped the grounds down with what she hoped was the right amount of pressure. Then she locked it back into the machine and set a small class cup underneath to catch the espresso.

"Good. Now pull the shot."

She pressed the button. The machine whirred, and dark espresso dripped into the cup in a slow, steady stream.

"Now set that aside and steam your milk."

Casey poured oatmilk into the little metal cup. Pulling the wand out, she stuck the cup underneath it, waiting for something to happen.

"You may want to turn on the steamer," Des said, pointing to the switch.

Casey flipped it, and the machine chugged. Steam quickly came whirling out of the spout, but the wand wasn't touching the milk, and so the milk spurted up, hitting Casey in the eye.

Tia winced. "Oof. Rookie mistake."

Des shook her head but didn't seem mad. "Better than burning a pot of coffee. At least we don't all have to suffer. Try again."

The second attempt was better, but the milk overflowed.

"You put too much cold milk in. You have to give it room to move and foam up when you steam it."

The third was almost perfect. She poured the espresso from the tiny cup into a larger mug, then added the steamed milk. She looked at Des, ready for her taste test.

Des raised an eyebrow.

"Oh! Cinnamon!" Casey said, reaching for the little canister and shaking it over the drink.

Des took a sip and gave her a rare nod of approval. "Not bad. Keep practicing, or I'll make you drink the crappy ones."

By noon, the café was packed again, and Casey was running purely on adrenaline. Table nine wanted extra syrup. Table four needed a check. Someone's kid knocked over a glass of orange juice. Luca shouted a ticket number that no one seemed to claim. Des slid her a heaping plate of scrambled eggs and bacon without looking up. "Take this to the guy in the corner—he looks like he hasn't eaten in a decade."

Casey had no time to think—just move. And by some miracle, she was keeping up. At one point, Marco, the server from her night with Jake came in.

"Rough morning?" Casey asked as she darted past him with a tray.

The part-time surfer-turned-server yawned, sunglasses still on. "Full moon. The ocean was calling."

Casey just shook her head, laughing. "Must be nice."

"It is. You should try it sometime. I know you're new here, but that's kind of the point of being here," Marco said with a lazy grin before grabbing a notepad and heading toward a table.

After another two hours of near-constant motion, Casey was clearing a table when she felt a presence beside her. She turned to see Luca, arms crossed, studying her like she was an ingredient he wasn't sure belonged in his kitchen.

"You didn't drop anything today," he said.

Casey blinked. "Uh… thanks?"

"Don't thank me. I'm just surprised."

Casey nodded. "I'll take it."

Luca grunted and walked away.

Tia appeared beside her, whispering, "That's basically a glowing review."

Casey exhaled, realizing just how much she had been waiting for some sign that she wasn't screwing everything up. Maybe she wasn't just surviving—maybe she was actually doing okay.

By 5:30 p.m., the chaotic rhythm of the day had finally started to slow. The morning coffee crowd had long since cleared out, the lunchtime rush had dwindled, and now the café was filled with a calmer, more relaxed energy that would end by the 7 p.m. dinner rush—but Casey would be out of here before then.

A few locals lingered at their usual tables, sipping iced coffee or finishing slices of pie. Outside, the golden light of the early evening cast long shadows over the patio, and the ocean breeze carried the faint scent of salt and sunscreen through the open doors of the café.

Casey wiped down the counter, rolling her shoulders and letting out a breath. Her feet ached, her hair was sticking to the back of her neck, and she was pretty sure she had espresso grounds somewhere on her face—but she'd survived.

Not bad for day one.

She was just about to grab a drink of water when movement caught her eye. She turned to see Jake stroll in, guitar case slung over his back, looking like he had just stepped out of a surf documentary. His damp hair curled slightly at the ends, and there was a hint of salt on his tanned skin.

Casey shook her head, smiling to herself. Some people just fit their surroundings.

Jake spotted her immediately and made his way to the counter, leaning one elbow on the polished wood.

"Hey, new girl," he said, smirking. "Survived your first shift, I see."

"Barely," Casey said, placing a hand on her hip. "I think my legs might actually fall off."

Jake chuckled. "That's how you know you did it right."

Before he could order, Casey grabbed a cold brew from the fridge and placed it in front of him.

"Rum-spiced cold brew and a slice of banana bread, right?"

Jake raised an eyebrow, clearly impressed. "Damn.

Either you're a mind reader, or I made a bigger impression than I thought."

Casey shrugged, wiping her hands on a dish towel. "I have a good memory."

He took a sip of the cold brew and let out a satisfied sigh. "This is why MoonDog is the best. They know how to make a drink that doesn't taste like regret."

Casey laughed. "That's… quite the review."

Jake tapped the edge of his glass. "Stick around long enough, and you'll understand what I mean."

She wasn't sure if he meant Key West, MoonDog, or both.

They lapsed into a comfortable silence for a moment as he dug into his banana bread, and Casey leaned against the counter, letting herself finally be still.

Then Jake glanced at her and tilted his head. "So… what's the plan now?"

Casey blinked. "Plan?"

He smirked. "Yeah. First day down, first shift survived. How are you celebrating?"

She let out a dry laugh. "By going home, taking the longest shower of my life, and probably collapsing into bed."

Jake tsked, shaking his head. "No, no, no. You don't *crash* after your first shift—you *celebrate*. Otherwise, you just wake up tomorrow and start the cycle all over again."

She raised an eyebrow. "And what exactly do you suggest?"

Jake leaned in slightly, the playful glint in his eye unmistakable.

"The Green Parrot. Tonight. You in?"

Casey hesitated, but before she could answer, Des walked by. "She's off at six," she said without missing a beat. "Take her out, show her how the locals unwind."

Casey groaned. "Are you *encouraging* bad decisions?"

Des shrugged. "I'm encouraging you to actually enjoy this town instead of just working in it. That ain't what you came here to do."

Jake grinned. "See? Even Des thinks it's a good idea."

Casey sighed, wiping down the counter again just to avoid looking at him. "You're persistent, you know that?"

"Guilty," Jake said, holding up a hand. "C'mon. One drink. You've earned it."

She glanced at him, silently acknowledging the easy, laid-back confidence that he carried.

What's the harm?

With a shake of her head, she sighed. "Fine. But if you start playing bad covers of 'Margaritaville,' I'm walking out."

Jake laughed. "Deal."

He took another sip of his cold brew, then slid a ten-dollar bill across the counter. "Keep the change, new girl. I'll see you tonight."

And with that, he was gone, strolling out the door like he had all the time in the world.

Casey exhaled, shaking her head. What had she just agreed to?

The night air wrapped around Casey like a warm embrace, a range of floral scents lingered on the heat. Casey was grateful for the long shower she'd just had, scrubbing off the sweat of her first MoonDog shift and readying herself for a night at the Parrot. As she stepped onto the quiet sidewalk outside her bungalow, she took a deep breath, feeling an unfamiliar feeling: anticipation. Key West had a different pulse after dark. It wasn't just the tourists spilling out of Duval Street's neon-lit bars or the distant hum of live music floating on the breeze. It was something deeper, something unspoken. An *energy* that made the island feel alive in a way she hadn't quite figured out yet.

With each step, the sounds of the town grew louder—the laughter from open-air patios, the rhythmic strum of a busker's guitar on a street corner, the occasional burst of applause from a hidden courtyard. The whole place pulsed with the easy, unhurried heartbeat of people who had nowhere else to be.

She let herself settle into that rhythm. She walked slowly, sipping the iced coffee Tia had given her earlier, her sandals tapping lightly against the pavement.

A part of her still couldn't believe she was here.

That she had actually done it—left, started over. *I wonder if I should send a letter of resignation or if they've figured it out.* She shrugged.

The thought made her chuckle to herself as she turned onto a livelier street, following the music and neon signs toward the Green Parrot. A few people were already spilling out onto the sidewalk, laughing, drinks in hand. She spotted Jake leaning against the bar's white siding, mid-conversation with someone, but the moment his gaze landed on her, a grin spread across his face.

"You actually showed up," he called over the music.

Casey shrugged. "I said I would."

Jake raised an eyebrow. "Yeah, but I figured you'd come to your senses before you got here."

"Guess I'm still feeling reckless," she said lightly.

Jake chuckled. "Careful, Case. That's how Key West keeps you."

She tilted her head, considering the words as the bar doors swung open behind them, spilling golden light onto the street, the sound of bluesy guitar and laughter curling into the night.

She didn't overthink it.

Didn't second-guess.

Didn't try to plan ahead.

She just stepped inside.

CHAPTER 4
LANDSHARKS AT NIGHT

The green glow of the neon lights bathed the sidewalk in a radioactive hue as Casey stepped up to The Green Parrot. The bar was already spilling over with life—patrons crowded under the overhang, drinks in hand, laughter rolling out into the humid night air. The scent of rum, citrus, and the faint salt of the ocean clung to the breeze, mingling with the sound of a bluesy guitar riff from the band inside.

Jake walked ahead of her, weaving through the crowd with ease. He glanced back, flashing a grin.

"C'mon, newbie. You gotta at least pretend to be excited."

Casey rolled her eyes. "I *am* excited."

Jake snorted. "You say that like you're convincing yourself."

She rolled her eyes but followed him. The Green Parrot felt even more alive than her first night in Key West when Jake brought her here after those killer sandwiches at MoonDog. A lot of the good things that had happened had been Jake-inspired, now that she thought of it. Her job at MoonDog, for one. She was still struggling to remember the names of her regulars, but she felt like she was already forming a little community on this island.

Then she looked up, and for a moment, she forgot entire train of thought. The ceiling above the main bar was covered in a massive, billowing parachute, its faded fabric rippling gently from the circulating fans. It stretched across the space like an oversized canopy, the way those colorful parachutes in elementary school gym class had trapped pockets of air underneath. Something about it made her smile. It was strange and unexpected, and yet, it fit.

Jake caught her staring and smirked. "It's a thing."

"What kind of thing?"

"A Parrot thing. You'll get used to it."

They stepped inside, and the atmosphere swallowed them whole.

The main bar was shaped like a square, taking up most of the center space. The bartenders moved between all four sides, their hands a blur as they poured drinks and passed out beers. The wooden counter was worn and smooth from years of use, every inch of it bearing the marks of countless hands and elbows, spilled whiskey, and late-night conversations.

Beyond the bar, a small stage in the back hosted the night's entertainment—a local band playing a slow, swampy blues track, the kind that settled into your bones and made even the most reluctant dancers tap their feet.

To the right, a side bar stretched along the wall with a more traditional setup of bottles stacked high on wooden shelves, casting amber reflections in the dim light. This appeared to be where the quieter drinkers tended to gather, the ones looking for a deep conversation rather than the roar of the main floor.

Casey took it all in: the thrum of the bass vibrating beneath her feet and in her chest, the sound of drinks clinking, and the occasional whoop from the crowd near the stage. It was chaotic but effortless—a place where nobody was in a hurry, but everything moved.

Jake led her toward the main bar and leaned against the counter as he flagged down the bartender with a quick nod.

"What's your poison?" he asked.

Casey glanced up at the chalkboard menu, scanning the selection. She had no idea what the house special was, and she wasn't in the mood to overthink it.

"A rum punch," she decided. It felt right—a drink that often accompanied beachy scenes like her new home and what she was drinking when she first met Jake at Captain Tony's.

Jake grinned. "Solid choice."

"Your usual?" the bartender asked Jake. He nodded.

The bartender—a woman with sun-streaked hair and a sharp but kind expression—slid their drinks across the bar with practiced ease.

"New girl?" she asked, eyeing Casey.

"She's learning the ropes," Jake answered before Casey could respond.

The bartender gave Casey an approving nod. "Then welcome to the island. Just don't try to keep up with the regulars on your first night."

Casey laughed as she took her drink, the first sip sweet but with an undeniable burn of rum. "I'll keep that in mind."

Jake clinked his glass against hers. "To surviving your first shift at MoonDog."

"To not dropping any trays," Casey said.

They both took a drink as the music swelled in the background, the night stretching out ahead of them—unknown, electric, and waiting.

Jake nudged her shoulder, tipping his chin toward a group gathered near the big bar.

"C'mon, let's introduce you to the people who actually run this town."

Casey arched an eyebrow. "I thought you ran this town."

Jake smirked. "Nah, I just make it sound pretty."

He led her toward a table where three people were casually drinking, their laughter easy and unforced. They were the kind of people who looked like they had been here forever—like they belonged to the island as much as the palm trees and the ocean breeze.

"Y'all, this is Casey." Jake said. "Casey, this is Rory, Ava, and Danny. Rory bartends over at the Schooner Wharf; Ava's an artist—she sells her stuff on Duval; and Danny plays music, usually here, actually."

Rory was the first to acknowledge her. Rory was decidedly androgynous with a deep tan and salt-and-pep-per hair that gave them the look of someone who had been kissed (or maybe slapped) by the sun a few too many times.

"So, you're the new girl Jake's been talking about," Rory said, tipping their beer toward her in greeting.

Casey shot Jake a look. "Oh? He's been talking about me?" Casey shot Jake a sassy look. She wasn't sure she should be flirting with him—a surfer boy island rock star? Not usually her type. But then again, what was her type? It certainly wasn't the suit-and-ties back home.

"Nothing but glowing reviews," Rory teased. "You must've made quite the impression."

Ava leaned forward with interest. She had dark curls piled in a bun on top of her head and a single paint-smeared finger-nail, as if she'd just walked away from a canvas.

"I love when fresh blood shows up," Ava said, looking Casey up and down like she was a blank canvas.

"Fresh blood?" Casey repeated, raising an eyebrow. "Jake, did you bring me to some vampire cult and forget to mention it?"

Jake smiled—or was that a smirk? The corner of his mouth curled up in a way that, in that moment, Casey really liked. He looked mischievous, like he was looking for trouble. Or maybe he was the trouble.

Ava's response broke the brief gaze between Casey and Jake.

"You've still got that newcomer glow. And you're funny. I like you." Ava's eyes sparkled and she smiled. Now that was a smile. Big and warm, like the sun itself.

"Is that a good thing?" Casey asked.

"Depends. You planning to stay?"

Casey hesitated. Was she?

"I don't know yet," she admitted. "I don't really have a plan."

Ava nodded as if she had expected that answer. "Then you'll fit right in."

Danny joined in. His hair was sun-bleached, his jeans ripped at the knees, and was the kind of guy who always looked like he had just walked off the beach. She could see how Jake fit in with these people.

"So what's your story?" he asked, leaning back in his chair. "People don't just land in Key West by accident."

Casey shrugged, glancing at Jake before answering. "Spontaneously bought a train ticket. Kept heading south."

Rory whistled low. "Now that's a proper Key West answer."

"I approve," Ava added.

Casey exhaled, some of the tension in her chest loosening. They weren't interrogating her, just feeling her out.

"So, how did you two meet again?" Ava asked, eyes flashing between Jake and Casey.

"Oh, I thought he told you all about me?" Casey laughed.

"He did," Ava said. "But I just want to make sure your stories add up" Ava laughed.

"Hey, are you calling me a liar?" Jake jokingly jumped in.

"Oh c'mon, Jake. She's beautiful. You're you. I just want to hear her side of the story."

"What's that supposed to mean?" Jake said, mock offended.

"Okay! Okay!" Casey said, waving her hands as if to quell the pretend argument. "I think Ava is due what she's asked for. "We met at Captain Tony's."

"And?" Ava said.

"Well, that's it," Casey said. "You asked how we met!"

"That's *where* you met. Not how. C'mon Casey, give me the story. Was Jake playing guitar and your eyes locked from across the room?" Ava gestured dramatically.

Casey almost spit out her rum punch.

"On that note, I'm going to the bathroom. Be right back," Jake turned away from the group.

As the conversation continued down other paths, Casey saw a familiar figure slide in beside her. "Look at you," Tia teased, her voice full of mock surprise. "Didn't even need me to hold your hand."

Casey laughed. "I'm adjusting."

Tia nodded toward her drink. "Rum punch? Solid move. And out for drinks after your first shift? Looks like you're even learning island time."

"Careful," Rory warned. "That's the first step to never leaving."

The group laughed, but Casey felt the truth behind the joke. There was something intoxicating about this place—the warmth, the way time stretched and twisted, the feeling of being outside the real world.

Could she really get stuck here?

She didn't have time to dwell on the thought because the energy at the table suddenly shifted. It wasn't something obvious, just a subtle pull in the air, a weight Casey hadn't noticed before. Ava was the first to react.

"Ohhh," she murmured, hiding her expression behind her drink. "And now it gets interesting."

Casey frowned. "What?"

Ava nodded toward the entrance.

Casey followed her gaze—and that's when she saw him.

Phillip from the tattoo parlor had just walked in. Even without meaning to, he commanded attention. He was dressed sharp but effortless, in a way that made Jake's casual charm look boyish. His piercing blue eyes scanned the bar, taking in everything without giving anything away. The green glow of the neon outside cast sharp shadows on his face, making him look like he had stepped out of another world entirely.

And then—his gaze landed on her.

Even though The Green Parrot was full of people, it was like there was no one else in the room. Phillip altered his path, no longer heading toward the bar. Instead, he walked straight toward her.

The group noticed. Casey could tell by the way Danny tensed, Tia fidgeted, and Ava nearly shook with excitement: something dramatic was happening, but she had no idea what it was.

Phillip stopped just short of the group.

"I see you're making yourself at home," he nodded toward Casey.

Casey tilted her head, feeling the weight of his attention. "Something like that. It's good to see you—" Before Casey could finish her sentence she heard Jake's voice behind her.

"Didn't know this was your scene."

Jake gave a lazy shrug. "Didn't know it was yours either."

"I'm here, like, all the time, dude," Jake retorted. "Danny plays here every week."

"And I work around the corner and come in often too."

Ava, who had been watching the exchange with thinly veiled interest, let out a low, knowing hum into her drink.

"Oh, I love this," she whispered as she took a slow sip. "I really do."

There was no outright hostility, but there was something unspoken there—a quiet measuring of space, of territory.

And Casey was right in the middle of it.

She barely knew Phillip, but there was something about him that made her feel like he saw through her. Like he knew she hadn't figured herself out yet—and that amused him. She wasn't sure if she found it annoying or sexy.

Tia nudged her elbow, whispering just loud enough for only Casey to hear.

"Careful, sweetheart. The sharks are circling."

Phillip didn't make a move to sit or leave—he just lingered, comfortably at ease, as if he were giving Jake space to react.

Jake, for his part, didn't rise to it. Instead, he let out a slow chuckle, tipping back the rest of his drink before looking back at Casey.

"It was good to see you, too, Casey," Phillip said in a mild-mannered tone. "I hope you're settling in well." It was the first time he had used her name—and she felt it like the brush of fingers against skin.

Phillip turned to leave, when Jake asked in a loud voice, "What do you think, Casey? You settling in?"

She met his gaze, noting the way he wasn't looking at Phillip—but still, the question was meant for him. Casey lifted her drink slightly, letting the ice clink against the glass. "So far, so good."

She turned to look at Phillip, but he was already up at the bar, his back to them. Had he even bothered to listen to Jake's exaggerated question? What kind of game were they playing here?

"I need another drink; anyone else?" Jake didn't actually wait for a response before turning toward the bar.

"Jake, don't you—" Tia began in a mothering tone.

"Relax, I'm just going to get another drink. Rory, Danny, care to join me? I apparently need handlers. The two rose from the table and followed Jake up to the bar, one on either side, seeming to escort him to the side of the bar where Phillip was sitting.

The moment they were gone, Ava and Tia both turned to Casey, eyes gleaming with mischief. Ava let out a low whistle. "Ohhh, sweetheart. You have no idea what you've just walked into."

"I told her the sharks are circling," Tia said.

"Fins to the left, fins to the right," Ava said with a slyness about her.

Casey rolled her eyes, but there was no real annoyance in it. Because she knew.

She had felt it from the moment Phillip's eyes met hers.

She had felt it in Jake's shift in posture around him.

She had felt it in the way the air around them had grown heavier—not hostile, but charged. She was standing at the center of something she didn't ask for, but she was curious about it, nonetheless.

"So is anyone going to tell me what is happening?"

"Girl, I don't think it's ours to tell, but just know there is beef between Jake and Phillip. Serious drama."

Before Casey could ask another question, Jake returned with a new drink, and as if he knew they were talking about him, he chimed in, "You should be careful with that one."

"Funny. I was just thinking the same thing about you," Casey retorted. Why was she still flirting with him? Hadn't she just learned to step away from him?

Jake met her eyes, and for a second—just a second—his smirk faltered into something real. Then, he clinked his glass against hers once more.

"Touché."

CHAPTER 5
FINS TO THE LEFT, FINS TO THE RIGHT

The morning air was thick with the scent of brewing coffee and fresh pastries as Casey stepped into MoonDog Café. She was off today, but she'd become accustomed to the vibe of the place, and truth be told, really wanted one of those delectable pastries for breakfast. The café was already buzzing—locals perched at their usual spots, conversations murmuring between sips of espresso. This certainly wasn't a Cincinnati coffee shop—not a laptop in sight.

She was getting used to this—the rhythm of the place, the warmth of it. The clatter of mugs, the hum of the espresso machine, the way Des barked orders without looking up from the register.

It felt… natural.

And yet, something was different today. Was it the lingering weirdness from last night? She'd only been in town less than a week, and she certainly didn't want any drama—island or otherwise—taking away from her newfound home. Casey pondered the feeling while gazing into the treat container.

Tia was on the other side of the counterrolling silverware into napkins, grinning like she knew something that Casey didn't.

Tia leaned against the counter with her arms crossed.

"So," she said casually. "How does it feel to be the most interesting thing to happen to this town in weeks?"

Casey snorted. "What are you talking about?"

"Oh, come on," Tia said. "First, Jake is suddenly all up in your orbit. And now, Phillip? You've been here, what, a week? That's impressive."

Casey rolled her eyes, but her stomach did a tiny, annoying flip at the mention of both their names.

"Less than a week. And it's nothing," she said, stacking the last of the rolled silverware in the bin. "People are just friendly here."

Tia raised an eyebrow. "Friendly? Maybe. But not *that* friendly."

Before Casey could argue, the bell above the door jingled—and Jake strolled in.

Jake moved through MoonDog like he owned the place. But didn't he do that everywhere? He was the kind of guy who people naturally turned to watch, his presence effortlessly magnetic.

He looked like he had rolled straight off a boat and into the café. His guitar case was slung over his shoulder like usual, and he was wearing a white T-shirt that was slightly wrinkled from what Casey assumed was the adventure he'd already had that morning.

He slid onto a barstool, grinning as Casey walked up. "Morning, new girl."

She tried not to smile, and went behind the counter to grab a cold brew from the fridge and set it in front of him before he could even ask.

Jake raised an eyebrow. "Damn. You really are good at this job."

Casey shrugged. "And I'm not even on shift."

Jake took a sip, his grin never wavering. "Then what the heck are you doing at work? Shouldn't you be actually gonna enjoy Key West?"

Before she could answer, the bell above the door jingled again.

Unlike Jake, Phillip didn't command attention.

He didn't have to.

He moved quietly, stepping inside without a glance toward anyone else. He wore dark sunglasses, his usual black button-down rolled to his elbows, his pace unhurried as he took a seat at the far end of the counter. Casey caught herself noticing him immediately—and the second she did, she felt Jake noticing her noticing him.

Jake smirked, tipping his coffee toward Phillip in greeting. "And here I thought I was your only regular."

Phillip removed his sunglasses and shrugged, his expression unreadable. "The espresso is good." It was a simple statement. But from the way he said it, Casey guessed it wasn't about the coffee at all. Casey grabbed a cup, moving toward Phillip. "Espresso?"

Phillip nodded, watching her as she worked. His gaze wasn't flirtatious or obvious—but it held something steady, something that made her heart beat just a little faster.

She handed him the cup. "No cream or sugar?"

"I don't like things too sweet."

Across the counter, Jake made a sound in the back of his throat—somewhere between a scoff and a laugh.

"You know he only drinks espresso and judgment, right?" Jake said, grinning at Casey.

Phillip didn't react—but there was an almost imperceptible twitch of amusement at the corner of his mouth. Casey exhaled, shaking her head as she grabbed a rag to wipe the counter. She had barely been here a week—but she was already caught in something she didn't quite understand.

And the worst part?

She wasn't sure she wanted to escape it.

The next day, the sun hung heavy in the bright blue Key West sky, the breeze carrying the scent of salt, sunscreen, and sizzling seafood from the open-air grills that seemed to be at every house. Casey had the day off, so when Tia dragged her out to a beachfront bar where Jake was playing a set, she didn't argue.

She told herself she was just going for the view, the

drinks, the music—but the truth sat unspoken somewhere in the back of her mind. She wanted to see Jake again… and if she was being honest with herself, maybe she wanted to see if Phillip would show up too. The island was small, she was learning. And anyone could be anywhere on any given night. The island is only four miles long and one mile wide, and most people who lived here had walked it drunk.

When they arrived, the place was packed.

"Is there some kind of event going on?" Casey asked Tia.

"Yeah, that's actually why Jake is playing. This is a little fundraiser for Joe's dog, Charley. He got hit by a tourist on a damn moped and they had to amputate his leg."

"Oh my god that's horrible." Casey said. "I'd be pissed if that were Marley."

"See, dog parents gotta stick together," Tia laughed.

"Damn straight," Casey said.

"So this is actually one of the only real 'beach bars' on the island. There's not much sand here; it's basically rocky beaches," Tia explained. "But Charley really likes the bit of sand here, and Joe bartends on weeknights, so this was the natural place for the fundraiser."

The beach bar was exactly the kind of place Casey imagined herself so many times—open, airy, and filled with barefoot patrons sipping drinks as the waves lapped lazily against the shore. The makeshift wooden stage stood at the edge of the sand, the ocean a perfect backdrop behind it.

When they arrived, Jake was already playing. His guitar was slung low and his voice was smooth and effortless as he sang to a crowd that was half-drunk and fully enchanted. He spotted Casey and Tia immediately, his gaze lingering just a second too long before he grinned at them, through the lyrics.

Tia made a face. "Oh, girl, you're in trouble."

Casey rolled her eyes, but she could feel it—the weight of his attention, how easy it was to fall into the pull of his charm. They grabbed a high-top table near the sand, ordering frozen daiquiris as Jake wrapped up his set. By the time he slung his guitar off his shoulder and headed toward them, the MC was thanking Jake for donating his time and talent and moving on to introduce the next performer. Casey didn't catch his name because that was precisely when Jake arrived at their table.

"Ladies," he greeted, his voice warm, teasing, but focused entirely on Casey. "Enjoying the show?"

Casey lifted her drink. "I'll let you know after I finish this."

Jake chuckled, wiping sweat from his brow. "So, that's how it is?"

Tia leaned in. "Oh, it's definitely how it is."

Jake smirked back. "Good thing I'm persistent."

And just like that, Casey was caught in his current again.

The conversation was easy, the way it always was with Jake. He was all laughter and sun-drenched confidence, the kind of guy who knew how to make anyone feel like they were the most interesting person in the world.

But then Jake's shoulders straightened slightly, and he seemed to start looking past Casey. Tia, who had been laughing a second ago, suddenly nudged Casey under the table. Casey followed their gazes—toward the bar.

And there he was.

Phillip.

Phillip didn't seem like a beach bar kind of guy. And yet, there he was—standing near the edge of the crowd, wearing his usual dark button-down, the sleeves rolled up just enough to make him look effortlessly composed despite the heat.

He wasn't looking at Jake. He was looking at her.

"Oh, this is getting good," Tia muttered under her breath, taking a slow sip of her drink.

Jake exhaled through his nose, shaking his head with a smirk. "Man, you really do pop up everywhere. Like an iguana falling out of a tree."

Phillip didn't rise to the bait as he approached with slow, deliberate steps, his gaze never leaving Casey as he slid onto the empty stool beside her.

"Small island. Plus Joe is a client of mine. And I have a soft spot for dogs."

Jake let out a laugh, leaning back in his chair. "Right. Of course."

The contrast between them was impossible to ignore. Jake—sunlit, easygoing, warm—was still grinning, but Casey could feel the slight edge in his posture. Phillip—cool, controlled, unreadable—wasn't smiling at all, but seemed totally calm. And Casey was sitting right between them.

Jake looked at Phillip, then back at Casey, his smirk widening. "So, what do you think, new girl?"

Casey arched an eyebrow. "About what?"

Jake leaned forward on his elbows. "You've got me on one side and him on the other. If this were a movie, this is the part where you'd have to pick a leading man."

Phillip finally spoke, his voice quiet, steady. "Good thing life isn't a movie, then."

Something flickered between them—unspoken but undeniable. Tia, watching the entire thing like it was the best entertainment she'd had all week, muttered into her drink, "I love this town."

Casey exhaled, shaking her head. "You're both ridiculous."

Jake grinned, lifting his beer. "And yet, here you are."

Phillip said nothing.

But Casey noticed the small, knowing tilt of his lips—just enough to let her know he was enjoying this in his own quiet way. That's when she realized she might actually be in trouble.

Jake returned to the stage, leaving Casey with Tia and Phillip. He seemed to be doing fifteen-minute set transitions between bands. And Casey knew it was fifteen minutes exactly because she kept checking her phone. For fifteen whole minutes, Phillip said not a damn word. The three of them sat in silence listening to Jake, and when he finished his set, Phillip even clapped. Did he even like her? Aside from a few stray glances, Phillip wasn't putting in much of an effort to win her over. Was she just imagining his interest in her because he clearly had a feud with Jake?

Another band of beach boys took the stage, and the late afternoon sun slanted over the beach bar, casting everything in a golden glow. The music had picked up, people were dancing in the sand, drinks flowed freely, and the ocean breeze made the air just cool enough to take the edge off the heat.

And yet, all Casey could focus on was the silent tension growing between Jake and Phillip—two completely different kinds of energy pressing in on either side of her. Jake—bold, warm, inviting—leaned in close, his easy charm filling the space like sunlight. Phillip—cool, observant, unreadable—didn't have to move to command attention. He simply existed in a way that pulled her focus like gravity.

It was an unspoken battle, and Casey was the prize. Or was she? Did Phillip even like her? Tia and Ava seemed to think he did.

Jake tried to be nonchalant, but it was obvious to Casey and Tia—and probably Phillip too—that he was incredibly annoyed. He downed the rest of his beer, set the bottle on the table with a satisfying thud, and stretched, throwing a lazy, knowing smirk toward Phillip.

"So, tell me, man," Jake said, his tone casual, but the undercurrent clear. "You ever actually been in the ocean over here?"

Phillip arched an eyebrow, his expression unreadable. "Not here in particular, no."

Jake grinned. "Figures."

Phillip didn't rise to it, just took a slow sip of his drink. "Why?"

Jake shrugged, standing up. "Because it's about time."

Tia immediately caught on. She gasped, grabbing Casey's arm. "Oh, my God, please tell me you're gonna make them do this."

Casey blinked. "Make them do what?"

Jake turned to her, eyes twinkling with mischief. "Take a swim, new girl. Make it fair. You're the only one who can referee this."

Casey hesitated, glancing at Phillip, who simply stared back, impassive as ever.

The worst part? She wanted to see what he would do.

"Doesn't that seem a little childish?" Phillip finally protested.

Jake scoffed. "Maybe you're just afraid. Can you even swim, Frenchie"

Phillip took a deep breath and sighed like he wanted to continue protesting, but instead, he rose from his seat, gesturing toward the water, calm as ever.

"After you."

Before she knew it, they were all heading toward the rocky shore, kicking off shoes, rolling up pant legs. The sand of the beach turned into a bunch of small rocks the further they got from the bar and the party, making it less comfortable to walk on for Casey, but the others seemed to be doing just fine.

Casey glanced at Tia looking for answers, but Jake was already in the water, laughing as the first wave rolled up to his knees, running a hand through his salt-damp hair. His clothes sat on a pile on the beach. *How had he gotten in the water so fast?* Casey thought.

Phillip, though? He took his time. He unbuttoned his sleeves first, rolling them up with slow, precise movements. He pulled off his button down methodically, revealing a physique Casey hadn't expected from someone who sits in a chair all day. She examined the tattoos on his chest and back until she realized that she must look like she was staring at him pulling off his jeans. She quickly averted her gaze to Tia, who saw the whole thing and chuckled, shaking her head. Then Phillip stepped forward, the waves licking at his ankles, his posture controlled—measured in a way that was so completely different from Jake's wild, carefree energy.

Casey tried, but she couldn't stop watching.

Tia nudged her. "Oh, yeah. You're doomed."

Without acknowledging Tia, Casey said, "Okay, to the buoy and back. On your mark, get set, go!"

And they took off. It was remarkable how fast they each were. Casey assumed Jake would be the clear winner with all of his time in and around the water. He seemed like he'd basically be a fish. But Phillip was keeping pace with him just fine. In fact, Phillip almost had more precise strokes, disturbing less of the water than Jake.

They were back before Casey knew it. Jake came up laughing. Shaking the water from his hair, looking every bit like the golden-boy musician who belonged on a tropical poster.

Phillip was calm and deliberate, surfacing and running a slow hand over his wet hair, dark and effortless as he pushed the water away from his face.

"Alright, so who wins," Jake asked, turning to Casey. Phillip was silent; he didn't even look at Jake, only Casey. She was honestly surprised he got in the water to begin with. He didn't seem like the type to give in to Jake's antics, but yet, they were both standing in front of her, dripping saltwater and staring into her soul. That's when she realized that Jake had all the charm in the world, but Phillip didn't need it. He was something else entirely.

"Uh, well, it was really close," Casey said. "But I think Jake did reach the shore—"

"Woooo!" Jake interrupted, jarring Casey a bit.

Phillip looked unbothered. As they both waded back onto shore, the air was different between them. Jake was still grinning, still cocky, still Jake. But Casey wasn't thinking about Jake anymore. And Phillip knew it.

As they reached the bar, the group started splitting

off—Tia heading inside for another drink where she could see Ava waving to her and hear Rory arguing with one of the bartenders about not putting oranges in a certain kind of drink. *Man did they miss a show*, Casey thought.

Casey needed a break from the tug-of-war between Jake and Phillip, so she slipped away from the group, making her way toward the storm-worn dock that stretched out into the water. She stepped onto the wood, the old planks creaking under her weight, and leaned against the railing, looking out at the endless horizon.

She hadn't been alone for more than thirty seconds before she heard the footsteps. Wet flip flops squeaked and squelched on the dock.

"Hell of a show today, right?" Jake asked with the kind of shit-eating grin that was always plastered on his face.

She turned slightly to see him standing beside her, hands resting on the railing. "You're ridiculous, you know that?" she said.

Jake laughed, running a hand through his damp hair. "Yeah, but you like it."

He said it playfully, but there was something else beneath it—a thread of realness, a quiet confidence. Jake knew his effect on people. And he wasn't blind. He saw the way Phillip looked at her.

And Jake?

Jake wasn't the kind of guy who let things slip away without a fight.

Before Casey could answer, another set of footsteps

echoed on the dock. Jake's gaze flicked past her, his smirk twitching at the corner.

"And here we go."

Casey turned, as if she didn't already know.

He wasn't rushing. Wasn't stepping in like he had any claim to her. But he also wasn't avoiding this moment.

Jake let out a soft chuckle, shaking his head. "Man, you've got perfect timing."

Phillip shrugged, his expression unreadable. "Didn't realize this was a private dock."

Jake grinned, turning back to Casey. "You know, this is usually the part where you make some kind of choice."

Casey scoffed. "A choice?"

Jake leaned in slightly. "Yeah, you know. The charming musician or the broody tattoo artist."

Phillip exhaled through his nose, his gaze steady. "You assume she has to choose at all."

Jake breathed out heavily, as if trying to control a burst of anger lurching forward within him. Phillip stood stoically, waiting for Jake to pounce. The tension was almost hostile. Casey could feel it pressing in on her from both sides, the silent push and pull of two completely different forces.

Jake smirked, stepping back. "Well, I'll let you two figure that out."

And with that, he turned, walking back toward the bar, leaving Casey and Phillip alone on the dock.

The silence stretched between them, the water lapping gently against the pilings.

Phillip didn't move, didn't push. He simply looked at her and said, "You handled yourself well today."

Casey let out a breath she hadn't realized she was holding. "You say that like I was being tested."

Phillip's mouth quirked at the corner. "Weren't you?"

She exhaled, shaking her head. "You and Jake are both impossible."

Phillip didn't argue. He just tilted his head slightly, like he was considering something.

Then he stepped closer, just enough for her to notice. "Goodnight, Casey."

And before she could respond, he stepped away and started heading back down the dock.

As she stood there alone, staring blankly at the waves stretching endlessly before her, the weight of anticipation and intrigue pressed against her ribs. *What the hell was that?* she thought. The longer she stood on the dock, the more confused she became. How did she get in the middle of this feud? Hadn't she come here to escape a life of stress? Why was she allowing herself to be pulled into a rip tide of a fight that wasn't hers to begin with?

But she knew the answer. Back in Cincinnati, she didn't get this kind of attention. Sure, she'd gone on a few dates here and there, but she didn't have the time to dedicate to anyone in particular. Now she was here, in Key West, with a clean slate—and two hot guys whose attention she didn't dislike. She sighed, trying to steady her breath against the thick air and her own racing thoughts. The distant crash of the surf mingled with the fading laughter from the bar, and for a long, suspended minute, she felt untethered—adrift in a sea of both promise and trepidation.

She had come here to disappear. To find peace, not… whatever this was. A rivalry? A love triangle? A test?

It was supposed to be simple. New town. New job. A few months to herself before she figured out what came next. But it wasn't simple. Not anymore.

Now it felt like she was constantly treading water—Jake pulling her one way, Phillip pulling her another, and her own heart caught somewhere in the middle, unsure which way to swim. Or whether she even wanted to swim at all.

The waves lapped lazily beneath the dock. A breeze rolled off the water, warm and sticky, and still, she couldn't shake the feeling that it was all about to get more complicated. Because maybe she hadn't just escaped Cincinnati. Maybe she had also escaped herself. And now… she was starting to wonder if she could outrun either.

She turned away from the railing, the dock creaking underfoot as she walked slowly back toward the lights of the bar.

CHAPTER 6
NO STRAIGHT LINES ON AN ISLAND

In the days that followed, Casey kept mostly to herself. She hung out with Marley at their little bungalow, wandered the quiet streets with a coffee in hand, and tried not to think too hard about what she was doing here. It was easier to focus on small things—sunlight warming the porch steps, the way Marley's ears perked at passing chickens, the smell of salt and hot pavement rising by midmorning.

Each morning, Betty was out early, sweeping her porch like it owed her money. She greeted Casey with a cheerful, "Mornin', sugar," and waved her over like they'd known each other for years.

Betty had this way about her—part busybody, part sage. Somewhere between a neighbor, a mentor, and a slightly chaotic life coach in denim capris and a sun visor. She'd offer advice with the same authority she used to direct tourists toward better fish tacos.

"You don't go to Blue Heaven on a Sunday, no matter what the guidebooks say," she told Casey one morning, leaning against her broom like it was a staff of wisdom. "Brunch lines'll stretch to Cuba. Go Tuesday, sit at the bar, get the lobster benedict and a mimosa. You'll thank me later."

Casey did. She always did. Every suggestion Betty gave—from the taco truck behind the gas station to the quiet sitting place tucked behind the old cemetery—was a tiny revelation.

"You got good taste," Casey told her once, sipping a café con leche from the place Betty insisted made it right.

Betty winked. "I know a good thing when I see it. That includes people, too."

It wasn't just the recommendations. It was the way Betty noticed things. The way she always asked how Casey was *really* doing, even when Casey answered with a noncommittal shrug. The way she looked at Marley like he was a full-fledged person. The way she dropped little pieces of her own story like breadcrumbs—enough to hint that she hadn't always lived this quiet porch-sweeping life.

"I came down here to start over, too," Betty said one morning, pouring Casey a splash of orange juice from the pitcher she kept in her mini-fridge. "Just took me thirty years and two husbands to admit I needed it."

Casey raised an eyebrow. "This your final form?"

Betty laughed, loud and full-bellied. "Hell no. I'm just in the intermission."

This morning was no different. Today Betty sent her and Marley to Marta's Bistro for lunch. Away from the hustle and bustle of Duval—a long way actually. Casey hadn't walked this far away from her place since she arrived there.

The bistro was tucked off a shaded side street, nestled behind a hibiscus-lined fence and guarded by a fat orange cat that barely lifted its head as Casey and Marley approached. A chalkboard sign leaned slightly to the left by the entrance, announcing the lunch special—conch fritters and citrus slaw.

Inside, the space felt like a dream—breezy, sun-dappled, filled with the scent of grilled seafood and ripe mangos. Ceiling fans stirred the air lazily, and a reggae version of a Fleetwood Mac song played softly in the background. Marta, a stout woman with kind eyes and a braid down to her waist, greeted Casey like an old friend even though they'd never met.

"You're Betty's girl," Marta said with a wink. "She called ahead. Said you needed a place to breathe."

Casey blinked. "She did?"

"She's not wrong," Marta said, leading her to a small table by the open window. "Sometimes this island's energy sneaks up on you. It looks like paradise, but it doesn't mean you stop feeling whatever you carried here."

Casey sat, momentarily stunned by how easily this stranger saw right through her. She nodded, brushing Marley's fur as he settled beside her under the table. After she ordered, she admired the art of the walls. It was eclectic but all looked like it belonged here. Marta caught her staring at one and stopped to tell her its story.

"Ahh, that one is by David. Amazing charcoal artist. Loves to draw manatees."

"Wow. He's way better than me."

"You're an artist? Bring your stuff by some time. Maybe it'll find a home on the wall."

Casey blushed.

"I could never. It's not good enough for that."

Marta smiled and shook her head. "Well, just bring it next time you come for lunch. I'd love to see the kind of work you do."

Casey nodded, and Marta went back to the kitchen.

Lunch arrived quickly—fritters still steaming, slaw crisp and bright—and Casey ate slowly, watching the lazy afternoon unfold on the street beyond the window. Locals walked by in no hurry, carrying grocery bags or surfboards or nothing at all. An old man pushed a cart of coconuts and called out something in Spanish to a woman across the road who threw her head back and laughed.

It should've felt peaceful. But inside, Casey's thoughts were anything but. She kept replaying the dock. The look in Phillip's eyes. The way Jake's smile had faltered at just the right moment. The way she'd felt suspended between them—wanted, but also trapped.

She took a sip of her drink, a homemade limeade Marta insisted she try on the house. Tart lime and sugar tickled her tongue. A breeze lifted through the bistro, carrying the scent of saltwater and something sweet Casey couldn't name. She closed her eyes, breathing it in.

Casey opened her eyes slowly, set her fork down, and scratched Marley's ears.

"Let's take the long way home," she whispered.

Marley thumped his tail.

Taking the long way home on an island that is 4.2 square miles had to involve some pit stops. Casey wasn't sure where yet, she figured she'd be a true islander and just walk until something spoke to her. She and Marley followed the sidewalk along the water. They passed the causeway, which had more vehicles than Casey had seen since she came to the island. It had to be the busiest driving area on the island, but still nothing close to rush hour in Cincinnati.

A sign advertised "Tiki Boat Adventures" and Casey could see a few tiki boats from the sidewalk. Each had a thatched roof bar surrounded by barstools on it. A pelican relaxed on a nearby pylon. Casey stopped to snap a photo before moving along.

It wasn't long before they were approaching Eaton Street, which meant they were getting closer to the heart of the island again and would not be directly along the water for at least a few blocks. Marley sniffed at the air.

"Whatcha smell, boy?" Casey asked, and then she inhaled. "Oh my god. What is that heavenly scent, Marley?"

They approached a simple white building with dark green shudders. An oval red sign read "Old Town Bakery." Casey peered in the window; she could see bakery cases full of pastries, pies, croissants, and more things she couldn't even identify. Marley started drooling.

"Aw dude," Casey said when she noticed. "You're drooling on my foot." Marley craned his neck to the left and to the right. Casey patted him on the head. A rooster bauked on a nearby bench, startling both Casey and Marley.

"Well I can't bring you in there, and I certainly can't leave you out here with him," Casey said to Marley, pointing at the rooster. She added it to her list of things she wanted to do from her first day here: try the po'boys at Maggie's Kitchen, peruse The Salty Spine Bookstore, and, now, get a pastry from Old Town Bakery.

Casey and Marley kept walking a few blocks before making a right onto William street to walk along the water again.

Unexpectedly, she was walking directly towards the Schooner Wharf Bar. Casey didn't realize how close to all the popular bars and restaurants it actually was.

"Hey Marley, I think that's where Rory works. You haven't met Rory yet. Want to see if they're around?"

She wasn't really in the mood to drink, but she approached the entrance to take a look around. *Ring. Ring.* A cool little street bike pulled up beside her, complete with a basket on the front. The rider who was ringing their bells was Rory, clocking in for their shift evidently.

"Casey! What brings you over here? Coming to have a drink with me on my shift?"

"Oh, hey, Rory!" Casey said, surprised at the convenience of her arrival time. "I was just taking a walk. Had lunch over at Marta's Bistro and figured I should do more exploring."

"Don't let me stop you then! Explore away!" Rory smiled a wide and happy smile. "Although, I don't think it's me who is stopping you." Their smile moved to a knowing look, inquisitive but not pressing or harsh.

"Well—"

"You don't need to explain yourself to me," Rory interjected before Casey could even begin her sentence. "I mean I'm not judging anything. I shouldn't have even said that. I just—well, I think everyone deserves to experience this place through their own eyes, not just how someone else wants them to see it."

Casey nodded, unsure of how to actually respond.

"Sorry," Rory shrugged. "I was a philosophy major. I overthink things." They chuckled.

Casey smiled. "It's okay."

"So who's this good boy?" Rory asked, squatting down to give Marley scratches.

"This is my buddy, Marley."

"Hey Rory, are you coming to clock in or do you have better things to do today?" A bald man called from inside the bar area.

"Looks like that's my cue. I'll see ya around, Casey."

Rory grabbed their back and headed to work. *Damn, did everyone know everything on this island?* Casey thought back to the first regular she served at MoonDog. *What was that she said? I'll hear it on the Coconut Telegraph sooner or later? Is this what she meant? Was every islander getting gossip updates in a daily magazine?*

Casey tried not to be consumed by these thoughts while she and Marley continued walking down Lazy Way, a little pedestrian-only walkway along the water. On their left was Shrimpboat Sound Studio, Jimmy Buffett's recording studio. If you didn't know what you were looking at, you'd think it was a trailer plastered with stickers at first glance. A small collection of items fashioned a memorial for the late, great artist—handwritten notes and poems, broken flip flops, autographed pictures of Andy Devine, and a number of other trinkets that Casey didn't quite understand.

They continued through the little courtyard next to the studio and up Elizabeth Street. Making a right onto Caroline Street, Marley trotted along. Casey yawned.

"Seems like it's time for a hammock nap. Whaddya say, Marley?"

He wagged his tail in agreement. They turned left onto Whitehead Street, which meant they'd be passing the Green Parrot. But before they got there, Marley paused in front of a gigantic tree. *How have I not noticed this before?* Casey wondered. They weren't far from home, and this thing was huge. It looked like multiple trees making up one giant tree? Or maybe it was one giant tree with a lot of holes in its trunk? *No, that can't be right,* Casey thought. And on the branches there were leaves but also…other branches? Or were those vines hanging off of it? *What the heck is that tree?* Casey was examining the tree, but it wasn't the tree that Marley had stopped for. He was looking at a gigantic iguana on the pathway near the tree. With one big leap, Marley pulled Casey forward as he lunged at the lizard.

The leash slipped from her hands, and Marley was loose, bounding after the iguana as he scurried toward the confusing tree. Marley barked, darting toward the base of the tree as the iguana shot upward with terrifying speed for something that looked like it should've retired decades ago. The massive lizard disappeared into the thick tangle of roots and vines while Marley circled the trunk, barking like a dog possessed.

Casey scrambled after him, heart pounding, fumbling to grab the leash as it snaked across the sidewalk.

"Marley! No! Leave it! Get back here!"

Casey finally lunged and caught the leash just as Marley tried to wedge himself into a hollowed-out crevice at the base of the tree. She yanked gently, breathless.

"Oh my god, oh my god, what if that thing's protected? What if there's like a law? The roosters are practically sacred around here—what if the iguanas are, like, holy too?" she said aloud, partially to Marley and partially to the tree.

She looked around, panicked, half-expecting a park ranger or island police officer to materialize out of the leaves and write her a ticket for *assaulting local wildlife with a golden retriever mix.*

She was already mentally drafting an apology to whatever environmental commission protected this Jurassic lizard when a shirtless man passing by, holding a coconut with a straw sticking out of it, paused and looked up into the tree. He squinted, unimpressed.

"Damn iguanas," he muttered. "Fall outta trees when it gets cold. Land right on your damn head. Nuisance if you ask me."

Then he kept walking.

Casey blinked.

"That's it?" she said out loud. "That's the commentary?"

Marley panted happily at her side, completely unbothered. She looked back up into the tree, now seeing at least three more iguanas lounging lazily in the branches like little green gods of chaos.

Casey shook her head, rubbing her temples. "I need a drink. Or a nap. Or maybe just…ooo I know. Let's go visit Tia at work and get a coffee."

She gave Marley a look. "You're lucky you're cute, but you're still not off the hook. No whipped cream for you; the last thing you need right now is sugar."

Marley whined, as if he understood perfectly well that he would not be getting his sweet treat at the cafe. Leash secured firmly in hand, they continued down the sidewalk toward the Green Parrot, the still-unknown tree behind them—silent, ancient, and apparently full of lizards no one gave a single damn about.

To get to MoonDog, Casey had to pass Angela Street,

where her place was. She figured Marley had had enough excitement for today—and she knew that she had—so she dropped him off in the backyard before continuing on to MoonDog for an iced coffee and chat with Tia.

The cafe was dead when she arrived, and Tia was leaning against the counter, scrolling lazily on her phone.

"Hey, babe!" Tia called to Casey when she saw her come through the door. "You look like you've seen a ghost. Or a tourist in socks and sandals."

Casey let the door swing closed behind her with a soft jingle. "Worse. Iguana. Marley chased it into some kind of eldritch horror tree. I thought I was going to get arrested for disturbing the sacred reptiles of the island."

Tia snorted. "Girl, please. Iguanas are the unofficial menace of Key West. The real danger is one falling out of a tree and landing on your mimosa."

"That's… oddly specific."

"Ask me how I know."

Casey grinned despite herself and walked to the counter, leaning against it. "Anyway, I dropped Marley at home. He's cut off. No puppuccino for him today."

"Poor guy," Tia said, mock sympathy in her voice as she reached for a plastic cup. "Iced coffee? Cold brew? Emotional support espresso?"

"Surprise me," Casey said, resting her head briefly on her arms. "Honestly, I just needed to be somewhere with air conditioning and no sentient lizards."

Tia set to work behind the bar, pulling shots and

pouring oat milk like she was born doing it. "Rough morning, huh?"

"I don't know," Casey mumbled. "It was a good lunch. Betty sent me to Marta's, which was incredible. But then I ended up spiraling about lizard laws and thinking maybe I'm slowly losing my mind."

Tia slid a finished drink across the counter. "You're not losing your mind. You're adjusting."

"Adjusting to what, exactly? Tropical chaos?"

Tia gave her a look. "Island life. You're in the weird part of the honeymoon phase where the magic's still there, but now you're starting to see all the oddball bits that come with it. You either settle in or run screaming."

Casey took a sip of the drink—sweet, rich, and way more caffeinated than she probably needed. "And which one are you?"

"Settled in, babe," Tia said with a wink. "With flair."

Casey smiled, tapping her fingers against the cup. The caffeine was already waking up the parts of her brain she'd left behind in the strange tree.

"I think I'm still figuring it out," she admitted. "Some days I feel like I belong here. Other days it's like… what am I even *doing*?"

Tia nodded, her expression softening. "You don't have to have it figured out yet. You just have to show up. And maybe avoid chasing reptiles into banyan trees."

Casey blinked. "Wait—that's what that was? A banyan tree?"

Tia leaned on the counter, clearly pleased to be the bearer of island trivia. "Yeah, girl. They're wild, right? Technically, it's one tree—but it grows all these aerial roots that drop down and form new trunks, so it *looks* like a whole tangled forest. The one up the street is the biggest one on the island."

"Okay, that's both magical and terrifying."

"Pretty much sums up Key West," Tia said with a smirk. "Especially the part where iguanas just move in and take over."

"I feel like I was nearly recruited into their lizard cult."

"Honestly? Wouldn't be the weirdest thing to happen here."

They shared a laugh, and then stood for a moment in the calm hum of the café, the overhead fans spinning lazy circles above them.

"You wanna hang out after my shift?" Tia asked casually. "I think Ava's off tonight too. We could do something low-key. Sunset beers, beach walk, or—if you're feeling chaotic—rooftop tarot with margaritas."

Casey laughed. "Those all sound dangerously perfect."

"Good," Tia said. "We like danger."

Casey took another sip, the cold brew sharp and energizing, like a jolt of clarity.

"Okay," she said. "I'm in."

Tia grinned. "That's the spirit."

The pink neon glow of 801 Bourbon Bar bled into the sidewalk like cotton candy sunset, casting a soft blush on everything and everyone around it. As Casey followed Tia and Ava through the door, the wave of air conditioning and glitter hit her all at once.

Inside, the bar was a fever dream of flair and fabulousness. Mirrors lined the walls, sequins sparkled from the rafters, and the soundtrack was one part disco, two parts power diva.

Behind the bar, an impossibly thin man with perfectly sculpted platinum blonde hair and glitter-dusted cheekbones whipped a cocktail shaker through the air like a baton. His nails—long, almond-shaped, and painted chrome—caught the light with every flick of his wrist.

"Angels!" he called, spotting Tia and Ava. "You're late and underdressed."

Ava blew him a kiss. "You love us anyway, Beau."

"Regretfully," Beau said, already pulling down bottles. "Who's the fresh meat?"

Tia pulled Casey forward. "Be gentle—she's new."

Casey offered a shy smile. "Casey."

Beau gave her a once-over like he was designing a runway look in his head. "Cincinnati girl, right?"

Casey's mouth dropped. "How—?"

"Honey, I've been doing this since the Clinton administration. And you've got that newly untangled look. Like you just escaped your big city job and haven't figured out whether this is a reset or a breakdown."

Casey blinked, then burst out laughing. "Honestly? Same."

Beau winked and slid three drinks across the counter—one garnished with edible glitter, another with a slice of dragon fruit, and a third with what appeared to be a cocktail umbrella *and* a flamingo stirrer.

"Enjoy, girls. Show tunes start at nine, and don't let any island men steal your joy before then."

They made their way to a booth beneath a glowing sign that read *Come for the queens, stay for the cocktails.* The plush vinyl stuck a little to their legs in the humidity, but the drinks were cold, and the conversation—like the atmosphere—was electric.

"So," Ava said, sliding into the booth beside Casey, "how's the settling-in going? Still thinking of running for the hills, or are you starting to feel like one of us?"

Casey sipped her drink—sweet and citrusy with a spicy kick at the end. "I don't know. I still feel like I'm in a dream. Like, at any moment, someone's going to tell me my time's up and I have to go back to real life."

Tia nodded. "That's how you know it's working."

"It is?" Casey asked.

"Oh yeah," Tia said. "If you're not at least a little confused for the first few weeks, you're doing it wrong."

Ava grinned. "Besides, you've got your own soap opera going already. Jake and Phillip? Please. It's like watching *The Bachelor: Key West Edition.*"

Casey groaned, covering her face. "Don't remind me. I came here to escape chaos, not be the center of it."

"Girl," Ava said, lifting her glass, "chaos *is* the culture."

Tia clinked glasses with her. "And you're thriving in it."

Casey shook her head, laughing. "I don't know if 'thriving' is the word I'd use."

"Well, give it a few more weeks," Ava said, settling back. "You'll be planning your island hop."

"My what?"

Ava shrugged. "Everyone does it. You live here long enough, and suddenly you're craving the next horizon. Some people go up the coast to little beach towns. Others head to Cuba for a weekend if they've got the passport hookup. If you're patient, you find someone sailing to Jamaica or Antigua."

"Antigua?" Casey echoed. "I *just* got here. I can't even afford another conch fritter right now, let alone a tropical getaway."

Tia grinned. "Don't worry. You don't have to *pay* for it."

Casey raised an eyebrow. "Excuse me?"

Ava leaned in, her voice a little lower. "People barter all the time here. You've got a skill, someone's got a boat—it's the island economy. I once painted murals for a guy in exchange for a round-trip charter to the Bahamas."

Tia nodded. "And I know someone who offered guitar lessons in exchange for three days crewing on a sailboat. Just depends what you're willing to trade."

Casey stared at them, stunned. "This is… a whole different world."

"That's kind of the point," Ava said, sipping her drink.

CHAPTER 7
ANTIGUA DAYDREAMIN'

The smell of espresso and cinnamon scones filled the air at MoonDog Café, wrapping around Casey like a familiar hug as she slid behind the counter and tied on her apron. Marley had barely lifted his head when she left that morning, clearly still recovering from his lizard-hunting escapade.

Tia was already on shift, humming something from last night's drag show while restocking the pastry case. Her hair was twisted up in a red bandana, and she wore earrings shaped like tiny pineapples.

"You survived the glitter hangover," she said without looking up.

"Barely," Casey replied, grabbing a fresh rag to wipe the counter. "I think Beau sprinkled fairy dust directly into my cocktail."

"Sweetheart, that's not glitter—it's island performance enhancement."

Casey laughed, but her thoughts were already drifting. She moved through the motions of morning prep, but she wasn't really *there*. Not entirely.

Tia noticed. Of course she did.

"What's up, Daydream Barbie?" she asked, leaning on the espresso machine like she had all the time in the world. "You've got that thousand-yard stare that says either you're falling in love or planning your escape."

Casey hesitated, then shrugged. "Maybe both."

"Ohhh," Tia said, instantly interested. "Spill."

Casey glanced around—no customers yet—and leaned a hip against the counter. "I couldn't stop thinking about what you and Ava said last night. About island hopping. Antigua. I went home, sat in the hammock with Marley, and just… stared at the sky thinking about it."

Tia tilted her head, curious.

Casey continued, "There was this one time back in Cincinnati—I'd just finished booking flights for my boss's honeymoon to Italy, and Booking.com sent me this promo for a solo trip to St. John's. Just me, a discounted plane ticket, and a beachfront cottage. I had it in my cart. Finger hovering over the *purchase* button."

"But…?" Tia prompted.

Casey let out a breath. "But I didn't do it. I told myself it was impulsive, irresponsible. I had too much going on at work. But the truth is, I was scared. I'd never gone anywhere alone. Never done something like that just because I *wanted* to."

Tia walked over and bumped her shoulder gently. "Maybe it's time you finish the booking."

Casey gave her a sideways look. "You think so?"

Tia shrugged. "Maybe it's a sign. You thought about Antigua before you even got here. Then it came up last night. You can't tell me that's just coincidence."

"But I *just* got here. Isn't it too soon to leave?"

"Casey," Tia said, gently but firmly, "Key West will be here when you get back. It's not like it's going anywhere. People come and go from here all the time. That's part of the rhythm."

Casey chewed her lip, weighing it.

"And besides," Tia added with a grin, "island life is all about indulgence. We live for it. Good food, good music, good drinks, a little sunshine, and an occasional reckless decision. If you don't indulge once in a while, what's the point of living here?"

Casey gave a soft laugh. "You make it sound so easy."

"Not easy. Just *worth it*."

The bell over the door jingled, and a couple walked in with their sandy flip-flops and sunburned shoulders, breaking the spell.

Tia winked. "Think about it. Maybe tonight after work, you go home, pour yourself something cold, and start looking at flights."

As Casey rang up a coconut cold brew and two croissants, her heart beat just a little faster. Antigua. It sounded ridiculous. Spontaneous. Unnecessary.

But it also sounded… possible.

The bright early afternoon light streamed through the windows of MoonDog Café. The café had a late breakfast rush, and things seemed to slow down when there would normally be a hectic lunch crowd. Luca went outside to smoke since there were no orders to prepare. Casey wiped down the counter, lost in the rhythm of maintenance tasks, when a familiar voice broke through the quiet.

"Tell me you don't have plans tonight."

She looked up to see Jake leaning lazily against the counter, his signature grin firmly in place. His hair was still damp from the ocean, his skin bronzed by the sun; there was just something undeniably easy about the way he existed in the world.

"What if I do?" she replied.

Jake tilted his head, mock-serious. "Then cancel them. Because you're coming to the beach."

She raised an eyebrow. "The beach?"

Jake slid onto a stool, resting his arms on the counter. "Bonfire. A little music. A little dancing. Maybe some questionable decisions." His grin widened. "Basically, a perfect night."

Casey let out a laugh, shaking her head. "That sounds like trouble."

Jake leaned in slightly. "Good trouble."

Before Casey could reply, Tia—who had been eavesdropping from the back—appeared at her side, drying a mug with exaggerated slowness.

"Oh, she's going."

Casey shot Tia a look. "I haven't agreed to anything."

Jake spread his hands. "I mean, you're in Key West now, baby. Might as well live a little."

Casey hesitated. Part of her knew exactly what this was—Jake's way of pulling her closer, keeping her in his orbit. And maybe… she wanted to be there. Maybe she wanted to let herself enjoy this, to not overthink it for once.

"Babe, these bonfire parties are so fun. And besides, once you've been to one of these, I can give you an official blessing to go island hopping, so long as you promise to return to me."

"Island hopping?" Jake jumped in, inquisitively. "Leaving so soon?"

Jake tapped the counter with his fingers. "Where were you thinking? Cuba? Bahamas? Or are you going full-on Hemingway and sailing off to Antigua to find yourself?"

Before Casey could answer, Tia scoffed. "I don't think Hemingway did that."

Jake raised an eyebrow. "Did what?"

"Sail to Antigua to find himself," she said, sipping from her water bottle. "He mostly found himself drunk and problematic."

Casey snorted. "Honestly, that tracks."

Jake chuckled. "Fair. But you get what I mean."

"Sure," Tia said. "But maybe let's not romanticize self-destruction as a travel plan."

Jake held his hands up in surrender. "Okay, okay. No

Hemingway comparisons. You're just Casey. Contemplating some well-earned island indulgence."

Casey smiled faintly. "Exactly."

Jake studied her for a beat. "Well, before you set sail anywhere, how about one more night of being right here?"

Casey sighed a comically dramatic sigh. "Fine. But if this turns into some kind of ridiculous swimming competition or an impromptu drinking contest, I'm out."

Jake winked. "No promises."

Casey wanted to roll her eyes, but part of her wished she could be that reckless or that spontaneous. Jake leaned in slightly, his voice dropping just enough to make it feel like they were in on something together.

"We could just grab a boat, you know. Make a run for it."

Casey laughed, shaking her head. "You're unbelievable."

But for just a moment, she let herself imagine it.

Tia had clocked out at three on the dot, blowing Casey a kiss and promising to "pre-game the bonfire with outfit changes and existential questions." Jake had left shortly after, teasing Casey on his way out that she better not bail or he'd come to steal Marley because he's "a dog who knows how to party."

Now, with only thirty minutes left in her shift and no real customers needing much, Casey moved through the closeout rhythm in her head—restock napkins, wipe the menu boards, check the pastry case inventory. She wasn't technically responsible for the changeover, but Marco, the actual closer, was already fifteen minutes late and couldn't be counted on to make sure things were ready for the morning.

She glanced at the door, half-expecting him to saunter in with some half-hearted apology and a sunburn. But instead, the bell jingled and a very different kind of regular walked in.

Phillip.

Casey straightened automatically, brushing her hands down the front of her apron. She hadn't seen or spoken to him since that night at the docks.

He stepped inside with his usual unhurried elegance, a paperback tucked in one hand, his sunglasses in the other. Today he wore a slate gray linen shirt, unbuttoned at the collar, sleeves casually rolled. He met her eyes and gave the faintest nod. "Afternoon."

"Hey," she said, trying to sound casual. "You're lucky. Marco's late again. I was about to lock the doors and flee."

Phillip smiled faintly, stepping up to the counter. "Can't imagine you're much of a flight risk."

"You're right," Casey admitted. "Des would kill me if I closed early."

They both laughed. Casey found herself a little relieved he hadn't shown up when Jake was still there. The attention was amusing, but she wasn't sure she could take the weird tension between them—over her?—while she was at work.

"So, uh, espresso?" Casey asked. *Why did he make her so nervous?*

"Please," he responded simply. Before she could start making it, the door jingled again. Marco finally strolled in, a pair of crooked sunglasses on his head and a smoothie in hand.

"Hey, sorry, traffic was nuts," he said, not sounding remotely sorry.

"Traffic in Key West," Casey said dryly. "That sounds fake."

Marco gave her finger guns. "You got me. I overslept. Again."

"Great. Well, you're just in time to make Phillip his espresso."

"Aren't there other customers that need serving?" Marco retorted.

"Both of those tables over there have been cashed out for hours, Marco. They're just chillin. So if you want any tips at all, make Phillip his espresso. And actually, while you're at it, make me an iced latte too. Add vanilla."

"You don't even pay for drinks. You work here."

"I will still tip you, dude. Just make the damn drinks," Casey said, rolling her eyes.

Marco scoffed as he moved behind the counter, slamming the fridge door louder than necessary as he pulled out the milk.

Casey muttered under her breath, "I honestly don't know how you still have this job."

Marco froze mid-pour. "Excuse me?"

Casey blinked, surprised he'd even heard her. "I said I don't know how you still have this job. You're late half the time, rude the other half, and you act like doing anything remotely in your job description is a personal attack."

Marco turned sharply, jaw clenched. "You know, just because you're new here and Des likes you doesn't mean you get to talk down to me."

"I wasn't talking down," Casey said, lifting her hands. "I was stating a fact. You were late. Again."

Marco stepped toward her, too close for comfort, his voice rising just a notch. "Maybe if you weren't always trying to be Employee of the Month, people wouldn't feel the need to walk on eggshells around you."

"I don't even think we *have* an Employee of the Month board, Marco."

"Then maybe they should make one—put your smug face on it so you can finally shut up—"

"That's enough." Phillip's voice cut through the café like a knife.

Marco paused, turning slowly toward him. "Sorry, what?"

Phillip didn't raise his voice. He didn't have to. There was a sharpness in his tone that made even the overhead fans seem to still. His expression was calm, but there was no mistaking the tension in his jaw, the controlled way he set down his espresso cup as if to keep from shattering it.

"I said that's enough," Phillip repeated. "You're embarrassing yourself."

Marco opened his mouth to argue, but Phillip continued, standing up from the counter, not threatening—just *unflinching*. "You're late, you're loud, and you're clearly under the impression that bullying someone who's doing their job better than you will somehow make you feel less small. It won't."

Marco looked between the two of them, scoffed again, and muttered, "Whatever. Do you want your drink or not?"

"No, I'm good," Casey replied curtly before hastily undoing her apron, tossing it behind the counter, and heading for the exit. Phillip threw a ten dollar bill on the counter and followed. He didn't speak until they were outside and up the street toward

"Are you alright?"

Casey swallowed, heart racing a little—not from fear, but from the unexpected rush of being *defended*. No one had stepped in like that for her in… well, maybe ever.

"Yeah," she said quietly. "I'm fine. That was—uh. Wow."

Phillip gave the smallest of shrugs. "He was out of line."

"And you were very… composed."

"Trust me," he said. "That was the restrained version."

She smiled at that, as if none of it had rattled him. But Casey was rattled—in a good way. The way he had stepped in, not to dominate or escalate, but to interrupt something unfair with calm authority—it was incredibly sexy.

"You didn't have to do that," she said.

Phillip met her eyes. "I know."

"I should get home. I'm supposed to meet Tia and some other friends at a bonfire tonight," Casey said, deliberately leaving Jake's name out of it.

"Allow me to walk you home."

"Oh, uh, sure."

They fell into step easily. They walked in comfortable silence for a moment, the late afternoon golden hour casting a soft glow over the cracked sidewalks and pastel-painted porches. When they reached Angela street, Casey turned right and nodded to Phillip.

"I'm just down here."

"You're in a good spot," Phillip said, nodding toward the direction they were heading. "A few blocks from work, couple more from the Green Parrot. That's about as Key West as it gets."

Casey chuckled. "Yeah, it's pretty ideal. Honestly, I wasn't even that picky—I just wanted somewhere with a working fridge and space for Marley. But Betty hooked me up."

Phillip gave a small smile. "Betty doesn't rent to just anyone. She's well-connected… and very particular about who she likes."

"Yeah?" Casey looked over at him, curious.

He nodded. "If she let you into her space, that says a lot."

Casey wasn't sure what to say to that. Something warm flickered in her chest—recognition, maybe, or the simple relief of feeling seen.

"She's been kind," Casey said after a beat. "Like, suspiciously kind. I'm still not convinced she isn't a retired fairy godmother."

"Oh, she is. But with sharper elbows."

They shared a laugh as they turned past a conch house with peeling paint and a hand-painted *BE NICE OR LEAVE* sign on the porch.

"What about you?" Casey asked. "Where do you live?"

"Stock Island," Phillip said. "Behind one of the older marinas."

Casey arched a brow. "That's kind of far, isn't it?"

He shrugged. "A couple miles. Not bad. Walkable if you've had the right amount of rum."

She snorted. "So… like a drunk pilgrimage?"

"Exactly. But it's shorter on my bike—only fifteen-twenty minutes."

"I never pictured you as an avid cyclist," Casey laughed.

"My motor bike," Phillip corrected himself, laughing.

She smiled. "I haven't made it over to Stock Island yet."

"It's rougher around the edges compared to the beautiful, touristy Duval," he said. "But there's good food. Good fishing. Fewer people trying to sell you souvenirs."

"I'm sold already."

At the sound of Casey's voice, a bark echoed from the other side of her fence. Casey grinned. They reached her gate, the low white fence already rusted a little at the hinges. Marley was practically bouncing behind it, tail wagging furiously.

"Well," she said, reaching for the latch, "this is me."

Phillip nodded, taking a small step back. "You heading straight to your bonfire?"

"Yeah. Going to eat something, change into something less… espresso-scented. Then I'm meeting Tia and the others."

"You'll fit in," he said. "Bonfires are all smoke and overstated metaphors."

"That's what I'm afraid of."

They shared a smile. For a moment, it was just them—and the quiet knowledge that something had shifted since they started walking.

"Thanks for walking me," she said.

"Anytime."

He didn't linger. Just gave her a parting nod and turned, heading back up Angela Street with unhurried confidence.

Casey let herself into the yard, greeted by Marley's overjoyed barking and spinning.

"Okay, okay," she murmured, crouching to ruffle his ears. "I know, you missed me. But wait 'til I tell you who walked me home."

Marley licked her chin in response.

She stood slowly, glancing once more toward the street corner where Phillip had disappeared. She briefly wondered if she should've invited him—if he was waiting for an invitation by asking if she was heading over there. But she quickly realized that would be absurd. Jake literally invited her to the bonfire. She couldn't invite Phillip. What was she thinking?

And what *was* she thinking? Wasn't she just telling herself she shouldn't be in the middle of those two? And what was she doing now? Putting herself exactly in the middle of those two!

Casey scolded herself while she showered. Restaurant sweat was a different kind of sweat, and she always needed to wash her hair after a shift at the cafe. She was deep in her thoughts about all the ways she was screwing up this fresh start already when she heard her screen door creak open and slam shut. It was a small bungalow. The bathroom was right off the main room—everything was basically one big room, honestly. But there was a door for the bathroom. And that door was the one thing that stood between whoever just entered her home and her in the shower.

"Hey babe! It's me!"

Casey was immediately relieved. "My god, Tia. You scared the shit out of me! I didn't know you were coming over."

"I told you I'd be over pre-game! And I'm here!"

"It's like not even seven yet!"

"Island time babe. It's always party time."

Casey rolled her eyes, still rinsing conditioner from her hair. "Give me ten minutes!"

"I'll pour drinks!" Tia called back. "Don't worry, I brought the good stuff."

That could mean anything, Casey thought as she turned off the water and stepped out onto the mat. Rum, probably. Or that pink wine in a can she swore by. Either way, Casey wasn't going to complain. Her brain had been spiraling all afternoon and she needed something to take the edge off.

When she finally stepped out—wrapped in a towel, hair dripping—Tia was barefoot on the floor, legs crossed in front of Casey's low coffee table, already halfway through mixing a drink in a repurposed jam jar.

"I made you a rum spritz," she said cheerfully. "Also I brought these." She held up a small plastic bag filled with something suspiciously gummy.

Casey narrowed her eyes. "What are *those*?"

"Shark-shaped edibles," Tia said. "I got them from Rory's roommate. But don't worry. They're chill."

"I already got into a fight with Marco at work. I don't need to be high *and* emotionally compromised."

Tia laughed and patted the floor beside her. "Then just drink. Sit. Let's get you into a better headspace. Marco's an asshole anyway."

Casey plopped down next to her, tugging her towel tighter around herself. "I'm having a hard time not feeling like I'm already screwing this all up."

"Screwing what up?"

"This. Key West. The reset. I came here to escape the pressure, and somehow I'm tangled in some ridiculous love triangle, Marley is trying to fight the island wildlife, I almost punched Marco in the face, and now there's a bonfire party I'm half-excited, half-dreading."

Tia took a slow sip of her own drink. "First of all, welcome to the island. Second of all—this is what it's supposed to feel like."

"Like chaos?"

"Like *life*." Tia leaned back on her elbows. "No one moves to Key West for structure. We're here because we're either running from something, running to something, or trying to pretend we're not doing either."

Casey let that sit for a moment. "What were you running from?"

Tia smiled softly. "A girl I thought I had to be. Spoiler alert—she was exhausting."

Casey took a sip of her drink. It was sweet, bright, and definitely stronger than she expected. "So I should just lean in?"

Tia clinked her jar against Casey's. "You're not screwing anything up. You're just in the messy middle. Trust me. The good stuff always happens there."

Casey exhaled. She didn't totally believe it—but she *wanted* to.

"Now go put on something cute and slightly irresponsible," Tia said. "We're about to dance around a bonfire and say things we'll regret tomorrow."

Casey stood. "Cute and irresponsible. Got it."

Tia grinned. "And maybe wear that halter top. You know, in case *someone* shows up."

Casey gave her a sharp look.

"I didn't say who."

Casey groaned, disappearing into her tiny bathroom to change. Outside, the sun was dipping lower behind the palms. Inside, the air buzzed with possibility, drinks, and just the right amount of chaos. Tonight was going to be something.

CHAPTER 8
CLOSE ENCOUNTERS

When Casey and Tia arrived, the bonfire already blazed high, sending golden embers into the night sky as waves lapped gently against the shore. The smell of salt, driftwood smoke, and rum filled the air, as the sound of laughter, clinking bottles, and distant guitar strumming filled Casey's ears.

Casey felt the warmth of it all—the glow of the flames, the press of people, the energy of a Key West night unfolding around her. And at the center of it, like always, was Jake.

He was perched on an overturned crate, his guitar resting on his knee as he played something low and slow, a song Casey didn't recognize. His guitar was a light grain, almost sand-colored, with a tortiseshell pickguard.

Tia put a drink in Casey's hand, as she watched Jake play from a few feet away, trying to soak in the moment. She had spent so long living in her head, overthinking everything—but right now, here, under the wide-open sky, it felt easy.

And Jake? Jake made everything feel even easier. He finished the song and leaned slightly to see around other folks at the fire, his eyes landing on Casey.

"There you are." Jake's voice cut through the chatter and laughter, drawing Casey's attention as he stood and made his way toward her.

"Here I am."

He didn't stop walking until he was right in front of her, the bonfire flickering behind him.

"You having fun yet?" he asked, his voice warm, teasing.

Casey tilted her head. "I don't know. Is this a test?"

Jake chuckled, taking the drink from her hand and stealing a sip like it was second nature. Someone queued up a playlist and connected to a bluetooth speaker. Zac Brown Band started playing.

"It's only a test if you're failing," he quipped.

Casey rolled her eyes, reaching to snatch her drink back, but Jake pulled it just out of reach, grinning as she stepped closer. The space between them shrank, and suddenly, the playful teasing didn't feel so playful anymore. The firelight cast shadows over his face, highlighting the angles of his jaw, the easy curve of his mouth.

Casey wondered if she had been underestimating him. If maybe Jake wasn't just fun, or just charming. If maybe, underneath it all, there was something real waiting to be acknowledged. His normal grin softened, and his voice dropped just enough to make the air between them feel heavier.

"Dance with me."

It wasn't a question.

The music wasn't loud, and no one else was dancing, but Jake didn't seem to care. He took her hand, tugging her forward, and Casey let him. They moved together.

"How are you barefoot on these rocks?" Casey asked Jake.

"After a while, they just become a part of me."

Casey had no idea what that meant, but part of Jake's charm was that he didn't always make sense. But damn it if that Southern surfer boy twang didn't get her.

Jake's hands found her waist—not forceful, but steady. And before she could overthink what they were doing, before she could question whether she should, he leaned in.

The kiss wasn't rushed or forced. It was slow—the kind of kiss that unfolded like a slow melody with no hurry to reach the final note. The taste of salt and rum, the sound of the ocean just beyond them, the way his hands tightened slightly on her waist like he was afraid she'd pull away.

Casey let herself sink into it and believe that maybe this was exactly what she wanted. But just as quickly as it began, the kiss ended.

Jake pulled back a few inches, his forehead resting against hers, the firelight dancing in the space between them.

"That wasn't so bad, was it?" he murmured.

Casey opened her eyes. "You're definitely trouble."

He smirked. "Only the good kind."

She didn't answer. Instead, she looked past his shoulder

toward the shoreline, where the tide was starting to creep in closer. The moment was… nice. More than nice. But it also left her feeling strangely exposed—like the kiss had peeled back a layer she wasn't sure she'd meant to reveal.

Jake stepped back, just enough to break the spell but not far enough to let her go completely. "Come on," he said. "There's a cooler somewhere with your name on it."

She followed him back toward the fire, the music picking up into something a little more upbeat—Chris Stapleton or maybe Morgan Wade, she couldn't tell. People were gathered in small clusters now, laughing, drinking, passing around bottles and beach snacks. Someone had rigged up a string of twinkle lights along a driftwood post, and the effect was… cozy. Unexpectedly so.

Tia reappeared at Casey's side with a half-empty seltzer in one hand and a gummy shark in the other.

"Don't even say it," Tia said, popping the gummy into her mouth. "I saw."

"Saw what?"

"You know *what.*"

Casey laughed and took the seltzer from her, grateful for the way Tia always seemed to cut through any tension without making her explain herself.

They stood side by side, watching the flames crackle and pop, until Jake wandered off to join Rory and a few other locals clustered near the driftwood benches.

"Are you okay?" Tia asked gently, shifting her weight toward Casey without fully turning.

"I think so," Casey replied. "I mean, I didn't expect that. Any of it."

"Do you want it to happen again?"

Casey didn't answer right away. She took a long sip from the can, letting the bubbles distract her. "It felt good. But I don't know if that means it *should* happen again."

Tia nodded. "Welcome to island dating. It's all vibes until there's consequences."

Casey let out a laugh, short but real.

Just then, movement caught her eye.

Down the beach, past the circle of firelight, someone stood near the water—half-silhouetted by the moonlight, a little too still to be casual. She squinted.

No. It wasn't Phillip.

It was someone else. A guy with dreadlocks who looked vaguely familiar. She recognized him from MoonDog, maybe—one of the regulars who rarely spoke but always tipped in cash. He wasn't looking at her. He was just staring at the ocean like it might tell him something if he waited long enough.

Casey blinked and looked away. She wasn't sure why, but suddenly, she felt unsteady again.

Jake's laugh floated across the sand, familiar and easy, and Casey turned to find him mid-story, animated hands and all.

Tia touched her elbow lightly. "Wanna walk?"

Casey nodded.

They wandered toward the edge of the firelight, letting the noise fade behind them.

"You're not falling too hard, are you?" Tia asked.

Casey shrugged. "I don't think so. I mean… maybe a little. It's just that he makes things feel easy. I haven't felt easy in a long time."

"And you deserve easy," Tia said. "Just don't mistake easy for *right*."

Casey glanced sideways. "You always this wise when you're mildly buzzed?"

"Only when it counts."

They laughed together, and the sound felt like a tether—something to hold onto. Something grounding.

Later, back at the bonfire, Jake found Casey again, this time with two popsicles—neon red and electric blue, already starting to melt in the heat.

"Pick your poison," he said, holding them up like a peace offering.

Casey raised a brow. "Are you trying to bribe me into liking you more with frozen sugar?"

Jake gave her a mock-wounded look. "I don't have to bribe you. I'm just sweetening the deal."

She rolled her eyes, but took the blue one. "Thanks. It's like eighty degrees and somehow still getting hotter."

"That's just you," Jake said with a wink, then took a

bite of his own popsicle. They walked a little closer to the water this time, the waves tickling their toes as they wandered just out of earshot from the rest of the group.

Jake asked her about northern winters, what it was like growing up so far from the ocean, if she thought she would eventually miss it. She surprised herself by how easy it was to talk to him. And how often she caught herself laughing.

"Dare you to get in," Jake said, nodding toward the water.

Casey looked down at her dress. "I'm not wearing a swimsuit."

Jake shrugged, already tugging his shirt off. "Neither am I. It's dark. The ocean doesn't judge."

She hesitated, but only for a moment. Then, she peeled off her dress, revealing a bralette and shorts underneath. Jake gave a low whistle, but respectfully kept his distance.

They ran into the surf, the warm water crashing against them in waves that felt more like welcome than force. Casey shrieked as a wave hit, laughing as Jake dove under and came up beside her, splashing her in return.

She splashed him back, and they stood there, laughing in the surf, their clothes clinging to them, the fire glowing behind them on the shore. It felt like a memory already.

Then Jake swam a little further out and floated on his back, eyes closed. "This is it," he said. "The whole reason I live here."

Casey treaded water beside him. "Because of night-time swimming?"

"Because everything slows down here. The world's a mess, but here—when the water's warm, the music's soft, and the sky's clear—you get a break from all of it."

She let herself float beside him, staring up at the stars. "You're not what I expected."

He cracked one eye open. "What were you expecting?"

"Something louder."

Jake chuckled. "I can be loud. But only when I want to be heard."

They floated in silence a little longer, letting the night wrap around them.

Eventually, Jake drifted closer, and their hands brushed beneath the surface. Not deliberate. Not quite accidental either.

Casey didn't move away. Jake turned to face her, treading water so they were chest-to-chest.

"You ever think about staying?" he asked suddenly.

"In the water?" she teased.

"No. Here. Key West."

Casey blinked. She hadn't expected the question. "I don't know. Maybe. I came here to figure things out."

Jake studied her face, the moonlight soft on his features. "Well… I hope we're part of what you figure out."

She didn't respond with words. Instead, she let the moment linger, water rocking them gently in tandem. The fire was a distant flicker now, and the music from the speaker sounded fuzzy and far away.

Jake reached out and gently pushed a wet strand of hair off her face. His touch wasn't urgent. It was soft, like he was afraid she might disappear with the tide.

"You always this charming in the water?" she asked, half-smiling.

He smirked. "Only when the moon's watching. Makes me look better."

Casey laughed, but her voice caught slightly at the end. Something about this—about him—was getting under her skin.

From up the beach, a voice rang out: "S'mores time! Come on, lovebirds!"

Jake groaned theatrically. "And just when I was about to tell you all my secrets."

Casey snorted. "Maybe next swim."

They swam back toward the shore, their soaked clothes heavy as they waded in. Jake grabbed his shirt from the sand, wringing it out while Casey did the same with her dress.

As they approached the firelight, a chorus of whistles and laughter erupted.

"Look who took a moonlight dip!" someone called.

"Damn, Jake! She's still hanging out with you even after seeing you mostly naked?"

Jake bowed dramatically. "You're welcome, everyone."

Casey rolled her eyes, cheeks flushed, but she was laughing. Jake handed her a towel someone tossed over, and they settled near the fire again, steam rising faintly from their drying clothes as they took seats close enough to warm up and maybe a little too close for comfort.

But that was the whole point, wasn't it?

It was later now. The fire had died down some, and the crowd had thinned. Jake had switched from beer to rum, and Casey could tell—his jokes got louder, his touches lingered longer, and the easy charm started curdling into something else. He leaned too far into her when he laughed, nearly spilling his drink once, and fumbled his way through half-finished stories. When he stood, he swayed. When he sat, he slouched until his elbow knocked into her knee. He smelled like salt and sugar and too much Bacardi.

They were seated on a log near the fire when Jake slung an arm around her and slurred, "So, you and Phillip, huh? What's the deal there? He give you a free tattoo or just the sad puppy eyes?"

Casey stiffened, the warmth of the fire suddenly feeling too hot. "What?"

Jake laughed, but it was the wrong kind of laugh—sharp, mean-edged. "I mean, the guy's all broody and mysterious. You like that? Is that your type? Or is he just the backup plan if Key West gets boring?"

"Jake," Casey said, her voice low. "You're drunk."

"I'm honest," he countered. "Maybe more honest than usual."

She stood up, brushing sand from her damp clothes. "No, you're just being a jerk."

Jake raised his hands in mock surrender. "Whoa. Sorry I touched a nerve. Guess I shouldn't question your deep connection with Mister Intensity."

"You don't get to talk about him like that," she snapped.

Jake blinked at her, the alcohol making his expression hard to read. "So there is something going on."

Casey didn't answer. She just turned and walked away, the sound of the fire cracking behind her.

Casey walked and walked and walked, grateful her undergarments had almost completely dried before she left. She found herself walking straight toward Duval. She didn't need to go up Duval to get home. In fact, it would be faster not to. She wandered aimlessly for a while, cutting past bars she didn't want to enter and clubs where the music pulsed with an energy that grated on her nerves. Neon signs bled pink and blue into the damp sidewalk, puddles shimmering like oil slicks under the glow. A couple stumbled out of a bar laughing, arms wrapped tightly around each other, carefree and dizzy with rum and flirtation. Casey tightened her jaw.

She kicked at a loose shell on the curb, watching it skitter and bounce toward the gutter. Jake's voice echoed in her head—"*So, you and Phillip, huh?*"—and a flush of embarrassment surged under her skin. Why had he said that? Why had he ruined a perfectly good night with one petty, territorial jab? Was he that insecure? Or was she that naïve?

She kept looping the block, pacing up and down the street, telling herself she needed more time to cool off, but she knew she was lying to herself. It was two in the morning and she was hoping beyond hope Phillip was pulling a late-night session. He told her once he worked better at night, so maybe he'd be there.

When she reached the studio, the lights were still on. She peered in the window, looking past the art she had been captivated by on her first time by the studio. And through the window, she saw him. Phillip.

He was sitting at his work desk, bent over a large sketch pad, a pencil moving steadily across the paper. His brows were furrowed in concentration, his hand gloved, the other supporting the edge of the paper as he refined a floral mandala along the curve of an imagined shoulder blade. A few reference photos and previous sketches were scattered on the table beside him, along with a half-drunk iced coffee sweating onto a napkin.

Casey hesitated for half a second.

Then, before she could think better of it, she stepped inside.

The inside of Southernmost Tattoo was nothing like its neighboring beach bars or tourist shops that lined Duval. It was quieter, still, personal. The walls were covered in bold sketches, delicate linework, intricate full-sleeve designs. The scent of ink and antiseptic lingered in the air, mixing with the faintest trace of salt from the open door. Phillip glanced up from where he was wiping down his station, his expression cool, but definitely surprised.

"Casey."

She wasn't sure if she liked the way he said her name.

Or maybe she liked it too much.

"Hey," she said, moving closer to the counter. "Didn't mean to interrupt."

Phillip arched an eyebrow but didn't comment. "You're out late."

Casey shrugged. "Could say the same to you."

He wiped his hands clean with a towel before tossing it onto the counter.

"I work late," he said matter-of-factly.

Casey leaned against the glass display case, scanning the sketches inside—intricate florals, delicate script, a compass drawn with incredible detail.

"I didn't expect to see you tonight. Weren't you at a bonfire party?"

"I left," she said. "Needed some air. Ended up walking this way."

He nodded once, like that made perfect sense. "Rough night?"

She hesitated, then walked farther inside, letting the door close behind her. "Something like that."

"You want to talk about it?"

Casey glanced at the sketch. "I don't want to interrupt."

Phillip followed her gaze, then closed the sketchbook gently. "It'll keep. It's just a mock-up for a hibiscus sleeve—client comes in tomorrow night. I've got time."

Casey lowered herself onto the edge of a low leather bench. The shop smelled faintly of antiseptic, ink, and something citrusy—clean but lived-in. Comfortable.

"I don't know what I want to say," she admitted.

"You don't have to say anything. You can just sit."

So she did.

And for a long moment, they sat in silence. The only sound was the gentle hum of the air conditioning and the faint bass of music from the street outside.

Then Casey exhaled slowly. "Do you ever feel like you're not sure what version of yourself you're supposed to be?"

Phillip turned his body slightly to face her. "All the time."

She looked up, eyes meeting his. "How do you deal with it?"

"I try to be the version that feels the least like pretending."

Casey smiled faintly. "That's harder than it sounds."

Phillip gave a small nod. "Yeah. But the more you practice, the more real it becomes."

She let that sink in, the quiet weight of his words settling somewhere deep.

"Thanks," she said finally.

He didn't ask what for. He just nodded again and re-opened the sketchbook, his pencil resting lightly in his fingers but not moving yet.

"You're always welcome here, you know," he said. "Even when you're not sure why you showed up."

Casey let herself lean back against the wall, eyes on the sketch he was drawing. The hibiscus design was intricate, but soft. Gentle curves met deliberate lines, like it was caught between blooming and unraveling. There was something soothing about the way Phillip worked—measured, precise, but with a looseness that suggested instinct more than calculation.

Her gaze drifted to the wall behind him. There, framed in glass, was a piece she hadn't noticed before. It was older, faded slightly. Not the bold blacks and grayscale of newer designs, but something a little less polished—an elaborate compass rose, almost filigree in detail, surrounded by faint script in French. It looked more like something from an antique map than a tattoo design.

Phillip followed her line of sight. "That one's old."

"Did you draw it?" Casey asked, tilting her head.

He nodded. "Years ago. One of the first pieces I did after I moved here. Not really a good tattoo design. Just pretty art, I think."

Her brows lifted. "It looks… different. Not just style-wise. It feels like it came from somewhere else."

Phillip set the pencil down again, the corner of his mouth quivered, like he was debating how much to say.

"It came from France," he said matter-of-factly.

"And how did it get here," Casey asked, knowing she wasn't really asking about the drawing.

"I left France looking for adventure," he said finally, standing with his hands in his pockets, posture effortlessly composed. "A friend told me to come to Key West. Said I'd like it here."

She waited, sensing there was more.

"He left a year later," Phillip added with a faint chuckle, dry but not bitter. "I stayed."

Casey studied him. The cool gray T-shirt stretched across his shoulders, the half-finished sketch beside him, the quiet steadiness in the way he watched her. "Why?"

His jaw shifted slightly, like the question wasn't new but still didn't have an easy answer. "Because it suits me."

She tilted her head. "You don't exactly scream 'beach bum.'"

That ghost of a smile flickered again. "No. But I like it here. The ocean, the space, the way time moves differently. It keeps you untethered, and that's… something I needed."

Casey's eyes drifted back to the compass rose. "So that's what the compass is for?"

Phillip nodded. "To remind me I didn't need to go back. That I wasn't lost—I just needed a new direction."

She let the words sink in. There was something vulnerable in the way he said them, even if his tone remained even. Like maybe he didn't say things like that out loud very often.

"You always this poetic at midnight?" she asked softly.

"It's way past midnight," Phillip said.

"Oh my gosh. I should get home for Marley," Casey suddenly realized.

"I'll walk you over there. I'm parked not far from there anyway."

Phillip gathered his things, cleaned up his station, and turned out the lights. Locking the door behind them, he and Casey walked the half block to Angela Street. Her place was only another half block down. Phillip was right the first time he walked her home. She really did luck out on location.

When they neared the house, they saw Betty on the front porch. She sat in her usual spot, a book in one hand and a mug of something steaming in the other—even in the Keys, some people drank tea at night like it was a sacred ritual. A small lamp glowed beside her, casting soft yellow light across her weathered face and white braid.

"Well, well," Betty called out as they approached, setting her book down on her lap. "Didn't think I'd see you out this late, Miss Casey."

Casey smiled sheepishly. "Hey, Betty. Sorry if we woke you."

Betty snorted. "Please. Marley's the one who woke me, whining at the door like you'd run off and joined the circus. Again."

Casey winced. "Shoot. I didn't mean to be gone this long."

"I figured you were fine when I saw who you were with," Betty said, tipping her head toward Phillip with a look that was half-appraisal, half-approval.

Casey glanced at Phillip, who gave a polite nod.

"Betty," he greeted.

"Hmph," she said, sipping her tea and then looking at Casey. "He's alright, you know," nodding toward Phillip, as if he wasn't right in front of her. "Quiet type. Thoughtful. Picky about your work and your company. Reminds me of my second husband. He was a keeper too."

Casey blinked. "You've had more than one?"

Betty grinned. "Only two. The first one was forgettable. The second one tattooed a wild orchid on my thigh when I was forty-two and never let me forget how good it looked."

Phillip raised his brows, clearly amused, but respectful. "He sounds memorable."

"He was. So you take care of this one," she said, looking at Phillip but speaking to Casey. "She's got good instincts. Even if she sometimes ignores them."

Casey laughed nervously. "Thanks, Betty. I'll take it from here."

Betty waved them off, picking her book back up. "Night, you two."

They walked the rest of the way to Casey's door in silence until she turned to face Phillip on her little porch.

"Thanks for walking me."

"Anytime," he said. Then added, "Really."

Casey nodded, suddenly hyper-aware of how close they were, of the quiet hum between them.

"Good night, Phillip."

He hesitated for just a beat—like he might say more—but then gave her a slight, knowing smile.

"Good night, Casey."

She stepped inside and closed the door behind her, leaning her back against it as Marley immediately padded up and pressed into her legs. She ran a hand through his fur, her thoughts tangled and buzzing.

She wasn't sure what she expected tonight to be. But it wasn't this.

CHAPTER 9
FOR ART'S SAKE

The porch swing creaked softly beneath Casey as she rocked forward and back, a half-drunk mug of coffee balanced on the armrest beside her. Marley was curled up at her feet, head resting on her paws, the tip of his tail twitching every now and then like he was dreaming about chasing lizards. The late morning sun filtered through the fronds of the palm tree by the front steps, casting shifting shadows across the porch floor. It was hot, already humid, and the world felt slow.

She wasn't hungover, not exactly. But something in her felt tender, as if her skin had thinned overnight. Maybe it was the bonfire. The kiss. The fight. The walk home. Or the way Phillip's voice had sounded in the stillness of the tattoo shop—measured, quiet, like he was telling her something without fully saying it.

Casey ran a hand through her hair and exhaled. She didn't have to work today. Tia was on shift at Moon-Dog, and Casey wasn't scheduled until tomorrow. She should've been glad to have the day off, to sleep in, to laze around. But instead, she felt itchy in her skin—restless, like something was waiting for her just outside the edge of her routine.

There was a pile of laundry somewhere inside that needed folding. Emails she should probably answer—it turns out her old job did notice and sent her severance papers to her personal email; did she really need papers? She knew she left. There were a dozen other things she could be doing besides that. But the idea of doing any of them made her stomach twist with low-key dread.

Marley let out a huff, as if echoing her thoughts.

Casey shifted, reaching to scratch behind his ears. "You ever get the feeling you're wasting something?" she murmured. "Time, maybe. Or a perfectly good day."

Marley gave no response, just blinked slowly at her and stretched a paw.

Her gaze drifted to the porch railing. Something colorful was wedged between the slats—a folded piece of paper fluttering in the breeze. She leaned forward, plucked it free, and unfolded it. It was a flyer for the street art market by Mallory Square. She recognized Ava's hand-drawn lettering immediately—loopy and uneven in a way that somehow made it feel more trustworthy.

Pop-up Creators' Market: Handmade Goods, Art, and Street Performers – Noon til Sunset, Seawall Row.

Casey read the words twice, then flipped the flyer over to find a tiny doodle Ava had drawn on the back: a mermaid with sunglasses, holding a paintbrush like a sword.

She smiled in spite of herself.

There were no plans. No pressure. But her fingers itched a little, and her sketchbook was still sitting on the counter inside, right where she'd left it after the last time she doodled half a page of palm fronds and then abandoned it.

She didn't have to make a thing of it. She didn't even have to stay long. But suddenly, the thought of sitting in Ava's orbit—watching tourists bumble by and letting her pencil move for no one but herself—sounded better than the alternative.

Casey reached behind her and pushed the swing to a stop. Marley stood as if he'd sensed her decision before she made it.

"I'm not promising anything," she told him, already heading inside for her sketchbook and a bottle of water. "But we're going out."

Mallory Square was already humming when Casey arrived. Vendors lined the seawall, their tables bursting with handmade jewelry, hand-painted coconuts, pressed t-shirts, carved fish, resin keychains, and signs declaring things like *Don't Worry Beach Happy* and *My Therapist Lives in the Ocean.* Musicians played island covers under umbrellas. A guy on stilts wobbled past juggling pineapples. A street poet with a manual typewriter shouted sonnets into the breeze.

And in the middle of it all, Ava.

She sat behind a low table covered in mismatched frames and bright watercolor prints, a wide-brimmed straw hat barely containing her curls. Her sunglasses were crooked, a paintbrush tucked behind one ear, and a portable fan clipped to her folding chair hummed like a dragonfly.

"Look what the tide dragged in," Ava called as Casey approached.

Casey grinned and leaned down to hug her. "Hey. I found your flyer."

"Oh, thank god. I put one on your porch because I figured you might be wallowing in your feelings or eating too much peanut butter straight from the jar."

"Rude."

"Accurate."

Casey pulled up an empty milk crate next to Ava and dropped her sketchbook into her lap.

"Not here to sell anything," she said. "Just… thought I'd draw."

Ava reached into her cooler and handed her a cold seltzer. "You don't need to sell to belong. Just sit, sketch, and people-watch. Honestly, it's the best way to spend a day."

Casey opened her sketchbook to a clean page and watched the flow of tourists. Some paused to admire the view, some moved with purpose toward the sunset pier, and some paused to look at the artists.

She started to draw. Slowly at first. A woman in a straw hat holding her toddler's hand. A tall man with a backpack who looked like he hadn't slept in a few days. A pair of teenage girls taking selfies by a seagull-ravaged popcorn stand. She didn't caricature them, not really—she didn't exaggerate their features or turn them into cartoons. She drew what she saw, but something more, too. She focused on expressions, on posture, on the way someone's shoulders tilted inward like a secret, or how their eyebrows furrowed even while they smiled.

Ava peered over her shoulder and let out a soft whistle. "Ooo I like what you've got going on. It's not like caricatures," she said. "Those are like… emotional portraits."

"I don't know," Casey shrugged. "They just come out that way."

"No, it's good," Ava said. "Better than good. You're not mocking people—you're seeing them. That's rare."

Casey looked down at the drawing she'd just finished—a middle-aged man sitting alone at the seawall, his hat pulled low, his hands clasped together like he was bracing for something. The sketch didn't make him look sad. Just… thoughtful. Real.

"It feels good," she admitted. "To just draw. No pressure. No rules."

"Exactly," Ava said, leaning back in her chair with a smug little nod. "Art for art's sake, baby. That's the dream."

The wind picked up a little, fluttering the corner of her sketchbook. Casey flipped the page and started again, her pencil moving faster now. She wasn't thinking about Jake or Phillip or the story she was supposed to be writing about her life. She was just… here. Sketching strangers. Letting the day stretch long and easy in front of her.

The sun was beginning to tip low in the sky, the edges of everything gilded in gold. The light made colors pop—Ava's paintings shimmered, the blue of the ocean looked like it had been freshly poured from a bottle, and the faces of tourists glowed with that dreamy, end-of-day warmth. It was the kind of light photographers chased. The kind of light that made everything feel important.

Casey was halfway through a sketch of a young couple slow-dancing to a steel drum band when she heard her name.

She didn't need to look up to know who it was.

"Casey!"

Jake's voice was unmistakable—laid-back, familiar, tinged with that casual drawl that made everything sound like a song lyric.

Casey glanced up anyway. There he was, in his usual uniform: sun-faded t-shirt, board shorts, and a grin that probably got him out of more trouble than it should. He held two drinks in his hands—plastic cups of something bright and boozy, lime wedges bobbing at the top.

"Brought you something," he said, walking up like he belonged there.

Casey blinked. "How'd you know where I was?"

"Ava told me you've been hanging with her today."

"Actually I told him not to interrupt you," Ava said dryly, not looking up from the watercolor she was touching up. "But he's got the self-restraint of a caffeinated raccoon."

Jake laughed and dropped down onto the milk crate beside Casey, way too close. "So this is what you do on your day off? Sit here and draw people? That's adorable."

Casey set her sketchbook down carefully and took the drink, but didn't sip it. "I wasn't really looking for company."

Jake didn't flinch. "Sure. But I was in the neighborhood, and it's not every day I catch you in your natural habitat." He glanced at her open pages. "These are really good. Like… legit good."

She raised an eyebrow. "Thanks. But again. I came here for some space."

Jake's grin faltered, just a fraction. "From me?"

Casey didn't answer. She didn't have to.

Ava, mercifully, chimed in. "Jake, why don't you go find Rory? I think they were setting up a fire juggler act near the end of the pier. Could use your help not catching on fire."

Jake hesitated. Then, with a theatrical sigh, he stood. "Alright, alright. I can take a hint. But hey, you free later? We could grab a drink or—"

"Not tonight," Casey said.

Jake nodded, a little too casual. "Cool. Another time."

And with that, he disappeared into the crowd, like driftwood caught by the tide.

Casey didn't move. Didn't speak. Just picked her pencil back up and started a new sketch.

This one didn't have a face yet. Just a posture. A kind of uneasy tilt. Like someone who didn't know how to take up space the right way anymore.

Ava didn't say anything until the lines started forming more confidently.

"You okay?"

Casey exhaled slowly. "Yeah. Just thinking."

Ava leaned over to peek. "You always draw what you can't say out loud?"

Casey gave a small smile. "Isn't that the point?"

The crowd at Mallory Square began to swell as sunset approached. Musicians played louder, children shrieked as they chased each other through the maze of vendors, and tourists began jostling for a spot with a view. The magic hour was near.

But Casey no longer noticed the ocean or the music. Her body was still there, sitting cross-legged on a woven blanket Ava had lent her, pencil in hand, sketchpad balanced on her knees—but her mind had drifted miles from the pier.

The space Jake left behind felt sticky, like salt clinging to skin. She hadn't expected him, and she hated how quickly his presence had clouded her clarity. Her hands had been steady all afternoon. Now they itched with something she couldn't name.

Ava packed up quietly beside her, giving her space. "I'm heading over to Hugo's before the rush hits. Want to come?"

Casey shook her head. "Think I'll hang here a little longer."

"You good?"

"I will be."

Ava studied her a beat longer, then nodded and left her to it.

Casey stared at the empty page in front of her. She didn't want to draw another couple. She didn't want to draw another whimsical face. Her fingers moved before she consciously told them to, tracing out a familiar jaw-line, a profile she hadn't realized she'd memorized.

Phillip.

His expression came together in fragments—a down-ward tilt of his eyes when he focused, the tension in his mouth when he was thinking, the gentle slope of his shoulders when he exhaled slowly, quietly, like he was trying not to disturb something delicate.

The sketch wasn't perfect, but it felt… right. Like the lines understood something about him that she hadn't quite found the words for. Not yet.

She added details slowly: the outline of his workbench behind him, the bend of his neck as he hovered over a sheet of paper, sketching something just out of frame. In her mind, he was drawing for someone else, but his posture—thoughtful, careful—still made her feel seen.

Her pencil stilled.

Last night, when he'd walked her home, Phillip hadn't pushed. He hadn't asked what had happened or why she'd shown up. He just let her be. She remembered his face as he said goodnight to her. God how she loved how he said her name. Was it the accent? His tone?

She looked down at the sketch and found she'd drawn him—his head turned slightly, as if looking back over his shoulder. Just like last night. Looking back. Not toward her. Just… back. Like he knew she was still watching him.

She closed the sketchbook, hugged it to her chest for a second, then stood and stretched. The sun was just touching the horizon, casting the water in fire.

Casey didn't stay to watch it.

She turned back toward home and began walking, the sketchbook tucked beneath her arm.

Some things were easier to draw than to explain.

By the time Casey reached the bungalow, the sky had slipped from molten orange to velvet blue. The cicadas were humming in full chorus. She unlocked the screen door and stepped inside, greeted immediately by Marley's soft chuff and the gentle thud of his tail against the floor.

"Hey, boy," she said, bending to rub his ears. "I'm home."

The place smelled like lemon soap and ocean breeze—the windows had been open all day, letting in the salt air. She flipped on the small lamp by the couch and kicked off her sandals, toeing them into the corner. The sketchbook was still tucked under her arm, warm from where she'd held it close.

She thought about setting it on the desk, but instead carried it out to the porch. The night air was thick but not unpleasant, and the porch swing creaked as she sank into it, Marley flopping down at her feet like he always did.

She didn't open the sketchbook right away. Casey let her head rest against the back of the swing and closed her eyes.

She thought about Jake. About how she had felt drawn to him, how easy he made things seem—until they weren't. Until the mess of real emotions came to the surface. She couldn't believe he would approach her so casually without even trying to apologize. Did he think he did nothing wrong? Was he so drunk he doesn't remember?

She thought about Phillip, too. The way he held space for things. The way he didn't ask her to be anything but exactly what she was in any given moment. The way he looked at her like she was already whole, even when she didn't feel it.

Opening the sketchbook, she flipped back to the drawing she'd made of him. It wasn't finished. The hand was wrong, and the lines on his shirt were too stiff. But it didn't matter.

She picked up a pencil and began to shade the edges. Light and soft at first, then darker—deeper—around the places where shadow would fall. As she worked, the tension in her shoulders softened, her breathing slowed.

This, she realized, was why she used to draw. Not to be good. Not to impress anyone. But to make sense of the feelings that never quite sorted themselves into sentences.

She didn't know what would happen with Jake. Or with Phillip. Or with anything, really.

But she had this moment. This night. This page.

CHAPTER 10
POSTCARDS FROM THE ROAD

Casey hadn't heard from either of the guys for a few days. The late afternoon sun streamed through the windows of MoonDog Café, casting a golden glow over the scattered tables. The café was quiet, the rush of the day having faded into the slow hum of evening. Casey was rolling silverware when she heard the door chime softly.

"Hey Case," Jake's voice cut through the stillness, lazy and warm.

She glanced up, trying not to look as surprised as she felt.

"Seriously Jake?" Casey said. "You better be here to apologize for that crap you pulled the other night."

"Actually came to say goodbye. I'm heading out for a bit."

Casey blinked, caught off guard. "You're leaving?"

He shrugged, like it was nothing. "Just for a couple weeks. Gotta hit a few spots on the road—Nashville, New Orleans, the usual."

The words hung between them, and Casey realized she didn't know what to say.

"Oh," she managed, leaning back against the counter. "Well, have fun, I guess."

Jake smirked. "Fun's a given. Don't miss me too much while I'm gone."

She rolled her eyes. "You're impossible, you know that?"

"Yeah, but admit it—life would be boring without me."

For a second, she thought he might kiss her again.

But instead he just rested a hand on the counter, his grin softening. "See you soon, Casey."

And then he turned on his heel and headed back out of the café.

Tia appeared at her side, leaning over her shoulder. "You sure you can handle being one of Jake's girls?"

Casey shot her a look. "I'm not one of Jake's girls."

Tia titled her head in disbelief. "You keep telling yourself that."

A week passed since Jake's abrupt departure, and Casey began to feel an uneasy absence. Phillip had also been keeping to himself. *Maybe he was busy at the shop*, Casey tried to convince herself. She was beginning to fear that as quickly as she'd been swept up in the romances of this island, she'd also be just as quickly washed away with the tide.

The heat of the afternoon was softened by a gentle breeze, and the hum of MoonDog had settled into its usual late-afternoon lull. Casey was taking a rare break, sitting at one of the outdoor tables with a cold iced tea, Marley snoozing at her feet. She'd begun bringing him to work when she realized she could tie him up in the shade and that the patrons were eager to pet him as soon as they realized he was there. She began flipping through her sketchbook, idly shading in the lines of a wave she'd been working on, when Tia dropped something onto the table in front of her.

"Mail for you, babe."

Casey looked up, frowning. "Mail?"

"Postcard," Tia said. "From your rockstar."

Casey's stomach fluttered involuntarily.

She picked up the card—a bold, vintage-style print of Nashville, with its neon signs and iconic cowboy boots. On the back, Jake's handwriting was scrawled in uneven lines, casual and rushed.

Casey—

You'd love it here. You should be here. Drinks are strong, music's loud, people are wild—just how you like it, right?

Back soon. Maybe bring you next time.

—J

Casey felt a small, involuntary smile tug at her lips, but it didn't quite reach her eyes.

The words were so Jake—light, charming, and a little reckless. But they felt like something written without much thought, as if she were just another stop on his endless tour. And he was still trying to brush everything under the rug. Casey couldn't let that happen.

"Cute."

Casey looked up to see Tia leaning against the table

"It's fine," Casey said, shrugging as she tucked the postcard under her sketchbook.

Tia raised an eyebrow. "Fine? Come on, he's clearly thinking about you. That's something, right?"

Casey hesitated, fingers brushing the edge of the postcard. "I guess."

But deep down, she couldn't help wondering: Was he thinking about her, or was this just… something Jake did?

Tia tilted her head, studying Casey. "You know what I think?"

Casey sighed. "Do I have a choice?"

"I think you're trying way too hard to act like you don't care."

Casey rolled her eyes, but before she could respond, Tia added, "I also think… he's saying a lot without actually saying anything."

The comment hit deeper than Casey wanted to admit. She glanced at the postcard again, the bright colors and rushed handwriting, and felt a knot of something she couldn't name tighten in her chest.

"He's just being Jake," she said finally, but even she could hear the uncertainty in her voice.

Casey slid the postcard into her apron pocket, picking up her sketchbook again, and tried to focus on the lines she'd been shading—it didn't work. She pulled out the postcard again, flipping it around in her fingers as Jake's words lingered in her mind—charming and fleeting, like they could blow away with the next breeze. And when the next breeze came, she smelled a familiar scent that she hadn't smelled in a few days. A cedarwood musk drifted faintly through the air, and before she could turn around, Phillip appeared.

"From your musician?" he asked, nodding toward the postcard as he pulled out the chair across from her.

"He's not 'my' anything."

"Does he know that?" Phillip asked. Not waiting for an answer, he placed the sketchbook he was holding on the table between them, the leather cover worn and soft. Casey eyed it curiously as he flipped it open to a page.

"Here," he said, sliding it toward her.

It was a tattoo design—simple and elegant, yet alive with motion.

Waves cresting and breaking, a horizon line disappearing into the distance, and above it was an open sky filled with sweeping lines and beautiful shadowing that gave the impression of freedom.

Casey blinked, caught off guard. "What's this?"

Phillip leaned back in his chair, his dark eyes steady on hers. "For you."

She frowned, her fingers brushing over the sketch. "Why?"

Phillip tilted his head, considering her for a moment.

"Because you like to imagine things you don't have yet."

Casey froze, his words hitting something raw and unspoken inside her.

"And I thought," he continued, his voice quieter now, "maybe you'd want something that stays."

She stared at the sketch, the intricate lines, the way the design felt like it belonged to her, even though she hadn't asked for it.

"You think I should get this tattooed on me?" she asked, her voice softer than she meant it to be.

Phillip shrugged. "Up to you."

His tone was calm, almost dismissive, but Casey could feel the weight beneath his words. This wasn't just about the tattoo—it was about what it meant.

About choosing something that lasted over something that was fleeting.

As Casey studied the sketch, Phillip's gaze flickered to Marley, who was now watching him curiously. He reached down, scratching the dog behind the ears.

"When I first started tattooing," Phillip said, his voice quieter now, "I didn't think much about permanence. It was just… lines on skin."

Casey looked up, surprised by the sudden vulnerability in his tone.

"But then I started seeing what it meant to people. How it became a part of them." He tapped the edge of the sketchbook. "You don't just give someone a tattoo. You give them a piece of something they carry forever."

Casey's throat tightened as she stared at the sketch again.

It felt like he had somehow given her something she hadn't asked for but truly needed. Phillip reached across the table, gently closing the sketchbook and tucking it back under his arm.

"Think about it," he said simply, standing and pushing his chair back while collecting his notebook from the table.

As he turned to leave, Casey found herself calling out. "Phillip!"

He paused, glancing back at her.

She held his gaze for a moment, searching for the right words. "Thank you."

He nodded once, a small, almost imperceptible smile flickering at the corner of his mouth. Then Casey was alone at the table, the postcard forgotten beside her as the weight of something more permanent settled in her chest.

Another week had passed since Jake had left, and MoonDog Café hummed with its usual rhythm. Casey had fallen into a comfortable routine—working shifts, walking Marley along the beach, and sketching ideas that rarely made it past the page. She wasn't expecting the second postcard when Tia dropped it onto the counter.

"Another one," Tia said, leaning against the espresso machine. "Your boy's consistent, at least."

Casey picked it up slowly, flipping it over. The front was a vivid image of New Orleans—jazz bands marching through the streets, brass instruments glinting under gas lamps. She turned it over, Jake's handwriting scrawled across the back, familiar and hurried.

Case—

New Orleans is dangerous. I think you'd like it.

See you soon.

—J

It was shorter than the first, the words light and playful, but there was something about them that felt… distant. Casey stared at the card, running her fingers over the raised edges of the print, searching for meaning in the few words he had chosen.

"Well?" Tia asked, propping her chin on her hand.

Casey shrugged, tucking the postcard into her apron pocket. "It's fine."

Tia raised an eyebrow. "Fine? That's all you've got?"

Casey exhaled. "What do you want me to say? He's having fun. Good for him."

"And you're over here acting like it doesn't bother you."

Casey's hand froze on the counter.

"It doesn't," she said quickly, but even to her own ears, the words sounded hollow.

Tia gave her a knowing look. "Sure it doesn't."

As Tia walked off to handle a customer, Casey eyes on her from the other side of the counter. She turned.

Phillip.

He didn't say anything, didn't even look directly at

her, but she knew he had seen the postcard exchange.

She busied herself with stacking mugs, trying to ignore the weight of his gaze. Finally, he spoke, his voice low, calm.

"Another one?"

Casey glanced at him. "What?"

He nodded toward her apron pocket. "Postcard."

She sighed, pulling it out and setting it on the counter between them. "Yeah. He's… consistent, I guess."

Phillip tilted his head, studying the card. "You don't seem convinced."

Casey frowned. "It's just… I don't know. He's out there, doing his thing, and I'm here. And these postcards…" She trailed off, searching for the right words.

Phillip finished for her. "They feel like an afterthought."

Her stomach twisted. "I didn't say that."

"You didn't have to."

Phillip tapped the edge of the postcard, his expression unreadable. "You deserve more than something that's mailed in."

The comment hit harder than it should have.

Casey swallowed, her fingers brushing the counter. "It's not like we're… anything serious."

Phillip's gaze sharpened, but his voice remained steady. "Then why does it bother you so much?"

The question hung in the air, and Casey didn't have an answer.

Instead, she turned away, tucking the postcard back

into her pocket, feeling the weight of Phillip's words settle into her chest alongside Jake's. She wondered if she was holding onto something that wasn't really there.

CHAPTER 11
BEHIND THE REEF

The following day, Casey had off and went adventuring through side streets she hadn't yet explored. The quiet side streets of Key West were a world apart from the energy of Duval. Sunlight filtered through the palms, casting shifting patterns on the weathered brick sidewalks. Marley trotted happily beside Casey, tail wagging, while she let her thoughts drift, her sketchbook tucked under her arm.

As she turned a corner, she saw him.

Phillip sat on the steps of a church, a small sketchpad balanced on his knee, a pencil moving with practiced ease. His dark hair caught the light, and his expression was focused with his eyes flicking between the page and something just beyond it.

Casey hesitated. She wasn't sure why.

Marley, however, had no such reservations. The dog bounded forward, tail wagging, pulling Casey a step closer. Phillip glanced up, noticing them instantly. A small smile tugged at the corner of his mouth.

"Bonjour, Marley." His voice was smooth, tinged with his light French accent, and he gave a subtle nod toward Casey. "Casey."

She felt a flicker of warmth at the way he said her name.

"Hey," she said, shifting her weight. "What are you working on?"

Phillip glanced down at his sketchpad, then turned it toward her.

It was a loose rendering of the shopfront across the street, the lines capturing its charm—the peeling paint, the small hanging sign, even the stray cat lounging near the door.

"Just something to pass the time," he said simply, though the detail in the sketch suggested otherwise.

Casey moved closer, her curiosity outweighing her hesitation.

"It's amazing," she said, genuinely impressed.

Phillip gave a small shrug, a faint hint of pride flickering in his expression. "Merci. You draw, don't you?"

Casey blinked, caught off guard. "How do you know that?"

He gestured toward the sketchbook she held. "You've been carrying it everywhere lately. Most people don't do that unless they use it."

She laughed softly. "Fair point."

Phillip set his sketchpad aside, leaning back on his hands. "Want to come to the shop with me? I can show you how that hibiscus piece turned out."

Casey didn't even hesitate. "Sure!" she blurted out

quickly, then wondered if it was too quickly.

Phillip stood, motioning the way. "After you."

They walked a few blocks back to Duval, chatting and playing with Marley along the way. When they arrived, Casey tied Marley's leash to a street sign.

"I won't be long, buddy!"

Marley wagged his tail and laid on the sidewalk. As Casey stepped inside the shop, taking her time this time to notice the mix of art and inspiration all over the walls: framed tattoo designs, intricate sketches pinned with tacks, and a few photographs of clients proudly showing off their fresh ink.

Casey followed Phillip toward the back of the shop, where his workstation sat. His leather chair gleamed in the soft light, and the desk beside it was covered with neatly organized tools, tiny ink pots, and a stack of sketchbooks. *Was he always this neat?* Casey wondered. Twice now his workstation has looked impeccable. She thought back to her messy desk in Cincinnati, relieved it was no longer her problem.

Phillip pulled out a shop tablet and flipped to the photos app. Apparently, all the artists took client photos on the shop's tablets so they were all saved in the same place.

He found the hibiscus tattoo he had been sketching and flipped the screen to show Casey.

"Oh wow," she said. "That's beautiful."

"Merci," Phillip said.

"When you were sketching it, I thought the grayscale was just for example and you would add color later, but you tattooed a hibiscus in gray? Can I ask why?"

He smiled a soft smile and pulled out one of the sketchbooks.

Casey perched on the stool. She watched as Phillip flipped through pages, each one revealing a piece of his mind laid bare. The sketches were nothing like the bold, colorful designs on the walls near other artists' stations. These were softer, more intricate, and intensely personal. Architectural drawings of Parisian streets, their cobblestones and lampposts rendered in painstaking detail. A ship cutting through rough waves, its sails catching an unseen wind. And then, more recent pieces—waves curling over coral reefs, delicate sketches of underwater life, the ocean captured in swooping, fluid lines. All in pencil.

"These are incredible," Casey said, leaning closer.

Phillip glanced at her, his expression unreadable but not unkind. "Merci."

Her fingers brushed the edge of one page, hesitating. "Can I…?"

He nodded, and she carefully turned the page, revealing a stark grayscale sketch of a compass.

"That's one of mine," he said, tilting his forearm to show her the matching tattoo etched into his skin.

"It's beautiful," Casey murmured, tracing the lines of the drawing with her eyes.

Phillip leaned back against the counter, crossing his arms. "It's the first one I designed for myself. Right before I left France."

"So that still doesn't answer my question: why no color?" Casey said, tilting her head as she ran her fingers over a page with a striking black-and-gray rendering of an ocean wave.

Phillip paused, glancing at her before shrugging lightly.

Casey raised an eyebrow. "Color can be so… vibrant. Expressive."

Phillip's lips quivered into a small, almost amused smile. "True. But it's also fleeting."

"Fleeting?"

He turned to face her more fully, resting an elbow on the edge of the counter. "Color fades. No matter how carefully it's done, over time, the vibrancy dulls. The lines blur. Black and gray, though? It ages with you. It stays sharp, clear. It grows into the story instead of fading away from it."

Casey considered this, her fingers absently tracing the edge of the stool. "So, it's about permanence?"

Phillip nodded, but there was something more thoughtful in his expression now. "Partly. But it's also about simplicity. Black and gray doesn't try to distract you. It doesn't rely on flash or brightness to make its point. It lets the lines speak for themselves. You can play with light in a beautiful way."

Casey's eyes dropped to the compass tattoo on his forearm, the fine details and shading giving it depth and dimension without a hint of color. "Like that?"

Phillip glanced down at his arm, a faint smile tugging at his lips. "Exactly like that."

"Do you ever miss using color?" she asked, curious.

He shook his head. "Not really. Black and gray feels… honest. It's raw. When someone chooses it, they're choosing to let the design stand on its own. No distractions, no embellishments. I'll still do color if a client really wants it, but it's definitely not my preference."

Casey looked at the sketch he'd just finished—another black-and-gray wave, the shading so detailed it felt like it might crash off the page.

"Honest, huh?" she murmured.

Phillip met her gaze, his expression steady. "Yes. Honest."

The weight of the word hung between them, and Casey felt her pulse quicken. It wasn't just about tattoos anymore—it was about how he saw the world.

"I like that," she said finally, her voice softer than before.

Phillip smiled faintly, closing the sketchbook. "I thought you might."

Another sketch caught her eye.

"This one's beautiful," she said, holding it up.

Phillip glanced over from his workstation, his pencil pausing mid-line. "The reef," he said simply, as if that explained everything.

"You dive?" Casey asked, setting the sketch aside. "I thought you told Jake you hadn't been in the ocean here?"

Phillip nodded. "I hadn't been in the ocean that lapped on that precise shore of the island—and I try not to give Jake more information than he needs. But I dive often. There's a reef just beyond the island that I visit when I can."

Casey raised an eyebrow. "Isn't that dangerous? Sharks and all?"

A faint smile tugged at his lips. "The sharks aren't the dangerous part. It's the silence."

"The silence?"

Phillip leaned back in his chair, resting his hands in his lap. "When you're under the water, it's quiet. All you can hear is your breath, the sound of the regulator. It's… isolating."

Casey tilted her head, intrigued. "That doesn't sound like something enjoyable."

"It's not about enjoying it," Phillip replied, his gaze distant for a moment. "It's about being in a world where nothing else matters. No noise, no distractions. Just you, the ocean, and whatever's in front of you."

Phillip turned back to the sketch he was working on—a more abstract interpretation of the reef, its lines flowing like currents.

"When I first moved here, I hated it," he admitted, surprising Casey.

"Really?"

He nodded. "It felt… empty. Too small, too slow. But then a friend convinced me to try diving. Said I needed to see what was beneath the surface."

Casey leaned forward, resting her chin in the palm of her hand. "And?"

"And I understood. The reef is like the island—it's not about what you see at first glance. It's about what's hidden, what you have to work for to notice. The small things that make it beautiful."

"Did you ever think about leaving?" she asked softly.

Phillip's pencil paused again, and he glanced up at her. "At first, all the time. But after that first dive… I started seeing the island differently. It wasn't just a place to pass through anymore."

"What was it, then?"

He hesitated. "It was home."

Casey wasn't sure what to say, and Phillip didn't seem in a rush to fill the silence.

"You should come diving sometime," he said casually, as if the idea wasn't monumental.

Casey blinked, surprised by the notion. "Me? I don't know the first thing about diving."

"You don't have to. I'll show you." His voice was so genuine. He was easy to trust. Yet, she hesitated, the idea was both thrilling and intimidating.

"I'll… think about it."

Phillip didn't press. He just nodded, the faintest hint of a smile appearing as he returned to his work.

The sun was low on the horizon when Casey stepped out of Southernmost Tattoo, the warm golden light spilling over the quiet streets. She undid the knot in Marley's leash and began their walk home. Marley trotted beside her, his leash slack in her hand, but Casey's thoughts weren't on where she was going. They were on Phillip's words, on the sketches he'd shown her, and on the reef he'd described with a kind of reverence she didn't expect.

She hadn't been able to stop thinking about his invitation.

"Come diving sometime. I'll show you."

The streets grew quieter as Casey neared her bungalow. The scent of saltwater and blooming flowers lingered in the air, and she found herself slowing down, her thoughts swirling. When Casey reached her bungalow, she didn't go inside right away. Instead, she settled onto the small porch swing with her sketchbook. Marley dozed at her feet, his tail flicking occasionally as the warm evening breeze rustled through the palmtrees. She was so lost in her thoughts that she didn't hear the screen door creak open from the main house.

"You've got that look again," teased Betty.

Casey glanced back to see her landlady stepping onto the porch, a glass of lemonade in one hand and a knowing smile on her face. Betty's silver hair was pulled into its usual bun, and she wore a faded blue sundress that looked as comfortable as it was practical.

"What look?" Casey asked, shifting on the swing as Betty handed her the lemonade.

"The same look you had when you first walked through

my door. The look of someone trying to figure out if they're running toward something or away from it," Betty replied, lowering herself onto the wooden chair nearby.

Casey smiled faintly, taking a sip of the cool lemonade. "You've been spying on me?"

Betty chuckled. "Sweetheart, I've been renting out rooms in this house for twenty years. I know the signs."

Betty's gaze drifted to the open sketchbook in Casey's lap. She leaned forward slightly, squinting.

"That's new," she said, nodding toward the design. "The reef?"

Casey hesitated, then nodded. "Yeah. Phillip was telling me about it earlier."

Betty's expression softened, a wistful look crossing her face. "That boy sees the world in a way most people miss. Always has."

"Oh you know him? He mentioned he came here with a friend," Casey said, testing the waters. "But the friend left."

Betty let out a small sigh, settling back in her chair. "I do, and he did. Came here looking for adventure, the same way most people do. But Phillip stayed. Said the reef changed something for him. I think it gave him roots in a way he didn't expect."

Casey glanced back at her sketch. "He said he realized he wasn't just looking for adventure. He was looking for somewhere to stay."

Betty nodded, her sharp eyes twinkling. "Smart boy.

He figured out something most people don't: you can't outrun yourself forever. Sooner or later, you've got to plant your feet somewhere."

Casey closed her sketchbook, resting her hands on the cover. "And this is the place people come to figure that out?"

Betty smiled. "Oh, Key West isn't just a place. It's a mirror. It shows you who you are when everything else falls away."

Casey frowned, her mind turning over the thought. "And what happens if you don't like what you see?"

Betty shrugged. "Then you decide to change it. That's the beauty of it, honey. The mirror doesn't lie, but it doesn't keep you stuck, either."

The porch fell into a comfortable silence for a few moments, the soft hum of cicadas blending with the distant crash of the waves.

Finally, Betty broke the quiet. "Phillip's a good one, you know. Different from the rest of the boys around here. He's not chasing the next thrill or trying to impress anyone."

Casey glanced up, her expression cautious. "I noticed."

Betty chuckled, standing up and smoothing out her dress. "Just saying. Sometimes the quiet ones see you better than the loud ones ever could."

She patted Casey's shoulder gently. "You'll figure it out, sweetheart. You've got that look of someone who's ready to."

As Betty disappeared back inside, Casey leaned back on the swing, sipping her lemonade and staring out at the fading light.

Sometimes the quiet ones see you better…

Casey felt like she was starting to see herself, too.

CHAPTER 12
STORM BREWING

The café felt different today.

Even though the fans above spun lazily and the late afternoon light filtered through the windows in golden ribbons, there was a heaviness in the air. A low pressure that made Casey's skin prickle. Outside, the sky had dulled from its usual azure brilliance to something flatter, heavier—a muted blue-gray that warned of something stirring offshore.

Inside MoonDog, the clink of silverware and the murmur of a few lingering customers provided a thin illusion of normalcy. Casey just finished her shift and was sitting at the bar, sketchbook open, a pencil smudging across the page as she tried to capture the motion of waves. But the lines kept coming out wrong—too jagged, too chaotic. Nothing flowed the way it usually did.

Tia appeared at her elbow with two iced teas, setting one in front of her.

"Don't take this the wrong way," she said, sliding onto the stool beside her, "but you've got hurricane eyes today."

Casey looked up. "What does that mean?"

"You're all stirred up. Something's spinning in there," Tia said, tapping her own temple. "And I don't think it's just the weather."

Casey offered a weak smile and flipped her sketchbook closed. "It's nothing."

Tia gave her a long look. "Storm's brewing. You feel it?"

Casey nodded before she could stop herself. "Yeah."

They both glanced toward the windows, where palm fronds danced more wildly than usual in the gusting wind. Tourists were still walking Duval like nothing was wrong, sipping drinks and pointing at landmarks, but the locals had started pulling in outdoor chairs and checking their phone alerts more frequently.

"You think it's going to hit?" Casey asked.

"Too early to say," Tia said. "But even if it doesn't, we'll get the sideswipes. Heavy rain, gusts, weird tides."

Casey drummed her fingers on the countertop. "Fitting."

Tia raised an eyebrow. "Storm metaphor, huh?"

"I'm not trying to be poetic. Just feels like everything's… about to shift."

Tia leaned forward, serious now. "This about Jake?"

Casey didn't answer right away. She didn't have to. The silence between them said enough.

"I haven't heard from him since that last postcard," Casey finally muttered. "He says he'll be back soon but… I don't know. It's all just words, you know?"

Tia sipped her drink. "And what about tattoo boy?"

Casey gave a small smile. "He doesn't say much. But somehow he says more."

The café door swung open then, letting in a blast of warm, unsettled air—and the buzz of conversation paused as a group of locals stepped inside, shaking off the wind and grumbling about barometric pressure. One of them, a weather-worn fisherman in flip flops and a Key West Conchs tank top, muttered, "Feels like '05 again. You mark my words, she's gonna spin."

Casey stood, tucking her sketchbook under her arm and grabbing her tea. "I'm gonna walk Marley before the rain starts."

"Text me if you see flying chickens," Tia called after her.

But Casey was already at the door, the heavy air wrapping around her like a warning. Outside, the first raindrops began to fall—big, warm, hesitant things that hit the pavement and sizzled into steam.

Somewhere out over the water, a storm was turning. And Casey wasn't sure if she was ready for what it might wash in.

The sky cracked open sometime after dusk.

Casey had just finished Marley's walk when the wind really started howling—sharp, sudden gusts that made the palm trees dance like they were trying to uproot themselves. The first sheets of rain came fast, not in slow warning drops like earlier, but all at once, like a faucet turned wide open.

By the time she reached the porch, both she and Marley were soaked. She fumbled with the screen door, laughing breathlessly as Marley shook water all over the steps. Her clothes clung to her, and her ponytail dripped down the back of her neck.

As she toweled Marley off, the lights flickered.

"Great," she muttered. She set her sketchbook on the kitchen table and headed to the bathroom to peel off her wet clothes. Thunder cracked overhead.

And then—a knock.

Not the wind. Not the rain. A real knock.

She paused, halfway into a dry sweatshirt.

The knock came again.

When she opened the door, her breath caught.

Jake.

Soaked to the bone, guitar case slung over one shoulder, his boots leaving muddy prints on the welcome mat. His curls were plastered to his forehead, and his T-shirt clung to his frame, his signature grin faltering slightly when he saw her face.

"Hey," he said.

Casey didn't move. Didn't speak.

Jake shifted his weight, running a hand through his dripping hair. "Thought I'd drop by. Guess I brought the storm with me, huh?"

"You think this is funny?" she asked.

His smile faded completely.

"I… no. Look, Casey—"

"You disappear for two weeks and then just show up in the middle of a damn monsoon like it's normal?"

"I sent postcards," he offered, lame and uncertain.

"You *sent postcards*," she repeated, incredulous. "Jake, you *kissed me*. Then you were super rude, which you never apologized for. Then you basically ghosted. And now you think you can just come back?"

"I didn't ghost you," he said quickly. "I needed space. Time to think. And I had an opportunity to open for a friend's band on a leg of their tour, so I just took it."

Casey stepped out onto the porch, arms crossed tight over her chest. "You just took it—without thinking about how your decisions affected anyone else. Besides, what did you need to think about?"

Jake looked away, then back at her, rain streaking down his face like it belonged there.

"Oh for goodness sake get it in here, you've been letting in the rain."

Casey pulled him inside and slammed the door shut. "So?"

"I needed to think about what I want. About you. About me. About how I mess up everything good that comes near me." He let out a bitter laugh. "And the whole time I was gone, nothing felt right. Nashville was loud. New Orleans was lonely. I kept picturing you sketching at MoonDog. Marley snoring at your feet."

He looked up, eyes searching hers. "So I came back. I came back for you."

Casey swallowed hard. Her heart thudded against her ribs, but her brain wasn't as easily swayed.

"You say that like you weren't coming back to Key West anyway," she said quietly. She looked past him, out at the street. The glowing porch light above them casting gold over the chaos.

"I think you should leave, Jake," Casey finally said. "I think now *I* need some time to think."

Jake left, closing the door softly behind him, moving slowly like a wounded puppy. When the door shut, Casey looked out the window to watch him return down the pathway to the street.

The storm kept raging outside. But inside, everything felt even quieter than before.

Casey stood in the center of the bungalow, arms crossed tight across her chest, her bare feet sinking into the worn rug as the storm pounded against the windows.

"I came back for you," she mimicked.

The audacity.

No apology. No real explanation. Just that boyish charm and wet curls and a half-smirk that used to make her stomach flip but now only made her want to scream. He thought he could drop two postcards in the mail and stroll back in during a hurricane like he was doing her a favor.

You don't just get to come back like that, she thought, pacing now. Her fingers curled into fists. The bungalow felt too small, too tight, like the walls were closing in. Marley was curled up in his usual spot, eyes watching her with quiet concern, head tilted like he knew she was unraveling.

She dropped into the armchair and sat there for a moment, the only light in the room coming from a storm candle flickering on the windowsill. The flame danced wildly in the breeze sneaking through the old wooden frame, casting shadows that stretched and moved with her breathing.

Her thoughts kept circling the same drain. Jake. The kiss. The fight. The silence. The postcards. The *timing* of his return—always on his terms. Like everything else.

She let out a growl and stood again. The storm outside had grown heavier, wind slashing rain sideways against the windows. But Casey didn't care. The pressure in her chest needed release, and Jake sure as hell wasn't the answer.

She marched to the bathroom, ran a brush through her hair, pulled on her rain boots, and tucked a few bucks and her ID into her back pocket. She grabbed her keys from the dish on the counter with a satisfying jingle and pulled on her hoodie from the peg by the door, adding a rain jacket over the top. Marley lifted his head as she passed, but she paused only to ruffle the fur on his head.

"Sorry, bud. Mama needs a drink."

He let out a soft whine but stayed put.

Casey yanked open the door, bracing herself against the wind. Rain hit her immediately, cold and soaking, but she barely flinched. She didn't care that her hoodie was already getting drenched or that her jean shorts would be heavy with water by the time she made it halfway down Angela Street.

She welcomed it.

Let the storm rage. Let the rain hit. Let the island drown if it had to.

She was going to the Green Parrot to drink until Jake didn't mean a damn thing to her. With thunder rolling like a drumbeat overhead and lightning flashing off the puddled pavement, Casey shoved her hood up and stepped out into the storm, one foot in front of the other.

She didn't look back.

The Green Parrot looked like a glowing beacon through the rain—windows fogged and warm, the faint sound of music and voices muffled behind the heavy storm door. Water dripped from the edge of the neon sign above, green light pulsing in time with each drop.

Casey stood across the street for a second, soaked to the bone, rain streaming down her face. She blinked it out of her eyes, half-laughing at herself. Only she would walk into a hurricane to prove a point. Only she would think a bar could drown out this kind of fury.

A car passed, sending up a spray of warm water from the curb that splashed her boots. She didn't even flinch. Just crossed the street and pushed through the door like a woman on a mission.

Inside, it was packed. A live band was playing something slow and gritty, a bluesy number that crawled down your spine and wrapped around your bones. People were scattered across the bar, clustered near the stage or huddled in booths, all seeking the same thing: shelter from the storm outside and maybe the one inside themselves, too.

Casey shook out her hoodie at the entrance, earning a few glances. She peeled it off and tossed it over her arm, rain dripping from her sleeves. The bartender caught her eye and gave her a nod of recognition—she was a regular enough now to get one.

She made her way to the bar and slid onto an empty stool near the end. The bar felt too warm at first after the wet chill outside, but she welcomed it. It made her feel human again. Like maybe she still had skin under the numb.

"What'll it be?" the bartender asked, wiping his hands on a towel.

"Something strong and not sweet," Casey said, her voice more bitter than she meant it to be.

He nodded and turned to pour her a dark rum on the rocks without another word. He clearly had seen a thousand broken hearts and had learned not to ask too many questions.

Her drink landed in front of her with a solid clink.

She took a sip. It burned, in a good way. The kind of burn that told you you were still here.

As the band shifted to a faster tune, the crowd roared in appreciation. Someone bumped into her from behind—dancing too hard or just too drunk—and she didn't even react. Just stared into her glass like it could offer answers. Here she was, in the middle of a hurricane, drinking rum like it could scrub Jake out of her system.

She drained the glass faster than she should've. Signaled for another.

The second drink hit harder. The buzz began to rise behind her eyes, and she let her shoulders drop just slightly, the music pulling at the edges of her consciousness. A man in a Hawaiian shirt started spinning an older woman on the dance floor. Someone hollered a request to the band. The world kept turning.

And for a moment, Casey let it. She let it blur. Let it melt.

She was soaked, spinning, pissed off, and more alone than she wanted to admit—but at least she wasn't home. At least she wasn't pretending Jake's presence didn't hurt.

Outside, the storm wailed against the walls.

Inside, Casey ordered another drink.

CHAPTER 13
THE EYE OF THE STORM

The Parrot was buzzing with storm-dodgers—locals who knew better than to fight the floodwaters and tourists who didn't have anywhere else to go. Casey sat at the bar, four drinks deep and not trying to slow down. Her cheeks were flushed, her curls damp from the walk, and her mood somewhere between rage and resignation. She was now nursing a rum and Coke with a pineapple slice floating, barely touched.

She didn't look up when someone approached—just reached for the drink again. But when the barstool beside her creaked, something told her to glance over.

Phillip.

Soaking wet, hair slicked back, calm as ever. He didn't look like he'd run through a storm, even if the water dripping from his coat said otherwise. His eyes met hers, steady and unreadable, and he settled in beside her like he'd been planning to all along.

"You stalking me now?" she asked, words slurring just slightly.

He raised an eyebrow. "The streets are flooding. Half the roads are impassable already. I couldn't get home if I wanted to."

She blinked at him, then looked toward the windows. Sure enough, the water was pooling across the road outside, streaming like a current toward the curb. A man waded through it ankle-deep just outside the door, shoes in hand.

"You walked through all that to come here?" she asked.

"I was at the studio," he said, shrugging off his jacket and draping it over the back of the stool. "Figured the Parrot would be open. Didn't expect to find you since you live so close."

Casey narrowed her eyes. "Well, here I am."

They sat in silence for a beat, the noise of the bar pressing in around them like a buffer.

"Drink?" she offered finally, raising her glass toward him.

Phillip gave her a faint smile. "No thanks."

"Suit yourself," she muttered, tipping it back.

She could feel his presence beside her—solid, unmoving, quietly watchful. It was oddly comforting. Or maybe just familiar. She couldn't tell the difference anymore.

"Rough night?" he asked after a moment, his tone casual but not unkind.

Casey snorted. "Define rough."

He didn't push. Just nodded, like he understood.

The band shifted into something slower, a song with a lazy, swaying rhythm. A couple near the door got up to dance, unbothered by the storm outside or the storm in Casey's chest.

Phillip folded his hands on the bar, glancing sideways at her. "You come here to drink until something doesn't hurt?"

Casey frowned. "Who says something hurts?"

He didn't respond.

She sighed, dragging her fingers through her hair and wincing as her ring got caught in a tangle. "Maybe I came to drink until I stopped thinking."

Phillip looked down at the puddle forming beneath his stool from his wet boots. "Let me know if it works."

She barked a short, surprised laugh. "What, and you'll try it next time?"

"Not really my method," he said. "But I'll keep you company while you test it out."

Casey leaned her elbow on the bar and looked at him through narrowed eyes. "You always this noble, or just when it's inconvenient?"

His gaze didn't flinch. "Just when someone needs it."

That shut her up.

Outside, the thunder cracked again, closer this time. Inside, the air felt heavier—like something was coming.

Casey was working on her fifth drink. The bartender—Pati, a woman with a sleeve of tattoos and the patience of a saint—had given her a raised eyebrow after the fourth, but hadn't cut her off yet. The Parrot wasn't exactly the kind of place where bartenders played mother.

Beside her, Phillip had ordered a soda water with lime. He sipped it slowly, his posture relaxed, but Casey noticed the way his eyes swept the bar now and then—watching people, keeping track. She wondered if he always did that. Like he couldn't turn off whatever mechanism inside him made him hyperaware.

Casey, on the other hand, was trying her best not to be aware of anything. Not the lightning slicing through the sky outside, or the way the floor seemed to tilt a little under her barstool, or the familiar ache crawling up the back of her throat every time she thought about Jake.

But then she heard a laugh—loud, low, and unmistakably Jake's—and all that effort unraveled like cheap thread.

She turned too quickly, and the room spun slightly before her eyes settled on him.

He was leaning against the back rail near the stage, drink in hand, grinning like the devil himself. He hadn't noticed her yet. Or maybe he had and didn't care.

Casey stiffened, and Phillip must have noticed, because he turned and followed her gaze.

Jake was surrounded by a few guys from another band—Casey vaguely recognized one of them from a night at Captain Tony's. His eyes were crinkled at the corners like he'd just delivered a killer punchline. His guitar was propped behind him onstage, still out of its case, which meant he'd probably played a set earlier.

She couldn't believe she hadn't noticed.

"I didn't know he was here," she muttered, more to herself than to Phillip.

Phillip's eyes stayed on Jake, but his voice was even. "Neither did I."

As if summoned by the attention, Jake peeled himself off the railing and ambled toward the bar. He didn't see them at first. Casey turned away sharply, trying to appear engrossed in the little paper napkin she was doodling on in pen.

Phillip didn't move.

Jake stopped at the bar just a few feet down from them, tapping the counter. "One more," he told Pati with a grin.

Then he glanced sideways and saw them.

His grin faltered. Just for a second. Then it snapped back into place like armor.

"Well, well," he said, sauntering closer. "Didn't expect to see the two of you here… together."

Casey's jaw tensed, but she didn't look up. Phillip, however, met Jake's gaze calmly.

"It's a public bar," Phillip said mildly.

"Didn't say it wasn't," Jake replied. "Just… cozy timing."

"Storm's got most people stuck," Casey muttered into her drink.

Jake leaned an elbow on the bar, looking her over. "You look cozy too. How many of those have you had, Case?"

She met his eyes, finally. "Enough to put up with this conversation."

Jake chuckled. "Still got that fire."

"She never lost it," Phillip said, his tone quiet but deliberate.

The two men locked eyes. Something in the air shifted—tense, electric. The noise of the bar faded behind it, thunder rumbling like a warning overhead.

Casey turned back to her drink, her hands clenching the sides of the glass.

She didn't know exactly how, but she knew what was coming.

And she didn't know if she could stop it.

The air between Phillip and Jake was thick and volatile, like air right before lightning splits the sky. The stool between them—where Casey sat—might as well have been the eye of the storm.

"You gonna sit there and brood all night?" Jake asked, his tone sharp enough to cut glass. "Or just keep pretending I'm not here?"

Casey stiffened. "Can you not do this?"

"Do what?" Jake said, raising his eyebrows in mock innocence. "Ask a question? Make conversation?"

Phillip didn't move, but his posture shifted slightly—more alert, more ready.

Jake leaned on the bar behind Casey, too close, the smell of bourbon clinging to him. "It's funny, really. You go on tour for a couple of weeks and suddenly the quiet guy with the tragic eyes swoops in?"

"Jake," Casey warned, voice low, "you're drunk."

"I'm *fine*," he slurred just slightly, waving her off. "You don't think it's weird, though? That he always seems to show up when I'm gone?"

Casey turned on her stool, trying to create space. "You left, Jake. You didn't say anything about us—you just *left*."

"I told you I'd be back."

"You sent *postcards*." The word stung as it left her mouth. "Like I'm some vacation stop you're checking off."

Phillip's jaw twitched. He set his drink down slowly. "Maybe you should walk it off," Phillip said.

Jake laughed, bitter and humorless. "Oh, *there* it is. Mr. Polite finally speaks."

"Jake—" Casey tried again, her voice cracking now. "Don't do this. Please."

But Jake was past reason. "Tell me, Casey. Did he sketch you something pretty? Promise you a tattoo with *meaning*?" He turned to Phillip. "That your move, man? Because I gotta say, the tortured artist angle is *rich*."

Phillip stood up.

The shift was subtle, controlled—but final. His height and presence cast a shadow over Jake's swagger, his voice calm but edged with steel. "You need to back off."

"Or what?" Jake barked. "You gonna draw me a warning?"

"Jake, stop," Casey snapped, getting between them. "This isn't you."

Jake's gaze slid past her, locked on Phillip. "You don't belong here. You don't know her."

"I know enough to see she deserves better than *you.*"

That did it.

Jake's fist came out of nowhere, wild and uncoordinated—but it connected with Phillip's cheek hard enough to jolt him sideways.

Gasps burst around the bar. Someone yelled, "Whoa!" as stools scraped and drinks sloshed. The band stopped cold.

Phillip righted himself with terrifying calm.

Then he struck—quick, deliberate. One sharp jab to Jake's ribs sent him doubling forward, coughing.

Pati, the bartender, shoved through the crowd. "*Jesus,* boys!"

Jake leaned against the bar, breath ragged. "He started it."

Phillip wiped his jaw, unfazed. "You threw the first punch."

"Both of you," Pati barked, pointing a finger between them. "Cut it the *fuck* out."

Jake straightened with a grimace. "What are you gonna do, Pati? Toss us out into a flood?"

"It's a goddamn monsoon and you're both regulars," she snapped. "So unless you want to mop up with your own clothes, *sit down* and behave."

Phillip didn't say anything. He stepped back and ran a hand through his hair, regaining composure.

Jake turned to Casey, eyes bloodshot and pleading. "You're really gonna stand with *him?* After everything?"

Casey stared at him, something inside her unraveling completely. "I'm not standing with anyone."

"You came here for *me*, didn't you?"

"No," she said, and it was like something inside her finally cracked open. "I came here to forget you."

Jake blinked, hurt flaring in his eyes. But Casey didn't flinch.

She turned, pulling on her still-wet hoodie and raincoat, grabbing her bag, her keys, the dignity she'd barely managed to keep intact.

"Casey, wait—" Phillip's voice was quiet but desperate.

"No," she said firmly, voice shaking but sure. "I won't be caught between the two of you. Not again. Not for another minute."

Pati reached for her, muttering, "Don't be stupid, girl—it's dangerous out there."

"Not as dangerous as staying here," Casey said.

And then she pushed through the door and into the storm.

Rain hit her like a slap—cold, hard, cleansing. The street was half-flooded, wind bending the palm trees, thunder rolling somewhere close. She didn't care. She kept walking, tears hot on her face, lost instantly in the downpour.

Behind her, the Parrot's lights glowed dimly through the sheets of rain, but she didn't look back.

Let them fight. Let the whole damn island drown in it. She was done.

Rain lashed against the windows of The Green Parrot like fists, thunder growling overhead as if the sky itself were furious. Inside, the bar had returned to a cautious hum, though everyone's attention still flicked occasionally toward the door Casey had just stormed through.

Jake sat hunched over the bar, cradling a new drink with a hand that trembled slightly—whether from the adrenaline or the booze, it was hard to tell.

Phillip stood a few feet away, arms crossed, soaked in fluorescent bar light and restrained rage. A bruise was beginning to form on his cheek where Jake had hit him. No doubt a bigger one was forming on Jake's stomach.

"She could get hurt out there," he said finally, voice clipped.

Jake snorted. "She's not a child."

"She's also drunk, pissed off, and walking into a *storm.*"

Jake turned to him slowly. "And you think *you're* the one to go after her?"

Phillip held his ground. "Somebody should."

Jake's laugh was hollow. "You think this makes you the hero now? You show up out of nowhere, hang around long enough to scribble something into a sketchbook, and suddenly you *know* her?"

Phillip's jaw tensed. "I don't need to know her whole life story to see when she's in danger."

"You don't get it," Jake snapped, standing now, too.

Phillip shook his head, exasperated. "This isn't about you."

"Like hell it's not," Jake said, jabbing a finger at him. "You think you're the calm, collected one, right? You think she's gonna run into your arms like some rainy romance flick because you *don't* yell back? Newsflash: that's not how she works."

Pati raised a warning eyebrow from the other end of the bar, but didn't say a word.

"Oh so you're an expert on Casey." Phillip said.

"I know more than you, buddy."

A gust of wind slammed against the door. Somewhere down the street, a transformer blew—lights flickered once, twice, then went out. The tension in the room didn't.

By the time Pati had turned on some portable lights and passed out flashlights, only one of their bar stools was occupied.

"Where'd he go?" Pati asked, receiving only a shrug in response.

Rain pummeled the pavement in relentless sheets, turning streets to rivers and sidewalks to slipstreams. The wind howled between the buildings, tugging at palm fronds and street signs alike, whipping through Key West with reckless abandon.

A figure moved through it all, hunched and determined, hood soaked through, hair plastered to his forehead. Head down against the storm, he turned onto a side street where pastel bungalows hunched behind garden fences.

Casey's house was just around the corner.

He picked up his pace, boots sloshing through ankle-deep puddles, rain running in rivulets down the back of his neck. The lights were off in her bungalow—only the faint porch glow of Betty's main house flickered faintly through the rain like a beacon.

Then he saw her.

Casey was slumped over the low white picket fence that bordered her garden, one arm looped loosely through the post like she was trying to keep herself from sliding off the earth. Her hair clung to her face in wet tangles, and her soaked lothes clung against her frame. Marley barked once from inside, muffled and frantic, but Casey didn't react.

"Casey," the man said, his voice low, urgent.

She turned her head slowly, blinking hard through rain that wasn't all from the sky. Her eyes were glassy, unfocused.

"Jake?" she slurred, squinting at him. "Phillip?"

She tried to stand straighter but lost her balance, collapsing sideways. He caught her before she hit the ground, his arms locking around her shoulders.

"Easy," he murmured. "I've got you."

She sagged into him, too drunk to argue, too tired to pretend. Her breath smelled like rum and regret.

"Couldn't… couldn't stay in there," she mumbled against his shoulder. "Too loud. Too much."

"I know," he said, voice steady despite the weight of her against him.

He guided her up the steps of her porch, fumbling with the spare key she said always kept tucked behind the chipped ceramic planter. Marley barked again, pawing at the door from inside.

He opened it gently, ushering her inside as Marley greeted them with frenzied relief. Casey half-collapsed onto the couch, her limbs heavy and graceless.

The man knelt to pull off her boats, setting them neatly on a drip mat by the door. He peeled off her raincoat and hoodie and jeans shorts in the most respectful way possible and hung them to dry. Then he knelt down beside her, brushing dripping hair away from her forehead. She shivered once, eyes fluttering shut.

"You're okay now," he whispered.

Marley whined and curled up at her feet as he draped a throw blanket over her body. She didn't stir. Her breath began to even; the storm outside continued to roar against the windows.

He stood there for a moment, drenched and silent.

Then, without another word, he turned and let himself out, the door clicking softly behind him.

The rain swallowed him whole.

CHAPTER 14
SHARKS THAT CAN SWIM ON THE LAND

Casey woke to the soft creak of the porch swing and the faint scent of salt still clinging to the breeze. For a long second, she didn't move—just lay there on the couch, blinking against the light filtering in through the half-closed blinds. Her head pounded in slow, rhythmic pulses, and her mouth felt like cotton and regret.

She groaned and sat up, clutching her temples. Everything ached. Her lower back, her knees, even her ribs. A full-body ache like she'd been tossed around by the sea—or by the night itself.

Marley lay curled on the rug in front of the couch, tail thumping lazily when he saw her move. At least one of them had slept through the storm.

"What the hell happened?" Casey whispered to herself, voice hoarse.

She remembered the rain, sheets of it, blinding.

She remembered walking to the Green Parrot, alone, determined to drink Jake out of her system. She remembered the sound of music blurring into noise, the warmth of bourbon on her tongue, the bartender with the amused smirk who kept pouring her another. She remembered Phillip showing up. His voice steady. His eyes hard to read.

And then… flashes. An argument. Jake's voice rising. Something crashing. Her body pushing up off the barstool. Yelling. And then—

Nothing. A blank space where the rest of the night should be.

She looked down at herself. She was still in yesterday's clothes—crumpled, stained, damp around the hem. But her hoodie and shorts were hung neatly by the door to dry. Her boots were likewise neatly placed by the door.

She didn't remember getting home. But someone had helped her. That much she knew. There had been a hand on her back, a shoulder supporting her weight when her knees buckled. Someone had walked her home. Made sure she got inside. Clearly helped her undress and even got her onto the couch.

She rubbed her arms, trying to piece together the voice. The scent. The touch.

It could've been Jake.

She frowned. He had been there. He had looked shocked, maybe even guilty, when she stormed out.

But it could've been—

She shook the thought off. No way to know. And no one had stayed. Whoever it was had left her here, alone, and locked the door behind them.

Just then, a gust of wind pushed against the bungalow's windows, and she flinched. The storm might've passed, but the headache it left behind was roaring.

She shuffled into the kitchen and poured herself a glass of water, taking small sips and trying not to gag. Her hands were still unsteady. She needed greasy food. A gallon of coffee. Maybe a few answers.

As if on cue, there was a knock at the door.

Casey turned slowly, heart suddenly thudding for an entirely new reason. She wasn't ready for this. Whoever it was—Jake, Phillip, a neighbor checking on the storm damage—she wasn't ready.

She set the glass down, took a breath, and opened the door.

Jake stood on the porch, hands shoved into his jacket pockets, rain still clinging to his curls and dripping from the hem of his sleeves. He looked less like the life-of-the-party Jake she was used to and more like someone who hadn't slept.

"Hey," he said, voice low, eyes searching hers.

Casey blinked at him, surprise giving way to something more guarded. "Hey."

"You look like hell," he said, then winced. "Sorry. That came out wrong."

She gave him a humorless smile. "Probably because it was true. So what do you want anyway?"

"I think I owe you an apology—and an explanation honestly." He hesitated. "Can I come in?"

She stepped aside, wordlessly, and let him pass. Marley lifted his head from the rug, growled once in a half-hearted warning, then dropped his chin back down like even the dog wasn't in the mood.

Jake stood just inside the door. He didn't take a seat.

"Look, I just wanted to check on you," he said. "Make sure you were okay. After last night."

Casey leaned against the arm of the couch, arms crossed. "Why? Guilt?"

"Maybe a little," Jake admitted. "But also because… I was worried."

She didn't say anything.

Jake rubbed the back of his neck. "You had a lot to drink. Storm like that, it's dangerous to be out alone. You could've gotten hurt."

Casey frowned. "I didn't get hurt."

"No," he said. "You didn't. I made sure of that."

She blinked. "Wait. You… got me home?"

He didn't answer right away. Just gave her a small, sheepish smile. "Yeah."

She stared at him. Tried to remember. But the night blurred at the edges. She remembered arms around her. A steady presence. But it hadn't felt like Jake. Then again, maybe it had. Maybe she was just so drunk she couldn't tell.

"…Thanks," she said finally.

Jake stepped closer. "I didn't do it for the thanks. I just didn't want anything bad to happen to you."

There was a moment of silence. Casey shifted her weight from one foot to the other. The rain was starting again, tapping lightly at the windows.

"Cut the small talk, Jake," she said, sharper than she meant. "You said you wanted to explain. So, explain."

Jake let out a breath, walked over to the couch, and sank down, elbows on his knees.

"Right. Okay. So, here's the thing: Phillip and I go way back. And it's… complicated."

Casey narrowed her eyes. "How complicated?"

Jake ran a hand down his face. "We both moved here around the same time. Kind of got tossed into the same orbit. But before that—back in Miami—we actually were friends for a few months. But there was a girl."

Casey's arms tightened across her chest. "A girl?" She was unamused.

Jake nodded. "Yea, Maria."

Casey studied him, trying to read between the lines. "And Phillip? He never forgave you for…something?"

Jake shook his head. "Not even close. And honestly? I don't blame him. What I did was wrong, and I'll own that. But there's something you should know about him."

Her brow furrowed. "What do you mean?"

Jake leaned back, his expression serious. "Phillip's not as calm and collected as he seems. When he gets mad— really mad—he's… unpredictable."

"Unpredictable?" Casey echoed.

Jake's voice dropped, tone conspiratorial. "I've seen him lose it before. After Maria, he… let's just say he wasn't the same guy. I'm not saying he's dangerous, but he's not exactly someone who deals with things in a healthy way."

Casey's chest tightened, her thoughts swirling. "So you're trying to tell me Phillip is dangerous now, Jake?"

Jake met her gaze, his voice softer now. "I don't want you to get hurt, Casey. Not by me, and definitely not by him."

The room fell into a heavy silence, broken only by Marley's soft breathing. Casey let out a long breath, shaking her head.

"I don't know, Jake," she said finally. "It sounds like there's more to this than you're saying."

"Maybe," he admitted. "But I'm trying to be honest with you. I don't want things to get messy again." His grin returned, softer this time. "And hey, I'm not asking you to forgive me or anything. I just… wanted you to know the truth."

"So what exactly is the truth, Jake?"

Jake hesitated, gaze dropping to the floor like the answer might be hiding there. When he looked up again, the grin had vanished.

"The truth is… I liked Maria. A lot. And she liked me. But it wasn't that simple. She and Phillip were on the rocks when I met her. They'd been fighting, breaking up, getting back together—one of those cycles you think'll break on its own but never does."

He scratched the back of his neck, eyes flicking briefly toward Marley before returning to Casey.

"She told me it was over. That she was done. And for a while, it seemed like she meant it. We started seeing each other. Quietly, at first. I was trying to give her space, trying not to get in the middle of anything. But Phillip didn't see it that way."

Casey didn't speak. She kept her arms crossed, her expression unreadable.

"He lost it when he found out," Jake continued. "Told me I'd crossed a line. That I'd taken advantage. But the truth is… I didn't chase her. I didn't manipulate her. She came to me."

Casey raised an eyebrow. "And you don't think that maybe, just maybe, it was a bad idea to get involved with someone who is in a situationship?"

Jake exhaled. "Of course it was a bad idea. I knew it even then. But I also knew what we had wasn't fake. Maria wasn't a game to me."

His voice softened further, guilt tightening his features.

"She left a few months later. Said she needed a clean break—from both of us. She moved back to Europe, and I haven't heard from her since."

Casey sat down across from him, rubbing her temples. "So what you're saying is… you and Phillip never made peace."

Jake shook his head. "Nope. Not even close."

"And you think I need to know this because…?"

Jake looked at her like the answer should've been obvious. "Because I've seen the way he looks at you. You're in this now, whether you want to be or not. I figured you should at least know what you're getting into."

Casey's chest tightened, unease curling beneath her ribs. It wasn't just Jake's words. It was the way he said them—half concern, half warning. Like he wasn't just trying to look out for her. Like he was trying to plant something.

She wanted to believe every word he said, but she couldn't remember any of it for herself.

"Thanks for telling me, I guess," she said quietly.

Jake nodded, leaning back, his grin fading into something more genuine. "Anytime, Case."

"Listen, I've got an idea," he said, his grin creeping back. "Let me make it up to you. Let's go sailing tomorrow."

Casey turned to him, surprised. "Sailing?"

Jake nodded enthusiastically. "Yeah. The winds are always perfect the day after a storm settles. There's nothing like it. Just us, the water, and the open sky. No drama, I promise."

She hesitated, unsure if she was ready to trust him again.

"You don't have to decide right now. But if you're up for it, I'll be at the dock at seven. No pressure."

He stepped out into the gray afternoon, and Casey shut the door behind him. Her pulse still thudded in her ears. She pressed her palms to the wood, closed her eyes, and let the silence of the bungalow settle back around her.

Somewhere in that silence, one question echoed louder than the rest: Who really brought her home last night? And why hadn't they stayed?

CHAPTER 15
CAUGHT IN THE CURRENT

The early morning air was crisp, the storm's lingering coolness softening the usual tropical heat but keeping it as humid as ever. The marina was quiet except for the occasional clatter of halyards against masts and the distant squawk of seagulls. Casey walked along the dock, her sandals echoing faintly on the wood, a knot of anticipation twisting in her stomach.

Ahead of her, Jake stood on a modest sailboat named *Sea Change*, his back turned as he adjusted the rigging. The boat wasn't flashy—its white hull streaked slightly with wear—but it had a charm that matched Jake himself: well-loved, a little rough around the edges, but still holding steady.

"Morning, Case" Jake called without turning, as if he'd sensed her approach.

Casey stopped at the edge of the dock, raising an eyebrow. "You always this chipper at sunrise?"

Jake turned, his signature grin firmly in place. "Only when there's a good wind and good company."

She couldn't help but smile, despite herself. "Nice boat."

Jake extended a hand, gesturing her aboard. "Come aboard. I'll give you the grand tour."

Casey took his hand, stepping carefully onto the boat as it swayed gently beneath her. The deck was tidy but lived-in, with a small pile of neatly coiled line near the mast and a cooler tucked under the bench on the starboard side.

"It's not much," Jake said, his voice softer now, almost self-conscious. "But she's mine."

Casey ran a hand along the polished wood of the tiller, nodding. "She's beautiful."

Jake's grin softened, and for a moment, he looked like he might say something more, but instead, he turned back to the rigging.

"We've got perfect conditions today," he said, his energy picking up again. "The storm cleared everything out. Smooth sailing from here."

Jake moved easily around the boat, untying lines and hoisting the mainsail with practiced ease. Casey watched him, fascinated by how natural he seemed in this environment—like the ocean was as much a part of him as his music.

"What do I do?" she asked, stepping closer.

Jake paused, looking at her with a glint of mischief in his eyes. "You're eager to help? I like that."

He handed her a line, guiding her hands to the proper knots. "Just tie this off here. Nice and snug."

Casey fumbled with the rope, her fingers clumsy

against the unfamiliar texture. Jake leaned in, his hands brushing hers as he adjusted the knot.

"There," he said, his voice low and close. "Perfect."

She glanced at him, feeling the intimacy of the moment, but he'd already turned away, checking the sails.

With a final shove off the dock, *Sea Change* drifted into the open water, the wind catching the sails and pushing them forward. The marina shrank behind them, replaced by the wide expanse of the ocean, shimmering in the morning light.

Jake leaned back against the bench, his hands on the tiller, looking completely at ease. "Not bad, right?"

Casey nodded, the tension in her shoulders beginning to loosen. "It's beautiful."

Jake's grin returned, softer now. "Told you. Nothing like it."

As the wind filled the sails and the boat picked up speed, Casey felt the thrill of the open water. She let herself relax as the ocean stretched out before them like a blank page waiting to be filled.

"Alright, Case," Jake said, handing her the tiller. "Time to see if you've got what it takes."

Casey hesitated, her hands hovering with uncertainty over the smooth wood. "You're trusting me with this?"

"I'm trusting you," Jake said simply.

And as she took the tiller and felt the boat respond beneath her grip, Casey couldn't help but smile, her heart lifting with the sails as they sailed into the horizon. The

Sea Change glided smoothly over the water, its sails taut with the steady morning wind. Casey sat, her fingers loosely gripping the tiller as Jake lounged nearby, watching her with an easy grin. The open ocean stretched endlessly around them, the sun casting golden ripples across the waves.

"Not bad for a first-timer," Jake said, tipping his head toward her.

"I'll take that as high praise."

"It is," Jake said. "Most people freak out the first time they feel the boat tilt. But you? Natural."

She glanced down at the water, where the shadow of the hull skimmed just beneath the surface. "I guess it helps that I don't have time to overthink."

Jake chuckled, leaning back against the bench. "See? That's the trick. Don't overthink it. Just feel the wind, feel the water, and trust yourself."

Casey gave the tiller a slight adjustment, watching as the sails shifted and the boat picked up speed. Jake whistled low.

"Careful there. Getting cocky already?"

She shot him a flirtatious look. "Just seeing what this thing can do."

"This 'thing' happens to be my baby," Jake said, mock-offended. "Show a little respect."

Casey laughed, the sound carried off by the wind. For a moment, the tension she'd been carrying since Jake's visit to her bungalow seemed to dissipate.

Jake stood and moved to her side, gesturing toward the lines and sails. "Alright, let's step it up. See that line there? That's your mainsheet. Give it a tug—gently."

Casey followed his instructions, the muscles in her arms straining slightly as she adjusted the sail. The boat responded immediately, the bow cutting through the water with renewed energy.

"There you go," Jake said, his tone warm with approval. "You're a natural, Casey. Might have to hire you as my first mate."

She rolled her eyes but couldn't help the smile tugging at her lips.

"You have to admit we'd have fun," Jake said with a wink.

As the boat settled into a steady rhythm, Jake took the tiller back and gestured for Casey to sit on the bow. She climbed over the cabin and stretched out, the salty breeze brushing her face as she looked out at the endless blue.

"So, Case, what's your real story?" Jake asked, his voice carrying easily over the sound of the water. "What really made you pack up and come to Key West?"

Casey hesitated, then shrugged. "It's not much of a story. I was burned out, stuck in a job I hated, in a city that didn't feel like mine anymore. I needed a change."

Jake nodded thoughtfully. "A sea change, huh? Guess that makes you and the boat kindred spirits."

Casey smiled faintly, the weight of her decision to come to Key West suddenly feeling lighter. "Something like that."

Jake leaned back, his hands resting loosely on the tiller. "You know, I wasn't much different when I came here. Bounced around a lot—different towns, different gigs. Always running, never settling."

Casey glanced over her shoulder at him. "And now?"

Jake shrugged, his grin softening. "Now? I've got the music, the boat… and I think I've maybe figured out how to stop running. At least for a while."

His words hung in the air, carried by the breeze, and Casey heard the shift in his tone—a vulnerability she wasn't used to seeing in him.

"It's not a bad place to figure things out," she said quietly.

Jake met her gaze, the corners of his mouth lifting into a small smile. "No, it's not."

For a while, they sailed in comfortable silence, the boat moving effortlessly through the water. Casey leaned back against the bow, letting the sun warm her skin, and Jake whistled a soft tune as he steered.

The moment felt perfect—free, unburdened, and alive with possibility. But beneath it, Casey couldn't shake the feeling that the calm wouldn't last forever. As the shoreline shrank behind them and the horizon stretched ahead, she wondered if she was truly ready to face what lay beyond.

The water darkened to a deeper blue beneath the afternoon sun as Casey sat cross-legged on the bow, her arms wrapped around her knees as the wind played with her hair. Jake had let the boat settle into a steady rhythm, the sails full and the tiller tied off for now. He joined her at the bow, sitting with his legs stretched out and a can of soda in his hand. For a while, they didn't speak, the silence filled by the sound of the waves lapping against the hull.

"This is peaceful," Casey said finally, her voice quiet, almost reluctant to break the moment. She'd never actually heard Jake this quiet before.

Jake nodded, his gaze fixed on the horizon. "Yeah. It's why I love it out here. Just you and the water—no noise, no distractions. You can't hide from yourself out here."

Casey glanced at him, frowning slightly. "Do you think you've been hiding?"

Jake let out a low laugh, though there was no humor in it. "My whole life, probably. Always moving, always chasing something… or running from it."

Casey tilted her head, studying him. "What are you running from?"

Jake hesitated, taking a long sip of his soda. "Failure, maybe. Disappointment. Myself. Take your pick." He sighed, leaning back on his hands. "I screw things up, Case. It's kind of my thing. But out here?" He gestured to the water around them. "It's like a reset button. A chance to forget for a while."

Her chest tightened at his words, the sincerity in his voice pulling at something inside her.

"You can't run forever, though," she said softly.

Jake turned to her, his grin faint but genuine. "That's

the thing about the ocean. It's vast and expansive. The perfect place to run forever."

They fell silent again, the gentle rocking of the boat lulling them into a quiet rhythm. Then Jake shifted, his tone becoming lighter, almost teasing.

"So, what about you? You've got this whole fresh start thing going on. What are you trying to find?"

Casey exhaled, leaning her chin on her knees. "Adventure. Maybe clarity. Or just… something different. I don't really know yet."

Jake chuckled. "Sounds like you're as lost as I am."

"Maybe," she admitted. "But at least I'm trying."

Jake nodded, his expression thoughtful. "I get that. But, Case… you've got to be careful who you let steer your ship. Not everyone out here has your best interests at heart."

Casey frowned, sitting up straighter. "And by 'everyone,' I'm guessing you mean Phillip."

Jake didn't respond immediately, his eyes scanning the water as if searching for something unseen.

"Look," he said eventually, his tone cautious. "I don't want to harp on it. But I've seen what happens when Phillip's involved in people's lives. He might seem like he's got it all together, but trust me—there's more to him than you know."

Casey narrowed her eyes. "And what about you, Jake? Are you as perfect as you're trying to make yourself sound?"

Jake laughed, the sound more genuine this time. "Perfect? Not even close. But at least I'm honest about my flaws."

The tension between them simmered, a subtle undercurrent beneath the conversation. Casey turned her gaze back to the horizon, unsure what to believe.

"You're painting Phillip as this... bad guy," she said after a moment. "But the truth is, I don't know who to trust. You're both holding back. And I'm stuck in the middle."

Jake's grin softened, and he leaned closer, his voice low. "You don't have to trust me, Casey. Just trust yourself. Out here, the ocean's always honest. It shows you exactly where you stand."

Casey met his gaze, her heart twisting with uncertainty. "I hope you're right."

Jake straightened, brushing off the moment with a small laugh. "Enough heavy stuff. You ready to take the tiller again?"

She hesitated, then nodded, letting the conversation fade into the background as she focused on the water, the wind, and the horizon ahead. But the weight of Jake's words lingered, pulling her deeper into the current of doubt and discovery.

As the Sea Change glided back toward the shore, the late afternoon sun cast bright, white-yellow rays across the water, painting the scene in warm hues. The earlier tension between Casey and Jake had eased, their conversation settling into quieter moments.

Jake stood at the tiller, adjusting the sails as a light breeze carried them along. Casey sat on the bench near the stern, her arms resting on the edge of the boat, letting the salty wind brush her face.

"You know," Jake began, his tone lighter now, "for someone who said she didn't know much about sailing, you handled yourself pretty well out here."

Casey's lips parted into a big smile, tilting her head toward him. "Are you saying I passed your test?"

"With flying colors," he said, grinning. "I might even let you take the boat out on your own someday."

"Generous of you," she replied, her voice laced with sarcasm.

Jake stepped away from the tiller, letting the boat coast as he joined Casey on the bench. The movement of the water was gentle, almost hypnotic, and for a moment, they sat in companionable silence.

Jake turned to her, his gaze steady. "Let me show you something."

He stood and pulled a small box from the storage compartment beneath the bench. Opening it, he revealed a compass, its brass edges worn but polished.

"This was my dad's," Jake said, holding it out for her to see. "He wasn't much of a sailor, but he always said a good compass would get you out of any trouble. It's not about finding the fastest route—it's about finding the right one."

Casey took the compass carefully, running her fingers over its smooth surface. "It's beautiful," she said. "Do you still use it?"

Jake laughed. "Sometimes. Mostly, it's just a reminder. You know, to trust the direction I'm heading."

Casey handed it back, her voice thoughtful. "I like that."

The marina came into view, its docks bustling with activity as locals and tourists returned from their day on the water. Jake returned to the tiller, expertly guiding the boat into its slip. As Casey stepped off the boat, Jake handed her the rope to tie off. She worked quickly, her earlier awkwardness with knots replaced by newfound confidence.

Jake leaned against the railing, watching her with a satisfied expression. "See? I told you you'd be a natural."

"Don't get used to it," Casey said.

Jake hopped onto the dock, stretching his arms over his head. "So, what do you think? Ready to set sail again sometime?"

Casey hesitated, looking back at the Sea Change, then at Jake. "Maybe. It was… different. In a good way."

Jake's grin softened. "That's all I wanted to hear."

Casey nodded, her thoughts swirling as she walked back toward the marina's main path. Behind her, Jake's voice called out. "See you around, new girl."

"Really? I'm still new girl?" Casey called back.

"You'll be new girl for a while."

That night, Casey lay wide awake in bed, the ceiling fan spinning a slow, lazy circle above her. The sea breeze drifted in through the screen, warm and damp, ruffling the curtains. Marley was curled at her feet, blissfully asleep, occasionally twitching a paw in some dream-drenched chase.

But Casey couldn't settle. Every time she closed her eyes, her mind replayed the same two scenes like waves lapping the shore: the easy laughter and warm sun on the boat with Jake—and the hollow space in her memory where the storm had left her the night before.

She turned over, pulling the sheet tighter around her, and stared at the blinking light on her phone. A new text. Her heart fluttered, but she couldn't decide if she hoped it was Jake saying what a great day he had or Phillip finally checking in from last night. She reached for it.

Phillip. *Hey, last night got a bit wild. Please let me know you are okay.*

She read the message twice, then a third time, her thumb hovering over the screen.

That was it?

Not *"I'm sorry."* Not *"I tried to find you."* Not even a question mark. Just a vague, passive check-in like he was talking about some concert or street fair they both barely remembered.

She didn't reply. She set the phone face-down on the nightstand and rolled onto her back, staring at the ceiling like it might offer answers the message hadn't.

If Phillip hadn't brought her home, then he really had just let her walk into the storm alone. And Jake—Jake said he had. Said he made sure she was safe. Said it with that soft, sheepish smile like it pained him to admit he still cared that much.

Could he have lied?

She wanted to believe he wouldn't. The way he'd stood in her doorway, soaked to the bone, just to check on her—the way he'd watched her all day on the boat, not with hunger but with hope. It all felt real.

But so had other things, once.

The memory of arms around her—strong, steady, careful—lingered just beyond her reach. She couldn't place the scent. Couldn't hear the voice. It could've been Jake. It could've been Phillip. Hell, it could've been a good Samaritan and she wouldn't have known the difference.

And wasn't that the worst part? That there were pieces of the night still missing, and the two men orbiting her were both capable of shaping the truth in their own image.

She squeezed her eyes shut and pressed the heels of her hands into them. "Stop," she whispered, too softly for even Marley to stir.

Her stomach knotted. Part guilt. Part suspicion. Part the slow, nauseating crawl of self-doubt. She remembered the way Jake looked at her on the bow of the Sea Change—like he saw something in her worth believing in. She wanted that to be real.

She *needed* that to be real.

But what if it wasn't?

Casey shifted beneath the sheets, trying to bury herself in the blanket, in the dark, in anything but this tangle of not-knowing. She tried to picture the ocean. The way it moved without explanation. Honest, Jake had said. The ocean never lies.

But people do.

She didn't text Phillip back. She didn't text Jake either.

She just lay there, her thoughts pitching and rolling, caught in a current of doubt.

Outside, the palm trees rustled in the night wind, casting shadows that flickered against the walls. Marley let out a sigh in his sleep, and Casey reached down to rest her hand on his back. Steady. Familiar.

She closed her eyes, finally, and let sleep take her—not gently, not fully, but in waves.

CHAPTER 16
LOOKING FOR SOME PEACE AND QUIET

The early morning light filtered through the slats of the window blinds as Casey sat on the porch, as usual, toying with the rim of her coffee mug. Her eyes were bleary from a restless night, her limbs heavy with doubt. The taste of sleep hadn't touched her, not really. Dreams had come in fits and starts, always dragging her back to the storm or the boat or the unreadable expressions of the men who haunted her waking thoughts.

Betty leaned against the doorway in her usual stance, arms crossed, cigarette already lit. Her gaze settled on Casey—not unkindly, but with that sharp, perceptive edge that could cut through most people's bullshit.

"You look like someone who spent all night arguing with the ceiling," Betty said.

Casey smirked, raising her mug. "The ceiling won."

"You're too young to be losing sleep over boys," Betty said, stepping onto the porch and lowering herself into the chair beside Casey. "Or too old, depending on how you look at it."

"I think I'm the perfect age for terrible decisions," Casey muttered.

Betty chuckled. "Ain't that the truth." She paused, tapping ash into a chipped ceramic mug she used as an ashtray. "Let me ask you something. If you could disappear for a few days, no questions, no complications—just sun and salt and time to think—would you do it?"

Casey tilted her head, intrigued. "Hypothetically?"

"Sure. Hypothetically."

"Then yeah. In a heartbeat."

Betty nodded as if that confirmed something she already suspected. "Good. Then this next part won't sound so crazy."

She stood and stretched, then looked out toward the sea. "Ray's heading out tomorrow," she said casually. "He's got a run to Montserrat, picking up supplies and whatnot. Said he's got space for one more if someone's willing to pull their weight."

Casey's eyebrows lifted. "Ray?"

Betty gave her a look. "I *know* I've mentioned him. Old friend. Captain. Runs a tight ship. Grumbles like a bear but has a heart somewhere under all that sea salt."

"Montserrat," Casey repeated, the word rolling off her tongue like a foreign promise. "That's near Antigua, right?" She still had no idea who Ray was, but if he was a friend of Betty's, he must be trustworthy. And besides, this sounded like a free ride to her dream island.

"Close enough," Betty confirmed, her gaze steady. "If you're looking to get away from the boys for a bit, this might be your chance. But you'll have to work for it—he doesn't take freeloaders."

Casey's heart skipped a beat. Antigua. The idea of a sudden solo trip felt both thrilling and daunting, but after weeks of feeling trapped in the currents of other people's lives, the thought of charting her own course was irresistible; it was what she originally left Cincinnati to do.

"Well, I'd have to talk to Des and see if she'd give me some time off…" Casey began to say, but Betty interrupted her.

"Oh don't worry. Des actually suggested it. When Ray and I were down at MoonDog, he was lookin' for some hands for the journey; she remembered you and your Antigua daydreams."

A bit taken aback, Casey didn't realize just how many folks on this island were talking about her and her daydreams.

"Des wasn't even paying attention when Tia and I were talking about that!"

"Honey, Des is always paying attention."

"So how long would I be gone for?"

"Well, the journey'd be longer than your stay, unfortunately. Ray stops off at different ports making runs for folks—get's paid good money too—but he'd drop you off at the port he frequents in Antigua, continue down to a few other ports and pick you back up in three or four days."

"So I'd be gone, what, a week and a half?"

"Ha! Dear, it's a two-week journey one way—and that's if Ray is quick at each port. The lodging on the boat will suck, you'll need to be prepared for that, but it's a free ride to Antigua."

Casey closed her eyes, counted to three, and let words spill out of her mouth without thinking.

"Okay, I'm in."

"Good. Pack light. No princess shit. And bring your sketchbook. You'll regret it if you don't. I'll take care of Marley while you're gone"

Casey nodded, her mind already racing with preparations. She had no idea what she had just agreed to. The bungalow felt quieter than usual as Casey moved through it, or maybe it was just that she could hear her heartbeat. Her duffel sat open on the bed, half-filled with lightweight clothes, a pair of sandals, and her sketchbook. Each item she packed had to be deliberate; she couldn't afford any excess physical or emotional baggage at this point. She hesitated at the sight of her hoodie—the one she'd worn the night of the storm—but left it folded on the dresser. Too heavy.

Marley trailed her every step, nails tapping a quiet beat on the hardwood floor. When she zipped the bag closed, he circled it twice before lying beside it with a sigh.

"You're staying with Aunt Betty," Casey said, kneeling down and wrapping him in a tight hug. "No barking at the mailman, no chewing the couch. You hear me?"

He licked her cheek once, then rested his head on her knee.

As if on cue, Betty appeared in the doorway, a mug of coffee in hand. "Ready to go?" she asked, her tone brisk but not unkind.

Casey nodded, standing and brushing off her knees. "I think so."

"Good," Betty said, setting the mug down on the counter. "I'll make sure this one gets plenty of walks and belly rubs." She gestured to Marley, who wagged his tail weakly, sensing the goodbye.

Casey knelt again, wrapping her arms around the dog's neck. "Be good, Marley," she whispered. "I'll be back soon."

When she straightened, Betty gave her a long look. "You're doing the right thing, you know," she said. "Sometimes you've got to step away to see things clearly."

Casey smiled faintly. "I hope so."

Betty's no-nonsense demeanor softened for a moment. "You'll figure it out. Just don't overthink it. And don't forget to enjoy yourself." With that, Betty handed Casey the keys to her truck. "Just leave it down at the dock; I'll take a walk and pick it up later," Betty said. Marley watched from the porch, his ears perked up as the engine rumbled to life.

As Casey pulled out of the driveway, she glanced in the rearview mirror, feeling a pang of both guilt and excitement. This wasn't just about leaving—it was about finding something she hadn't even realized she'd lost.

The drive to the dock was uneventful, the roads still slick from the recent rain. When she arrived, Captain Ray was already waiting, his weathered face splitting into a smile as he spotted her.

"Got everything you need?" he asked, hoisting her dufflebag aboard with surprising ease for someone his age.

Casey nodded, taking in the small but sturdy vessel. "I think so."

Ray clapped her on the shoulder. "Good. We set sail in an hour. Get yourself settled."

As she stepped onto the boat, Casey felt the first stirrings of anticipation take root. Finally, she wasn't thinking about Jake or Phillip, or the tangled mess she'd left behind. She was thinking about the horizon, and the endless possibilities it promised.

The boat creaked and groaned as it swayed gently in the water, the salty breeze tugging at Casey's hair. It was a larger boat than Jake's, but not by more than 15 feet. She kneeled on a seat in the cockpit, watching the dock grow smaller and smaller until it disappeared entirely. The open ocean stretched out before her, a vast expanse of blue that seemed to mirror the sense of freedom bubbling within her.

Captain Ray stood at the helm, his hands steady on the wheel. He had the kind of presence that came from years spent at sea, a calmness that made Casey feel both safe and at ease. "Wind's in our favor today," he said, glancing over at her. "We'll make good time."

Casey nodded, gripping the railing a little tighter as the boat tilted with the current. "Anything I can do to help?" she asked, eager to feel useful.

Ray chuckled, nodding toward the sails. "You can start by helping with the rigging. Pull that line tight and secure it. You'll get the hang of it.

She followed his instructions, her hands fumbling at first but growing more confident with each knot she tied. The physical effort was grounding, a welcome distraction from the swirl of thoughts that had consumed her in recent weeks. As the hours passed, she found herself settling into the rhythm of the boat—the snap of the sails, the hum of the wind, the steady pulse of the ocean beneath them.

During a break, Ray handed her a bottle of water and joined her at the railing. "First time on a boat like this?" he asked.

"Well, it's only my second time on any boat," Casey admitted with a laugh. "I've always lived near water, but I guess I've never really been on it."

"Well, you're a natural," Ray said. "Takes most folks a lot longer to find their sea legs."

The compliment warmed her, and she found herself smiling. "Thanks. It feels good to do something different."

Ray nodded, his gaze fixed on the horizon. "That's the thing about the sea. It's always changing. Keeps you on your toes but gives you space to think, too."

As the sun dipped lower in the sky, painting the water in shades of gold and pink, Casey felt a sense of peace she hadn't known in a long time. They sailed that way, mostly quiet unless they were working, for nearly three days, anchoring the boat and sleeping at night.

The morning after their second port stop, Casey stood on deck barefoot, a bar of soap in one hand and a plastic bucket in the other. Her hair was plastered to her neck with sweat, and her skin felt sticky from sun, salt, and whatever grime had collected during their last supply run.

Ray, perched on a stool in the shade of the cabin, looked up from coiling a rope and raised an eyebrow. "You look like you're about to do somethin' foolish."

"I'm about to try bathing," Casey said. "Which might be foolish, considering I'm not entirely sure how."

Ray chuckled. "We've got fresh water stored for drinking, not for princess rinses. You want clean, you learn to get creative."

He stood, walked over to the side of the boat, and dipped a larger bucket into the ocean. "Two saltwater rinses to scrub the worst of it off. One freshwater splash to finish. You'll be cleaner than a Sunday saint."

Casey followed his lead, and five minutes later, she stood near the bow, bucket poised above her head, bracing herself.

"This is going to suck," she muttered.

She dumped the bucket. The saltwater hit like a slap, and she let out a half-scream, half-laugh. Ray cackled from the other side of the boat. "You're officially a sailor now."

She scrubbed her arms, legs, and hair with soap that claimed to be "ocean-friendly," then repeated the rinse. When she finally poured the small ration of freshwater over her head, it felt like a baptism.

Dripping and grinning, she looked toward Ray, who handed her a towel without comment.

"Better?" he asked.

"Infinitely."

That evening, they dropped anchor in a quiet inlet—nothing but mangroves and moonlight for miles. Ray made strong coffee on a single-burner stove and poured two mismatched mugs. They sat on overturned crates, toes almost touching.

"You ever get lonely out here?" Casey asked, staring into the dark water.

Ray scratched at his beard. "Sometimes. But the sea's good company. Doesn't ask for much. Just respect and a bit of your soul."

"That's comforting," Casey said dryly.

Ray grinned. "Better than people. People lie. The ocean just is."

They sat in silence for a while, the mug warm between her hands.

"You believe in ghosts?" she asked suddenly.

Ray didn't hesitate. "Absolutely."

Casey looked at him sideways. "Really?"

"Girl, you've never heard the wind whisper through torn sails at three in the morning in the Bermuda Triangle. It'll make you believe in all sorts of things."

She laughed, but goosebumps rose on her arms.

"What about you?" he asked, voice softer.

"I think I've been haunted," she said. "Not by a ghost, but...by a version of myself I left behind."

Ray took a long sip of coffee. "That kind of ghost's the hardest to outrun. But it's also the one you're allowed to say goodbye to."

They were four ports in and seven days deep when the boat's rhythm and routain felt familiar. Mornings began before the sun—Ray insisted the sea deserved attention before it gave anything in return—and Casey, for once in her life, didn't mind the early hours.

She woke with the gulls, stretched her limbs on the narrow bunk, and made her way above deck, where the sky bled slowly from lavender to gold. Most days, Ray was already there, barefoot, mug of instant coffee in hand, the collar of his faded shirt open and flapping like a flag of surrender to the wind.

Casey joined him without needing to speak. They didn't need much talking before coffee. The silence between them had become something familiar. A shape she could lean on.

"You learn anything useful in those dreams of yours?" Ray asked one morning, his eyes scanning the horizon.

Casey blinked against the sun. "I dreamt about my mom's garden," she said. "Back in Ohio. I used to help her water the marigolds."

Ray nodded like this was the most reasonable thing anyone could say at sea.

Later that afternoon, when they were docked for supplies at a sleepy port with more goats than people, Casey lingered on the edge of the harbor market while Ray bartered for oil and rope. Her fingers grazed handmade soaps and knotted bracelets. A woman sold passion fruit from a basket. Children splashed in a tide pool while an older man played steel drums off-beat but joyfully.

Casey bought a mango and sat near the edge of the dock, legs swinging. The fruit was sticky and sweet, juice trailing down her wrist, and she let it fall without wiping it away. She pulled out her sketchbook, now dog-eared and salt-splattered, and started to draw the dock, the tin-roofed buildings, the way everything here looked like it was halfway between standing still and falling apart.

Ray joined her eventually, bags in hand. He offered her a bottle of something that tasted vaguely like ginger and molasses. "For the nausea," he said.

"I'm not nauseous," she said, taking a sip anyway.

"You will be once we hit the pass between here and Dominica. Currents twist like a corkscrew there."

She grimaced. "How do you know all this?"

Ray shrugged. "Thirty-five years at sea. You usually stop counting after twenty."

They sat in companionable silence for a moment, listening to the clang of bells and the calls of dockworkers. They set sail again that evening, the sun slipping behind the mountains in a haze of pink and flame. As Ray navigated out of the bay, Casey stood at the bow, wind tearing at her hair, and for the first time in weeks, she didn't feel like she was running.

She felt like she was arriving.

Later that night, Ray showed her how to use the stars to find her bearings.

"The North Star doesn't care who you are," he said, pointing to the small, steady light. "It'll still guide you home if you ask."

Casey lay back against the deck, her fingers tracing constellations she didn't know the names of.

"I don't know where home is anymore," she admitted.

Ray didn't respond for a long time. Then, finally:

"Good. That means you're looking."

The boat rocked gently beneath them, the kind of lullaby the land could never offer. Casey closed her eyes and listened—to the wind, to the waves, to the sound of her own heartbeat finding a steadier rhythm.

And somewhere in the vast dark, she realized she hadn't thought of Phillip or Jake in days.

By the time the island of Antigua came into view, a dark silhouette against the dusky sky, Casey's heart was racing with anticipation. The boat cut through the water, drawing closer with each passing minute. She could make out the lush greenery, the gentle slope of the hills, and the promise of something new waiting just beyond the shore.

Ray's voice broke through her thoughts. "There she is. Antigua. You ready?"

Casey turned to him, her eyes shining. "More than ready."

As they approached the dock, Casey felt a spark of hope flicker to life within her.

"I'll drop you here, and pick you up here in four days; first light. You got that?"

"I got that."

The boat glided into the harbor as the last light of day gave way to the deep indigo of twilight. The gentle rocking slowed as Ray expertly maneuvered the vessel toward the dock. Casey leaned forward, her hands gripping the railing as she took in the sight before her. Antigua's coastline glowed softly under the flicker of lanterns and lights from the scattered buildings near the shore.

"And here we are," Ray said, cutting the engine. The sudden quiet was filled with the sound of waves lapping against the boat and the faint hum of life on the island. "Welcome to Antigua."

Casey exhaled, her excitement tempered by a moment of hesitation. She'd spent weeks yearning for something—freedom, clarity, herself—and now, standing on the brink of this new adventure, she felt both exhilarated and unsteady.

Ray caught her expression and gave her a reassuring nod. "Take your time. No rush to step off until you're ready."

She smiled at him, appreciating his unspoken understanding. As he tied the boat to the dock, Casey gathered her things, slinging her bag over her shoulder and clutching her sketchbook tightly. The wooden planks creaked beneath her feet as she stepped onto the dock. The air was warm and carried the scents of salt, tropical flowers, and the faint spice of food cooking nearby. Each step felt like a declaration—she was here, on her own terms, ready to face whatever came next.

"You'll be alright," Ray called after her, his voice tinged with fondness. "You've got the sea in your soul now."

Casey turned back to him, her smile wide and genuine. "Thank you, Ray. For everything."

He waved her off with a chuckle before returning to his boat to continue on the 27 miles to Montserrat. As Casey walked toward the glow of the small village ahead, she felt the weight she'd carried for so long begin to lift. Antigua stretched out before her, a canvas waiting to be filled.

The gravel path crunched beneath Casey's sandals as she made her way toward the village, her steps slow, cautious, like she didn't want to startle the quiet. The last light of day stretched long shadows across the earth, casting the pastel buildings in a soft amber glow. Shutters hung open to the warm breeze, fluttering like tired eyelids at the end of a long day. Bougainvillea spilled over fences, their blooms bruised purple in the fading light. Somewhere, a rooster crowed too late or too early—it was hard to tell.

She passed only a handful of people: an old man sweeping dust from his stoop, a couple sitting side by side in silence, watching the sky darken. A child darted past her barefoot, the plastic wheels of a toy truck dragging behind him. It felt like the island was exhaling. The day was finished; night was gently taking over.

Casey reached a small café with its door propped open, the lights inside already dimmed to a golden hush. The smell of grilled fish and citrus lingered in the air. A soft, slow reggae tune floated from an old radio behind the counter—tired, maybe, but still swaying to its own rhythm.

She stepped inside.

The woman behind the counter—late fifties, maybe, with silver threaded through her thick braids—looked up and nodded in welcome. She didn't speak right away, just finished stacking a few cups, her movements easy and familiar.

"Hi," Casey offered, her voice hushed, not wanting to break whatever spell the evening had cast.

"You look like someone who could use something cold," the woman said after a moment, voice warm, low.

Casey gave a soft laugh. "That obvious?"

The woman smiled, grabbing a glass and a lime from beneath the counter. "Only to someone who's been there too."

She handed over the drink, and Casey carried it to a small table near the open shutters. The wood was worn smooth, and the air smelled of salt and something sweet she couldn't quite place. She set her sketchbook down but didn't open it. Not yet. Instead, she watched the slow quiet of the town—how everything seemed to settle into itself here, like it had nothing to prove.

Her drink was tart, fresh, grounding. It snapped something into focus—not everything, but enough.

Eventually, she opened her sketchbook. The first page was cluttered with Key West—Captain Tony's, Marley sprawled in the tattoo shop, an unfinished sketch of Jake half-hidden behind guitar strings, that portrait of Phillip she started drawing. She flipped past it all.

A clean page.

She began to draw the café: the soft curve of the archway, the woman behind the counter, the way the shutters threw shadows on the floor. Her hand moved slowly, then steadily, lines taking shape without judgment or hesitation. It felt good to see instead of remember.

She was halfway through shading the folds of the curtains when the woman approached, wiping her hands on a faded linen towel.

"You're quiet," she said, nodding at the sketchbook. "Like someone used to watching more than speaking."

Casey looked up, startled for a second, then offered a small smile. "Old habit."

The woman pulled out the chair across from her and sat without asking. "You got a name?"

"Casey."

"Well then, welcome, Casey. I'm Amani. This here's mine," she said, sweeping a hand toward the café's cozy interior. "And upstairs is yours, for a few nights. Room's already ready."

Casey blinked. "Wait—you're the one I'm staying with? And how did you know it was me?"

"How many young American females show up in the port of a small town in Antigua alone in the evening?"

Casey didn't know how to respond.

"Plus Ray called ahead, gave me a description, and

booked your full stay, paid in full by someone named Betty," Amani winked.

Casey smiled. "Thank you."

Amani stood, her chair scraping gently against the tile floor. "Well. You'll sleep good tonight. That room catches the breeze just right. Tomorrow, I'll make you something strong and sweet to get your head working again." Amani set the key in front of Casey. "The stairs are just outside."

"That sounds… amazing," Casey murmured.

Amani winked again and turned away, humming faintly to the rhythm of the radio. Casey sat still, her eyes lingering on the fading gold beyond the shutters, then back to her half-finished sketch.

The lines on the page suddenly felt like more than art. They were proof. Of being here. Of choosing to come. Of trying.

After a while, she wandered again—down a narrow path behind the café, where lanterns flickered above shop windows that had already closed for the night. She passed a church with a cracked bell tower and a group of older men playing dominoes by candlelight, their laughter low and steady.

No one asked her name. No one needed to know.

Later, in the small guest room above the café, she stretched out on a woven blanket, the window open to the stars. There was no ceiling fan, no distant bar noise, no memory of a storm.

Only the rustle of leaves. The distant hush of waves. The promise of sleep.

CHAPTER 17
TO SEE THE SUN AGAIN

Casey woke to birdsong. Not the shrill kind that jolted you upright, but soft, melodic warbling—so gentle it threaded itself into her dreams and pulled her awake like a tide. For a moment, she didn't open her eyes. She just listened, letting the breeze slip over her skin and the linen sheets lay loosely around her legs. The air smelled different here. Less like salt and sweat, more like citrus trees and woodsmoke and rain that hadn't fallen yet.

When she finally opened her eyes, the room was bathed in the kind of golden light that made everything look like it had been dipped in honey. The shutters were still open, letting in sunlight and shadow in equal parts. A lizard clung to the wall near the window, its tiny chest pulsing as it blinked at her lazily.

Casey sat up slowly, surprised to find her body didn't ache for once. Her limbs were still, not trembling or tight.

Her thoughts were quiet too—less like shouting voices, more like murmurs. Background noise. Bearable.

She swung her legs over the edge of the bed and stepped onto the cool tile floor. No Marley to greet her this morning. No coffee waiting in the kitchen. But she didn't feel alone—not in a bad way. She felt… unmoored. In a way that just might lead to something new.

Downstairs, the café was quiet. The scent of baking bread clung to the warm air, and from somewhere deeper in the kitchen came the soft clatter of pans. A kettle hissed gently on the stove.

Amani looked up as she entered, offering a nod.

"You sleep okay?" she asked.

"Better than I have in weeks," Casey admitted.

"Good," she said, sliding a mug across the counter. "Coffee. Strong. And I made coconut bread."

Casey blinked. "You didn't have to—"

The woman cut her off with a look. "You think I make it for you? I make it because it's Thursday."

Casey smiled, accepting the plate and mug with a grateful nod. She took her breakfast outside, settling into the same spot where she'd sketched the night before. The village was beginning to stir. A few children walked by in school uniforms, their laughter bubbling like birdsong. A man on a bicycle passed with a basket of plantains strapped to the back. There was no rush here. Everything moved at the pace of the sun.

She took a bite of the coconut bread—warm, slightly

sweet, crumbly—and exhaled.

Today, she would draw. Not because she had to. Not because it would distract her. But because it felt right.

She pulled out her sketchbook and flipped past the Key West pages again. The blank sheet greeted her like a friend, not a challenge.

She began with the trees across the road—twisted trunks, big leafy canopies, roots that seemed to know more than they let on. She sketched the uneven cobblestones, the wrought-iron café sign, the tilt of a dog sleeping under a chair.

She thought about shadows and light. And the lines that held everything together.

And then she turned the page and started something new.

By midday, the sun had stretched high into a cloudless sky, bright and indifferent. The café had just a few locals lingering over conversation or leafing through weather-worn newspapers. Casey had moved to a shadier table beneath the awning, sketching the contours of the same dog from earlier, now flopped onto his side in a different patch of sunlight.

She didn't notice Amani until the older woman set down a tall glass of something pale pink and sweating from the heat.

"Guava juice," Amani said simply, then nodded toward the sketchbook. "That dog belongs to nobody but comes around like he owns the place."

"He has a good face," Casey said. "A little lopsided, but good."

Amani snorted. "Most of the good ones are."

They sat in companionable silence for a moment. Casey took a sip—cool and slightly tart, the kind of drink that made you think of beach towels and sticky fingers.

Amani lingered by the table this time, folding her arms across her chest. "So," she said, not quite a question, "what brings you here?"

Casey set down her pencil, glancing out toward the street like the answer might be walking by. "Honestly? It started with a dream. I've been talking about coming to Antigua for years—and then I moved to the Keys and everyone said I should visit. And then, out of nowhere, Betty—this woman I've been renting from, the one who apparently paid for my whole stay—tells me her friend Ray's taking a supply run to Montserrat and has room on the boat and needs help."

Amani blinked once, then burst out laughing. A big, sudden, full-body laugh that made the nearby café cat flinch and dart away.

Casey stared at her, blinking. "What?"

"Oh, child," Amani said, wiping at her eyes. "Ray? That man's been sailing between those islands longer than I've been pouring coffee. You think a sailor with thirty-five years on that route needs help?"

Casey blinked, startled. "But—he said—Betty said—"

Amani raised a brow, grinning. "How long you been sailing, then?"

Casey sighed, cheeks flushing. "Well… that was my second time on a boat. Ever."

Amani cackled again, shaking her head as she walked off. "Ray didn't need help. Ray—or somebody—gave you an excuse."

Casey sat there for a moment, stunned. And then—despite herself—she started to laugh too. Maybe she hadn't sailed across the Caribbean to help anyone but herself. And maybe everyone else already knew that.

The sun had begun its slow descent by the time Casey finished her juice and packed up her sketchbook. The shadows stretched long again, the breeze off the water cool but fragrant—carrying with it the mingled scents of hibiscus, sea salt, grilled fish, and sun-warmed stone.

She hadn't planned to go anywhere in particular. That was the beauty of being somewhere new with no expectations—everything was an option, and nothing was an obligation.

The narrow cobbled street curved gently uphill, and Casey followed it on instinct, her sandals slapping softly against the uneven stones. Every so often, she passed bright wooden homes with tin roofs and sun-faded paint, where open windows let out the clatter of dishes or the murmur of a radio. One home had dozens of wind chimes dancing in the doorway, their music high and chaotic like birdsong. Another had a stoop full of painted buckets brimming with basil and thyme and lemongrass.

She passed a bright turquoise wall covered in peeling murals—waves, faces, fish that looked like gods. One of the figures had gold-leaf eyes that caught the sun and winked. It made her stop for a moment. She sketched a quick outline in the margins of her sketchbook.

As she turned a corner, a chorus of voices rose up—children, maybe six or seven of them, racing barefoot down the hill, shrieking with laughter. A few blocks later, she found what looked like a garden growing wild between two abandoned buildings. Banana leaves waved lazily overhead, and thick vines curled through rusted fences. In the center was a carved wooden bench, weathered but still whole. She sat for a while, letting the hum of cicadas and the low rustle of wind through leaves wrap around her like a lullaby.

She wandered toward the western edge of the village, where the houses thinned out and the sky opened wide. Just past a bend in the road, she found herself looking at the sea again—this time from high above, where the cliffs dropped steeply toward a crescent of white sand and aquamarine water.

Casey let out a breath she hadn't realized she was holding.

From here, the world looked curved and endless.

She sat down in the grass and let herself watch the

sun begin to dip, casting the sky in every color she didn't have words for. This wasn't the kind of sunset you caught by accident while walking home or waiting for a dinner reservation. This was the kind of sunset that demanded your full attention. The kind that made you feel like the world was showing you something sacred. The kind that made you feel like you found the sun again.

CHAPTER 18
BETWEEN HERE AND THE HORIZON

The scent of simmering cinnamon drifted in from the kitchen, but Casey stayed in bed a few moments longer. The linen sheets had tangled around her ankles in the night, and for once, she didn't mind the warmth. Her limbs were sore in that good way—used, sun-kissed, stretched. No panic jolted her awake. No storm. No missing pieces.

Just breath. Just birdsong.

When she sat up, the shutters were cracked open enough to show a sliver of early light, streaking gold across the terra-cotta floor. She dressed quietly and folded her spare clothes with care, slipping them into her duffel in practiced motions. The sketchbook went on top, pages now rippled from salt air and smeared with charcoal thumbprints.

Downstairs, Amani was behind the counter, already humming. She didn't say good morning. She poured coffee and slid a cup across the bar.

"You ready?" she asked.

Casey nodded, lifting the mug. "Not really. But I'm going."

"Same thing, most days."

They drank their coffee in silence, save for the soft knock of a spoon in a sugar jar and the breeze that rattled the screen door. Casey finished first, setting her mug gently on the counter.

"I think I'll miss this place," she said.

Amani smiled, but didn't soften. "Of course you will. But you weren't meant to stay."

Casey adjusted the strap on her duffel and hesitated. "Thank you—for the bread. The juice. The place to land."

Amani reached over and clasped her hand, firm and brief. "Thank Ray and that Betty woman, too. They gave you the chance. You just decided to take it."

Before leaving the cafe, Casey slid a small drawing—Amani behind the café counter, backlit by sunlight—into the inside fold of the register near the till. She didn't leave a note. It didn't need one.

Outside, the sun had barely cleared the rooftops. The village was still stretching, still yawning itself awake. A dog trotted past, one ear flopped inside out. A boy balanced a bucket on his head like it was a crown.

Casey walked slowly to the dock, her feet familiar now with the cobblestones, her body shifting into the rhythm of this place even as she prepared to leave it.

Captain Ray was already there, a silhouette against the glint of water, arms crossed as if he'd been waiting all night.

"Morning," he called as she approached.

"Barely," she replied, climbing aboard.

Ray hoisted her duffel with ease and dropped it into the cabin. "You sleep?"

"A little," she said.

He nodded. "Good. We sail with the tide."

As they untied from the dock, Antigua slipped away behind them, a watercolor dissolving at the edges. Casey stayed at the railing longer than necessary, watching the outline of the island blur into sea and sky.

She didn't cry. She didn't smile, either.

But somewhere deep inside her, something felt lighter.

The sails filled with the morning wind, taut and eager. The boat sliced forward cleanly, water hissing beneath the hull. Casey sat cross-legged on the deck beside the helm, watching Ray adjust the lines with easy familiarity. The sun was higher now, the heat beginning to hum against the back of her neck, but the breeze kept it tolerable.

They'd been sailing in near silence for close to an hour—Ray humming under his breath, Casey sipping from her water bottle, her sketchbook closed in her lap like a cat that hadn't decided yet whether it wanted attention.

Finally, Ray broke the quiet. "You leave anything behind?"

Casey glanced up. "Like… in the Antigua?"

He shrugged. "Anywhere."

She thought about it. "No," she said slowly. "I took what I needed. Left what I didn't."

Ray gave a small grunt of approval. "That's harder than people think."

Casey shaded her eyes with one hand and studied him. "What about you? You ever think about staying in one of those ports you stop in?"

He grinned without turning. "You mean quit sailing and open a juice bar or a hammock shop or something?"

She laughed. "I mean, it's not a bad life."

"Nah," he said, tightening a knot. "Too still for me. I don't trust land that doesn't move."

Casey mulled that over. "But don't you ever get tired of leaving?"

Ray's hands paused. He looked out at the horizon, his voice quieter when he answered. "Sure. But the sea always gives me something back. A new current. A new sky. You stay long enough in one place, you start mistaking your comfort for truth."

Casey leaned back on her elbows, letting his words settle. The sky stretched wide above them, clear except for a thin line of clouds far to the east. The water sparkled like crushed glass.

"Betty told me you were grumpy," she said, finally.

Ray snorted. "She would."

"But she also said you had a heart under all that salt."

"She would say that, too." He gave her a sideways glance. "And she's usually right, which is the most annoying part."

Casey smiled. "You know she paid for my lodging?"

"Of course she did," Ray said. "Betty always sees what people need long before they do."

"She told me I needed to get away. That it would help me see clearer." Casey looked down at her hands. "I think she was right. But it also just… hurt. Everything I saw when I stepped away."

Ray didn't answer right away. He adjusted the sail again, then rested his hands on the wheel.

"Hurt don't mean wrong," he said. "Sometimes the hardest thing is realizing you weren't crazy after all. You were just stuck somewhere that didn't want you to know the truth."

"Oh and speaking of truth," Casey said, trying to lighten the conversation, "Were you ever going to tell me you didn't really need help?"

Ray laughed—a slow, gravelly sound that rolled out of his chest like distant thunder. "What gave it away? Was it the way you learned to tie knots upside down?"

She raised an eyebrow. "Amani told me. Said you've been sailing longer than she's been alive."

Ray shrugged, eyes squinting against the sun. "Might be true. Betty thought you needed this more than I did."

Casey narrowed her eyes. "So this whole time, you've just been humoring me?"

"No," he said, shaking his head. "I've been teaching you. There's a difference."

She snorted. "Teaching me what, exactly?"

Ray's expression turned thoughtful. "That the world's bigger than whatever storm you just came out of. That your hands still work. That you can do hard things and not fall apart."

Casey was quiet for a moment, watching the water. A flying fish leapt out ahead of the bow, a flash of silver in the light before it vanished again.

"I don't know if I feel stronger," she said eventually.

Ray didn't respond right away. He adjusted the wheel, the sails rustling in response. Then he glanced at her, eyes clearer than she'd ever seen them.

"You don't have to feel strong to be strong," he said.

The words hit her somewhere deep in the chest. She looked down at her hands—sunburnt, a little calloused now. Her fingers bore faint smudges of graphite from her sketchbook. She'd stopped hiding them in her sleeves. She'd stopped hiding a lot of things.

She reached for her water bottle and took a slow sip, letting the wind do the talking for a few minutes.

"So…" she said after a beat, "Betty and Des and even Tia—they were all in on it, weren't they? This whole grand escape plan."

"Is Tia that cute young girl from Des's place?"

Casey laughed, "Yes, yes she is."

"Then yes, Betty and Des and Tia." Ray grinned. "Let's just say people notice when someone's drowning on dry land."

Casey winced. "Ouch."

He shrugged. "You made it aboard, didn't you?"

She nodded, the hint of a smile playing at her lips. "I guess I did."

The silence that followed wasn't heavy. It stretched easy between them, like a well-worn rope that didn't need to be pulled taut to hold strong.

Ray pointed to a smudge on the horizon. "Next port's still a few hours out. You got time to sketch if you want."

Casey stood, brushing salt from her shorts. "You know, I think I will."

She climbed down to the bench near the stern, sketchbook in hand, and began outlining the lazy arc of the horizon, the way the clouds leaned against it like tired elbows. Her pencil moved with the same rhythm as the sea—gentle, unhurried, sure.

Back at the helm, Ray hummed an old tune.

The boat carried them forward.

The late afternoon sun hung low, casting long golden streaks across the gently rippling sea. The sky had taken on a warm haze, and the coastline of Cuba sat like a faded mirage off the starboard side. The boat moved steady, purposeful, cutting through the glimmering water as if it knew exactly where it was going.

Casey stood near the bow, one hand resting on the railing, the other shielding her eyes as she squinted toward the horizon.

"Hard to believe we're almost back," she said, mostly to herself.

Ray, standing at the helm, looked over and gave a short nod. "Ninety miles from Key West."

Casey turned, eyebrows lifted. "That's it? After all this? We're only ninety miles away?"

Ray chuckled. "We'll be there in three, four hours—if the wind stays kind."

Casey let out a breath, somewhere between amazement and exhaustion. "I don't know why I thought Antigua wasn't that far. It felt like we went halfway around the world."

"That's 'cause you did it the old way," Ray said. "Wind, tide, time. No shortcuts."

She smiled faintly, still staring out across the water. "It's funny. I kept telling people I was going to Antigua like it was a quick little escape. Didn't realize the journey was the point."

"Ya can't trust everything Jimmy Buffett says," Ray snarked, a teasing glint in his eye.

"Huh?" Casey blinked, thrown by the non-sequitur. She thought of all the strange signs and tokens around Shrimp Boat Sound that she still didn't fully understand.

"Ya know, the song?" Ray continued. Without waiting for her to respond, he started humming, then singing in a gruff, off-key voice: "She sailed off to Antigua… took her three days on a boat…"

He swayed his hips awkwardly as he sang, throwing in a little shoulder shake for effect.

Casey laughed, shaking her head. "I definitely don't get that reference."

Ray winked. "Ya haven't been in Key West long enough. Give it time."

She rolled her eyes good-naturedly, then looked back toward the line of sea and sky, her smile softening.

"I think I get the spirit of it, though," she said. "This… whatever this was. It slowed me down enough to hear myself again."

Ray didn't respond, but the slight tilt of his head was answer enough. He adjusted the sails without a word, letting the silence stretch between them like the open water ahead.

Casey sat down on the bench near the railing, sketchbook in her lap. She didn't open it this time. Instead, she just watched the ocean.

CHAPTER 19
RETURN TO THE REEF

The warm, salty breeze swept through Casey's hair as she stepped off of the Ray's sailboat and onto the familiar shores of Key West. Everything looked the same, from the turquoise waters to the bustling streets lined with pastel-painted shops. Yet, something about it all felt different, as though the island itself was welcoming her home in a way it hadn't before. She adjusted her bag on her shoulder and took a deep breath, savoring the feeling of solid ground beneath her feet.

Her first stop was Betty's house. *I guess I can start calling it home now*, Casey smiled to herself as she weaved through streets that were unfamiliar to her just a few months ago. The bungalow looked just as she had left it, not that she expected a month to change much. The porch was still adorned with potted ferns but Betty added new wind chimes that tinkled softly in the breeze. Betty opened the door before Casey could get close to the house, her sharp eyes immediately softening as she took in the younger woman's relaxed posture and quiet smile.

"You look different," Betty said, stepping aside to let Casey in. "Good different. Like you finally figured something out."

Casey laughed, setting her bag down in the foyer. "Maybe I have, thanks to you."

"What did I do? I didn't do nothin'," Betty said, shrugging her shoulders in an exaggerated manner.

"The jig is up. Ray told me," she said. "Well—Ray and Amani, the woman who Ray sent me to stay with. I asked her if Ray really needed help on the supply run, and she just about died laughing."

Betty chuckled, not the least bit apologetic.

Casey took a sip of her tea. "You set me up."

Betty didn't deny it. "Not just me. Des. Tia. Even Ray, though he took a little convincing. The man's got salt for bones, but he's not heartless."

Casey looked down at the table, running a thumb along a faint water ring in the wood. "I should be mad, I guess. Or at least a little embarrassed."

"You gonna be?" Betty asked, leaning back in her chair, arms crossed but not unkind.

Casey met her eyes. "No. I think I'm just… grateful."

Betty's face softened, her sharp lines easing into something maternal. "You were drowning, sweetheart. All we did was toss you a line."

"I didn't realize how far gone I was until I got some distance. From everything. From myself."

"That's the trick," Betty said. "Sometimes you can't see

the shape of the storm when you're right in the middle of it. Gotta get to the edge before you even know what hit you."

Casey nodded slowly. "I kept thinking this trip would fix everything. But it didn't. Not really."

"Nope. And it wasn't supposed to," Betty said. "It just reminded you that there's more to you than what you ran from."

"I started drawing daily again," she said, almost shyly. "Not because I had to. Just because it felt right."

Betty grinned. "That's how you know it's working. You're finding your way back—not to what you were, but to who you are."

Casey felt the weight of those words settle gently in her chest. She reached across the table and placed her hand over Betty's. "Thank you. For everything. For the nudge. For the net. For the home to come back to."

Betty squeezed her hand. "Anytime, darling. That's what we do around here—we look out for our own."

"Not to ruin the moment, but where is my dog?" Casey asked.

"I like to think of him as *our* dog," Betty smiled. "And he's in the next door neighbor's yard playing with the kids."

"I'm gone a month and you got my dog a babysitting gig?"

"I wish it paid," Betty snorted.

Marley's bark interrupted them, the Labrador bounding into the room with his tail wagging furiously.

The neighbor boy opened the front door to let him in.

"He heard you come home and was whining at our fence to come back," he called, slamming the screen door and running back to his yard.

Casey dropped to her knees, wrapping her arms around him as he licked her face with unrestrained joy. "I missed you too, buddy," she said, her voice thick with emotion.

Betty watched the reunion with a knowing smile. "He's been waiting by the door every day. I'm glad you're back—for his sake and mine. Now, sit down and tell me everything."

They spent the rest of afternoon on the porch, Casey recounting her time in Antigua while Marley dozed at her feet. Betty listened intently, her occasional nods and wry comments encouraging Casey to keep going. When Casey described the clarity she'd found on the island, Betty's expression turned thoughtful.

"It's not easy, you know," Betty said, sipping her coffee. "Letting go of what doesn't serve you. But it sounds like you've done just that. Hold onto it, Casey. Don't let anyone pull you back into their mess."

Casey nodded, her resolve hardening. "I won't. I've got too much I want to do, too much I want to be."

As the sun dipped lower in the sky, Casey stood to leave, Marley's leash in hand. "Thank you for the kind words, Betty. "

Betty waved her off with a heartfelt smile. "Go on, now. Key West missed you. But not as much as you missed yourself."

Casey's first venture back into town wasn't to the usual haunts where she might run into Jake or Phillip. Instead, she went back to Marta's Cafe, where she'd planned to share her sketches for the first time.

"Casey!" Marta greeted her warmly from behind the counter. Her curly hair was pulled back into a loose bun, and her apron was dusted with flour. "You're back!"

"I am," Casey said, smiling as she set her bag down. She pulled out her sketchpad, its pages filled with images from Antigua. "And I brought these."

Marta's eyes lit up as Casey carefully laid out a series of sketches on the counter. There were vibrant market scenes, fishermen silhouetted against the sunrise, and detailed renderings of the lush hillsides. Each piece seemed to hum with the energy of the island.

"These are incredible," Marta breathed, her hands hovering over the sketches as though they were treasures. "The colors, the movement—it's like I can feel the sun and the sea."

Casey's cheeks warmed at the praise. "Antigua was...special. It felt like every moment was begging to be captured."

"Well, you did it justice," Marta said, looking up at her. "These are going to be perfect for the display. Unless, you would still rather keep them private?"

"If you think they are good enough, then who am I to argue?" Casey said with a smile.

"Great. Let's pick a few to frame and put up."

Casey nodded, her nerves settling into a quiet excitement as she and Marta began to sort through the sketches. They chose a mix of bold, colorful pieces and softer, more intimate scenes, some even in full grayscale. As Marta worked on framing and hanging the first sketch, she paused and glanced over her shoulder. "You know, Casey, this is more than just art. It's you—your perspective, your experience. People are going to feel that."

The words resonated deeply. Casey had always thought of her art as a private endeavor, something that existed more for herself than for anyone else. But now, seeing it in Marta's hands and soon on the café walls, she realized it could be something more—a way to connect, to share—and somewhere in the back of her mind she thought of how Phillip viewed tattoos.

Leaving the café, Casey carried that warmth with her. She didn't stop at the Green Parrot or wander toward familiar faces. Instead, she walked along the quiet streets, Marley by her side, letting the evening air fill her lungs.

As the stars emerged one by one, Casey found herself smiling. The island wasn't just a backdrop for her life anymore—it was a part of her story, and she was ready to write the next chapter on her own terms.

The bungalow came into view as she rounded the corner, its soft yellow paint illuminated in the pale glow of the moonlight. She hadn't been back inside since she got home. Just dropped her duffle bag at Betty's up front and went on her way to Marta's with Marley.

She paused at the door, her hand resting on the brass doorknob. For a moment, she didn't move, letting the night wash over her. The scent of salt lingered in the air, mingling with the faint trace of jasmine from the overgrown vine by the window. This was *home*. Marley nudged her leg with his nose, pulling her back to the present.

"Alright, boy," she murmured, twisting the knob and stepping inside.

The bungalow greeted her with a familiar warmth. The small living room was untouched, its mismatched furniture and eclectic décor exactly as she'd left it. A stack of books still sat on the coffee table, a throw blanket was draped over the arm of the couch, and a shell-shaped lamp—that she initially thought was tacky—cast a soft glow in the corner. Casey set her bag down by the door and reached to switch on the overhead light, but paused. She didn't need it. The moonlight streaming through the windows was enough, bathing the room in a serene silver hue.

Marley padded ahead of her, sniffing around the room as if reacquainting himself with the space after living in Betty's house for a month. He paused by the couch, his tail wagging furiously, before hopping up and curling into a contented ball. Casey chuckled softly, shaking her head as she slipped off her shoes and padded barefoot into the kitchen.

She opened the fridge and found it mostly empty, save for a bottle of water and a few takeout condiments. Grabbing the water, she twisted off the cap and took a long sip, leaning against the counter. The quiet of the bungalow wrapped around her, and realized it felt like a comfort rather than an emptiness like it would have before.

The bedroom was simple and uncluttered. The bed was neatly made, the soft gray quilt folded just so. Her small desk by the window was bare except for an empty vase, a forgotten remnant of a bouquet she couldn't remember. She placed her sketchpad carefully on the nightstand, alongside a small conch shell she'd brought back from Antigua. It felt right to have a piece of the island that was now part of her home.

Casey changed into a soft, worn t-shirt and a pair of shorts, her movements slow and deliberate. She pulled back the curtains, letting the moonlight flood the room, and climbed into bed. Marley followed, hopping onto the foot of the bed and stretching out with a satisfied groan.

Lying there, Casey stared at the ceiling, her thoughts swirling. The bungalow was the same, but she wasn't. Antigua had left its mark on her in ways she hadn't fully understood until now. She thought about Betty's words, about letting go of what didn't serve her. That resolve filled her now, a quiet but unyielding strength.

Her thoughts turned briefly to Jake and Phillip. Their faces flickered in her mind, but she pushed them aside for the moment. Tonight wasn't about them. It was about her—this new version of herself that she was still getting to know. The bungalow was quiet except for the soft hum of the ceiling fan above and Marley's rhythmic breathing at the foot of the bed. Casey lay on her back staring at the shadows shifting with the breeze outside, her body still but her mind restless.

She closed her eyes, inhaling deeply, letting the salty breeze from the open window fill her lungs. Her thoughts went back to Betty's words again—about letting go of what didn't serve her. It wasn't just a mantra; it was a challenge. Could she really let go?

Her mind wandered back to the café and Marta's encouragement. The sketches she'd left there were more than art—they were pieces of herself. Casey had never felt like she had something to offer the world that wasn't tied to anyone else, but now she did.

She opened her eyes. Tomorrow, she would face Jake and Phillip. But tonight, she would hold onto this moment of quiet clarity.

CHAPTER 20
NOW SHE FEELS LIKE A REMORA

Casey woke to the scent of bacon and waffles drifting through the open slats of her bedroom window. Outside, a rooster crowed in the distance.

She swung her legs over the side of the bed and stood, stretching until her spine popped. The scent of breakfast thickened in the air—Betty always cooked when she had something on her mind.

Slipping on a pair of soft shorts and a tank top, Casey padded across the cool floor, opened the screen door, and stepped outside into the yard. Dew clung to the grass, and the morning sun was just beginning to climb above the palms. She paused, tilting her face toward it, letting it warm her eyelids.

From the open kitchen window of the main house, Betty's voice rang out like a bell.

"Girl, you better not be standing out there pretending you're still in Antigua. Get your ass inside. Waffles are getting cold."

Casey smiled, that wide, involuntary kind of smile that comes when someone sees through you and doesn't mind. She crossed the small stone path to the back porch, slipping in through the screen door just as Betty was pouring syrup into a mismatched ceramic pitcher. The kitchen smelled like butter and cinnamon and echoed old radio music—Betty's kind of sacred.

"Thought maybe I'd sneak a few more minutes of peace before the island woke up," Casey said, easing into the chair at the table.

Betty snorted. "You're lucky I didn't set Marley on you. He'd have dragged you in by the pajama leg."

Casey laughed, eyes softening. "He'd probably just bring me the ball and wait."

"Well, so would I," Betty said, setting a plate in front of her. "But this time I brought waffles. Now eat."

Casey picked up her fork and took a bite—crispy edges, soft center, just the right amount of salt. Her eyes closed briefly in appreciation.

"God, I missed this," she murmured.

Betty poured coffee into two mugs and sat down across from her. "We missed you too. Now tell me what you're gonna do with all that clarity you found while pretending to help an old man sail."

Casey laughed into her coffee. "Still working on that part."

A soft chime buzzed on Casey's phone, vibrating against the wood of the kitchen table. A text from Phillip.

"Hey. It's been a while. You free to talk sometime?"

Casey stared at it for a second too long. Betty didn't say anything, but Casey could feel her watching. Waiting.

She set the phone down without responding. "He wants to meet up."

Betty raised an eyebrow. "Which one?"

Casey rolled her eyes. Her phone buzzed again. *"Saw Ray's boat in the marina. Didn't know you were back. Missed you. Drinks tonight?"*

Casey sighed and dropped the phone onto the counter. "Both of them."

Betty laughed heartily.

"That's all you, honey."

Instead of texting either of them back, Casey texted Tia. *Drinks?* Of course, Tia said yes.

They met just after sunset at The Lost Shaker, where the air still carried the heat of the day and the lights strung overhead blinked like tired fireflies. The bar had the easy hum of a Tuesday night crowd—just loud enough to blend into, quiet enough to talk over. Casey claimed a booth in the corner while Tia got them two mojitos.

When she slid in across from her, Tia gave her a look. "You have that 'I'm pretending everything's fine but it's not' face. Spill."

Casey snorted and took a sip of her drink. "I haven't even said hi yet."

Tia raised an eyebrow. "Girl, you said hi when you texted me. You brought me to the confessional."

Casey smiled into her glass. "Fair enough."

They sat for a moment, letting the ice melt slightly in their drinks. The tang of lime and mint cut through the heavy air. Music drifted through the open door—a guy with a guitar playing something mellow and familiar.

Finally, Casey leaned back and let out a long breath. "They both texted me. Jake and Phillip. Within minutes of each other."

Tia didn't flinch. She just stirred her drink slowly. "Yeah. I figured that'd happen. Word gets around when Ray's boat pulls in."

Casey glanced at her. "I mean they both had to be preoccupied for the month I was gone."

Tia nodded. "I mean, sorta. Jake's been… twitchy. He's been playing every bar that'll have him and snapping at the sound guy over nothing. And Phillip's been holed up at the tattoo shop like he lives there."

"They both want to talk."

"Do you want to talk to them?"

Casey didn't answer right away. She traced the condensation ring on the table with one finger. "I don't know. Part of me wants to run. Back to Antigua. Or maybe just hide behind Betty's hydrangeas and eat waffles forever."

"Tempting," Tia agreed. "But not a long-term plan."

Casey hesitated. "I don't know how I feel about either of them anymore."

"Yeah, but that's not the same as not feeling anything."

Casey gave her a tired smile. "You know, you're annoyingly wise sometimes."

Tia shrugged. "Comes with drinking my body weight in rum and watching every romantic disaster unfold in this town at least twice."

Casey swirled the straw in her glass. "Jake makes me feel lighter. Like everything was easy. But he also made me feel… twisted. Like I was being pulled into something I couldn't control."

"And Phillip?"

Casey frowned. "He makes me feel safe. But he can be so aloof; I can never tell how he's really feeling. I certainly don't have that problem with Jake."

Tia was quiet for a beat, then said, "Well, damn. You're really stuck between a rum punch and a hard place."

That made Casey laugh—a real one, the kind that unspooled something tight in her chest. "You're not mad? I mean… you're friends with Jake."

"Yeah," Tia said, sitting back. "Jake's a good guy. But he's complicated. Charming, but sometimes… slippery. You never know if you're dancing or drowning. And I've never been interested in him like that, so it's not weird. I want you to do what's best for you. Even if that's neither of them."

Casey stared at her, surprised by the clarity in that answer. Tia raised her glass. "To not being remoras. Swim your own damn path."

Casey clinked hers against it. "To freedom."

They drank in unison, letting the sweetness settle in their mouths and the salt of the air remind them both: tides come and go, but a girl in Key West still gets to choose her direction.

That night Casey laid still on the couch, eyes open, staring at the ceiling. There was no rush of anxiety in her chest, no second-guessing what needed to be done. She had already made her decision.

She padded into the kitchen, barefoot, the floor cool against her skin. Marley's tail thumped against the cabinets as he looked up at her, head resting on his paws.

"I know, buddy," she murmured, running a hand over his fur before grabbing her phone from the counter.

She scrolled past the notifications she didn't care about and went straight to her messages. She tapped out the same text to both Jake and Phillip, sending them separately.

Meet me at the benches by Shrimp Boat Sound at 8 tomorrow night. We need to talk.

She didn't elaborate. They could show up or they couldn't. That was their choice. But she was done playing by *their* rules. It was time they played by *hers*.

CHAPTER 21
THE BIG WHITE TEETH

Neither Jake nor Phillip responded immediately, but she wasn't waiting for their approval, so Casey went to bed with her mind at ease. She chose Shrimp Boat Sound because, while an island icon, it was pretty nondescript unless you had a Jimmy Buffett fan with you.

The next morning she filled Marley's bowl, poured herself a cup of coffee, and leaned against the counter, watching a cat stroll by outside her window. Key West had always been a place where time moved differently—somehow slower and faster all at once.

Today, though, she was in no hurry.

She wasn't nervous.

She wasn't uncertain.

She was ready.

By the time the sky faded into soft streaks of peach and lavender, Casey was already sitting on one of the worn wooden benches outside Shrimp Boat Sound. The salty breeze rolled in from the marina, carrying the faint scent of diesel fuel and fresh catch from the nearby docks. This place was far enough from the bars and tourist traps that she wouldn't have an audience—but open enough that she had *exit points* if things got out of hand.

Her back was straight, legs crossed at the ankle, her fingers loosely gripping a takeaway cup of rum and coke. She wasn't second-guessing herself. She was *ready*.

A lone pelican drifted across the water, diving suddenly and emerging with a wriggling fish clutched in its beak. Casey watched it, feeling a strange kinship with the quiet, predatory patience. *Sometimes you wait. Sometimes you strike.*

The sound of flip-flops slapping against pavement broke the stillness. She didn't turn immediately, but she could already picture Jake's easy swagger as he approached—*relaxed, cocky, like nothing could touch him.*

"Well, well," he drawled as he spotted her. "If this isn't the most mysterious damn text I've gotten in a while. And after a month of being gone, and not even a postcard."

Without waiting for an invitation, he dropped onto the bench beside her, legs sprawled out, arms draped over the back like he owned the place.

"You wanted to see me, babe? Should've just said you missed me. I would've made it easier on you."

Casey didn't dignify that with a response. Instead, she glanced at her watch. 7:59 p.m.

Right on time, Phillip arrived.

He approached the benches at a slower pace, taking

in the scene. Unlike Jake, he didn't immediately sit. He stood just a few feet away, hands in the pockets of his jeans, gaze steady.

"Guess I should've known," he muttered, eyeing Jake before turning to Casey. "You want me here for the same reason you wanted *him* here?"

Jake let out a bitter chuckle, shaking his head. "Unbelievable."

Casey finally exhaled, shifting her weight so she could face both of them. She didn't give either of them a chance to talk first.

"You're both here because I need to make something clear," she said, voice even, unwavering. "And I didn't feel like having this conversation twice."

Jake scoffed. "Oh, this oughta be good."

Phillip, to his credit, just tilted his head, waiting.

Casey took one last sip of her drink, then set it down on the bench beside her. She met their gazes, one at a time, making sure they understood that this wasn't a debate.

"I'm not going to be defined by either of you," she said simply. "I will see who I want, when I want, how I want. And if either of you have a problem with that, then you know where the exit is."

Jake tensed beside her, his jaw flexing. For the first time, his usual bravado didn't have an immediate comeback.

Phillip, on the other hand, just exhaled slowly, like he had seen this coming.

"And if we both walk?" he asked, his voice calm, measured.

Casey lifted her chin. "Then that's your decision."

Jake let out a sharp laugh, standing abruptly. "Right. So that's it? You get to play both sides? Until you get bored? Or *worse*—until you decide which one of us is the *runner-up*?"

Casey didn't flinch. "No, Jake. That's not it. This isn't a competition. That's the problem—you've been treating me like I'm something to win. And I'm not."

Silence stretched between them.

Phillip's gaze stayed on her, unreadable.

"And while we're at it, I have another question."

Casey exhaled and stood from the bench, her drink abandoned. She crossed the space between the two men, grounding herself. This was the moment. She had waited long enough. Her voice was calm, but there was no mistaking the weight behind it.

"I need to know something. And I want both of you to answer honestly."

Neither Jake nor Phillip moved.

She met their eyes, one at a time.

"That night, during the storm… I blacked out at the Green Parrot. Someone brought me home. Tucked me in. Left without a word. And I've been trying to figure out who it was ever since."

She watched them closely. "So tell me. Who was it?"

A beat of silence passed—and then, simultaneously:

"I did," they both said.

Casey blinked.

Jake looked smug, almost triumphant, like he'd won a prize.

Phillip looked confused. His brows furrowed.

"I did," Phillip said again, more firmly now, like he couldn't believe what he was hearing. "I found you outside, by the fence. You barely recognized me. You collapsed and I carried you in."

Jake scoffed. "Bullshit. I saw her stumble out of the Parrot. I followed her. Got her home, made sure she was safe, and left before it turned into a thing."

"You didn't even get up from the bar," Phillip said, tone flat but icy.

"I left right after her," Jake snapped. "Ask anyone."

Casey's heart was pounding.

Phillip stepped forward, slow and deliberate. "You're lying."

"Prove it."

"I don't have to. I was there."

Casey raised a hand. "Stop."

The air crackled with tension. She looked between them—Jake's eyes flashing with defiance, Phillip's steady and wounded.

"You both expect me to believe you. But only one of you is telling the truth."

Neither spoke.

Casey's breath caught in her chest. She wanted to believe Jake—God, she did. Why would he claim he helped her if he didn't. But Phillip had no reason to lie.

"I don't know what game this is," she said quietly. "But I'm not playing it."

Jake moved toward her. "Case—"

She stepped back. "No."

Casey's eyes burned. She didn't know who to believe, and that uncertainty felt worse than anything.

"Whatever this is between the two of you—your history, your pride—it ends now. Because I'm not some prize you win by being the most convincing."

She turned away, her chest tight, her throat raw.

"I'll figure out the truth," she added, quieter this time. "And when I do, I hope at least one of you has the decency to be ashamed."

She walked away then, leaving them both in silence under the Key West dusk, the soft hum of the marina the only sound between them.

Casey left the guys behind, hoping neither had the guts to follow her. She marched straight to the Green Parrot. Someone must've seen something.

The bar was quieter than usual for a Key West evening—only a few regulars slouched on stools, and a local band was tuning up in the corner. The low hum of conversation, the clink of glasses, the lazy ceiling fans stirring the muggy air—all of it felt familiar and strangely hollow.

Casey made a beeline for the bar, her sandals slapping against the worn wood floor. Pati was there, as always, wiping down the counter with a rag that had seen better days. Her sleeve of tattoos peeked out beneath a faded T-shirt, and her expression was as unreadable as ever until she caught sight of Casey.

"Well, well," Pati said, raising an eyebrow. "Look who blew in."

"Hey," Casey said, breathless. "Can I ask you something?"

"That depends. You here for a drink or the truth?"

Casey leaned on the bar, voice low. "Both, if you're offering."

Pati nodded once, pulled a short glass from beneath the bar, and poured her a shot of rum. Casey took it.

"That night—the storm. I was here. Drunk out of my mind. I left at some point and someone brought me home. I don't remember who. Do you know?"

Pati's face didn't change, but she stopped wiping the bar.

"Yeah, but you left alone."

"Are you sure?" Casey asked"

"Yeah," she said finally. "I remember."

"Huh," Casey pondered.

"But shortly after you left, someone went after you."

Casey's heart thudded. "Was it Jake?"

Pati let out a breath through her nose. "Jake was here. Loud, as usual. But no, it was the other one. He's a regular, but he's quiet. The one with the French accent. I can never remember his name."

Casey swallowed hard. "Phillip?"

Pati gave her a look. "Tall, quiet type? Showed up dripping wet, sat next to you like he was guarding Fort Knox? Yeah, I saw him. Wouldn't take a drink, just sat there watching you like you might shatter."

Casey gripped the glass. "Did you see him leave?"

"I saw Jake and him go at it, then you stormed off—literally into the storm. They continued to bicker once you left. Then the power went out. By the time I got the emergency lamps up, he was gone."

Casey's throat tightened. "So it was him."

"Yeah," Pati said. "That guy? He was worried. Not the 'I'm trying to get laid' kind. The real kind."

"I should've asked you sooner," she murmured.

Pati shrugged. "Sometimes we don't wanna know the truth until we're ready to believe it."

Casey nodded slowly, a wave of shame and relief crashing together in her chest. "Thanks, Pati."

"Don't mention it," she said, already turning back to restock the garnish tray. "But if you ever get in that state again, you better sit your ass at this bar until someone can walk you home. And you never go out in a storm like that unless you have to."

Casey smiled faintly. "You got it, Pati. But right now, I've gotta go."

Casey rushed out the door. Her legs were moving before she had made a conscious decision. The walk to Southernmost Tattoo was barely five minutes, but it felt like she couldn't move fast enough.

Duval Street was alive, buzzing with the seamless blend of tourists and locals, the night pulsing with neon lights and the steady hum of music spilling out from open-air bars. Groups of day drinkers, still going strong, wove in and out of crowds, margaritas sloshing in plastic cups. Couples strolled arm in arm, the scent of rum and fried seafood thick in the warm air.

Normally, Casey moved through these crowds with ease, ducking past bachelorette parties, avoiding the stumbling tourists who had clearly underestimated the potency of a Duval Street mojito. But tonight, it all felt loud. Cluttered. Too much.

She wasn't second-guessing her decision—she just wanted to be there already.

By the time she reached Southernmost Tattoo, her shoulders had tensed from the push of the crowd. She stepped off the street and burst into the shop, exhaling as the noise of Duval dulled behind the door. The sharp, familiar scent of antiseptic and ink filled the space, a stark contrast to the sweat and liquor outside.

The counter attendant was asleep on the couch meant for clients. He jumped awake, startled by Casey's forceful entrance. An artist Casey didn't recognize was working at one of the stations with bright, colorful work on the walls. The artist nor the client lifted their head to see who came in the door, both concentrated on their art or their pain, respectively.

"Is Phillip here?" Casey asked gasping for air as if she had just gone for a run.

The sleepy attendant shook his head no. "Just missed him. He stopped in and grabbed his bag and said he was going home for the day."

"Shit." Casey said, and she left just as forcefully as she had entered. She took off, actually running this time, toward Petronia street—the next side street over where Phillip sometimes parked his bike. Casey had never actually seen it, but he said he parked there a few times, so it was her last hope.

As she reached the corner, she saw Phillip revving his engine to take off.

"Phillip!" Casey shouted—but her voice was lost in the roar of his engine and the murmur of the street.

She dashed around the corner just as he accelerated into the road, her momentum too fast to stop in time. The world tilted—headlights flared, tires screeched, and a deep, guttural *thrum* of the bike's brakes howled as he yanked the handlebars left, narrowly swerving past her.

"Shit!" Phillip shouted, killing the engine as the bike fishtailed slightly and came to a stop just inches from her. "Casey!"

She stood in the middle of the street, heart racing, chest heaving, frozen in the wash of adrenaline. A car horn blared somewhere down the block, but all she could hear was the pounding of her heart in her ears and the metallic click of the bike cooling beneath him.

Phillip threw down the kickstand and jumped off, helmet still half-fastened beneath his chin. "Are you *out of your mind?*"

"I had to—" she gasped, then stopped, tears catching in her throat. "I had to find you."

He stepped forward, eyes blazing with confusion and concern. "You almost got yourself *killed.*"

"Yeah, well," she said, breathless, "it was a calculated risk."

His hands were on her arms now, checking if she was shaking from the near miss or from something deeper. Her skin buzzed under his touch—every nerve in her body had snapped awake.

"You ran into traffic, Casey," he said, voice low but edged. "What the hell is going on?"

"You," she said. "You happened. You brought me home that night. I *know* it was you."

Phillip blinked. "Pati told you."

Casey nodded. "I can't believe I didn't trust you. I can't believe I let him lie to me."

"I didn't want to make it worse," he murmured. "I didn't want to be another reason you hurt."

Her breath hitched. "But you weren't. You aren't."

They stood there, staring at each other in the golden wash of a streetlamp. A breeze fluttered the hem of her sundress, and the night around them stilled for just a moment.

Then she closed the gap.

Casey grabbed the collar of his T-shirt and yanked him down into her. Their lips crashed like waves against a seawall—messy, hungry, desperate. Phillip stumbled back a step from the force of it, catching himself on the handlebar as she nearly knocked him off his feet.

But he didn't let go.

His hands moved to her waist, gripping tight, grounding her as she kissed him like she was drowning and he was air. It was heat and salt and wind and something that had been waiting far too long to erupt.

When they finally broke apart, their foreheads touched, breath mingling in the space between them.

"I've wanted to do that since the day you showed up in front of the shop" Phillip said, voice ragged.

Casey laughed, breathless.

"You were the most beautiful girl I'd ever seen."

She let her eyes close, heart beating in time with his. "Take me somewhere quiet."

He nodded, gently brushing a curl from her cheek. "Hop on."

Without hesitation, she climbed onto the back of the bike. Her arms slipped around his middle, her cheek pressed against his spine. The engine growled back to life beneath them.

And then they were gone—slicing through the humid Key West night, two souls speeding away from the noise, toward something real.

CHAPTER 22
BENEATH THE SURFACE

Casey woke to the scent of salt air drifting through the open window, with warm sunlight creeping across the sheets. For a few long seconds, she stayed still, caught in that hazy space between sleep and wakefulness, where everything felt distant and weightless.

Then, she registered the slow, steady breathing beside her. The quiet warmth of another body.

Phillip.

Her eyes opened fully now, adjusting to the soft gold light of morning. The room around her was unfamiliar but comforting in its simplicity. A low bookshelf lined one wall, its contents a mix of art books, worn paperbacks, and sketchpads stacked with the absentminded precision of someone who used them often. A small desk sat beneath the window, cluttered with pencils, an old ashtray, and a half-finished watercolor of mangroves in moonlight.

Casey turned her head slightly. Phillip was lying on his stomach, arm slung over the pillow between them, hair tousled, breath even. The sheet had slipped low across his back, and the sight of him like that—unguarded, completely at peace—tugged at something deep in her chest.

She traced the shape of his spine with her eyes, remembering the feel of his hands on her waist, the way he'd murmured her name against her collarbone like a secret.

She hadn't meant to fall asleep here. They hadn't meant for any of it. But once they arrived last night—after the storm of emotions and actual traffic—they hadn't talked much. Phillip had made her tea. She hadn't touched it. She had touched him.

Now, in the quiet hush of his bedroom, it felt like something had shifted. Or maybe not shifted—maybe just surfaced.

Casey rolled gently onto her side, careful not to wake him. Her legs were tangled with his under the sheets, one bare foot grazing his calf. The intimacy of it—the normalcy—almost startled her.

For the first time in what felt like weeks, her body didn't ache from stress or too much alcohol. Her mind wasn't spinning with questions. She felt… soft. Still. Like she could just be.

But of course, that stillness didn't last.

Voices—internal, intrusive—began to stir. What now? What did this mean? Was this the start of something or just a perfect moment carved out of chaos?

She closed her eyes again, trying to press pause, but

it was no use. Her body might've relaxed, but her brain never learned how to sleep in.

Phillip stirred beside her. She felt it before she saw it—the shift of muscle, the subtle intake of breath as he returned from whatever place he'd wandered in his dreams.

His voice came low and rough with sleep. "You awake?"

"Yeah," she whispered.

He turned his head, blinking slowly as he met her gaze. "You okay?"

Casey hesitated. "Yeah. I think I am."

A soft smile tugged at the corner of his mouth. "Good."

They lay there like that for a long beat, eyes locked in the hush of early light. She reached out and brushed a curl of hair from his forehead. He caught her hand in his, kissed her palm, and let it go.

"I didn't mean for last night to happen like that," she said finally.

Phillip nodded, not pulling away. "Neither did I."

"But I'm not sorry."

He let out a breath that was almost a laugh. "Me either."

Somewhere outside, a boat engine revved in the marina, gulls calling across the water. The world was waking up, slowly. So were they.

Casey tucked closer, her head on his shoulder now. "So this is where you live," she said quietly.

Phillip nodded. "Pretty much. Quieter. Fewer tourists."

"I can see why," she murmured, fingers tracing lazy patterns on his chest.

He looked at her, and this time the softness in his eyes had weight. "You don't have to go back right away."

She kissed his shoulder, just once, and whispered, "Then I won't."

Phillip's hand grazed her face. "Come diving with me."

She blinked. "What?"

"I called my buddy yesterday when I was upset. So, I've got a boat for the day." He tilted his head slightly. "Unless you've got better plans?"

Casey scoffed. "I just woke up. I haven't had time to make worse plans."

"Good. Then it's settled."

She shook her head, still waking up, still trying to process the shift between last night and this morning. "Since when do you just have a boat ready to go?"

Phillip shrugged, pulling his shirt over his head. "Since always. I know how to sail."

Casey sat up. "Bullshit."

He gave her an unimpressed look. "Why is that the thing you don't believe?"

"You don't look like someone who—"

Phillip cut her off with a sharp laugh. "What does a sailor look like, Casey?"

She considered, then waved a hand. "I don't know. Older. With a beard. Probably wearing some ridiculous captain's hat. Or like Jake."

Phillip just shook his head, amused. "I grew up in Nice. Sailing since I was a kid."

Casey blinked. "Wait. Nice?"

Phillip raised an eyebrow. "Since when is this news?"

She threw up her hands. "I don't know; I thought you grew up in Paris or something."

"You just never asked."

Casey opened her mouth, then closed it. She hated that he had a point.

She crossed her arms, narrowing her gaze at him. "You're telling me you've been casually sailing the Mediterranean since childhood, and you've just been sitting on that information?"

"Some things are better revealed in the right moment."

She scoffed, flirtatiously. "And this is the right moment?"

"You tell me." He leaned in and kissed her, first softly, then deeper, lingering like he wasn't in a rush to be anywhere else.

Casey melted into it, her arms loosening from her crossed chest and curling around his shoulders instead. She leaned into him until she was practically in his lap, the sheets twisted at her waist, the salt air curling around them like a slow dance.

When they finally broke apart, breathless and smiling, Casey gave him a look.

"I don't understand you."

Phillip tilted his head, eyes glinting. "And yet, you're still here."

"Because I'm trying to figure you out."

"You could just ask."

She hummed, unconvinced. "Yeah, but where's the fun in that?"

He kissed her on her forehead—quick this time, and just once—then stood and stretched. The sunlight caught his silhouette as he crossed the room to the small kitchenette tucked into the corner of the open floor plan. Casey watched him rummage around a mini-fridge, still trying to believe she was really here, really in his bed, really about to go sailing with him.

She flopped back onto the mattress and stared at the ceiling fan turning lazily above. "So what's the plan? You take me out on the open sea, charm me with your mysterious past, and then what? We wrestle an octopus for a treasure chest?"

"Close," Phillip said, returning with a pair of bananas and two bottles of water. "But I was thinking something more along the lines of a reef dive and maybe a beer on the dock afterward."

"You're very casual about offering me one of the best dates I've ever been invited on."

"Maybe that's because I want you to say yes without thinking too hard."

She propped herself up on one elbow. "I mean, we already kissed like the world was ending and slept together. Feels a little late to start playing hard to get."

He offered her a banana with a shrug. "Can't blame a guy for trying to impress you."

Casey took it and peeled it slowly. "You kind of already did."

Their eyes met again, the spark between them not fading with daylight. She chewed thoughtfully, then asked, "So, this dive—how deep are we going?"

"Not far. A reef shelf off Sand Key. Clear water, good visibility, lots of fish."

She raised an eyebrow. "And you have gear for both of us?"

He nodded. "My buddy's got gear that will fit you on the boat. He owes me."

"For what?"

Phillip smirked. "Taught his girlfriend how to draw an anatomically correct octopus for her marine biology class."

Casey liked that. Phillip was talented and kind.

She got up and started collecting her things from where they'd landed last night—her sundress, her tangled hair tie from the corner of the nightstand. She moved slowly, her body sore in the best possible way, her heart still thudding in her chest with something she didn't want to name yet.

As she stood by the window, pulling her hair into a messy bun, she glanced out over the view—boats bobbing lazily in the marina, sun catching on water like scattered coins. She was distracted by the quaint view and didn't notice Phillip got completely dressed already.

"Ready to go?" he asked.

She turned to him, herself still disheveled.

"Well let me at least put the sundress back on."

"I don't know. I kind of like this look," Phillip winked.

She pulled on the dress, kind of wishing she could just leave it off and stay there with him all afternoon.

Phillip pulled smoothly into a spot near the marina, killed the engine, and kicked down the stand in one effortless motion.

Casey swung off the bike. "Sundresses were not made for motor bikes."

"You looked good anyway."

She rolled her eyes but didn't argue. The sun was already high, baking the lot with mid-morning heat and bouncing off the rows of white boats that bobbed gently in their slips. A few fishermen were cleaning their early hauls nearby, and the air smelled like salt, sunscreen, and the faint bite of diesel fuel.

"Which one's yours?" she asked, adjusting the strap of the bag on her shoulder.

Phillip pointed to a sleek thirty-footer near the end of the dock, blue trim along the hull and a shaded console gleaming under the sun. A man in board shorts and a long-sleeved fishing shirt was already aboard, waving them over.

"That's Terry," Phillip said as they walked. "Old friend. Dive instructor now."

Terry called from the boat, "Well, if it isn't the Frenchman."

Casey turned to see an older man in his fifties standing near a mid-sized sailboat, tying off a line at the stern. He was tanned and scruffy, with sun-bleached hair and the kind of face that had seen years of sun, salt, and adventure.

Phillip walked toward him. "Hi Terry."

The man shook his head. "Figured you'd be late." His sharp gaze flicked to Casey. "She dive?"

Phillip, without hesitation: "Not yet."

Casey interjected. "Not ever."

Terry snorted. "And you trust him to teach you?"

Casey crossed her arms. "I guess we'll find out."

"This should be fun." Phillip nodded to Terry.

"Well, you know your way around. Just close everything up for me when you get back," Terry said.

The dock faded behind them as Phillip steered the boat out into open water, the engine humming beneath their feet. The air smelled cleaner, fresher, untouched by the cocktail of sunscreen and fried food that lingered over Key West's tourist-packed streets.

Casey stood near the stern, arms crossed as she watched Phillip move effortlessly around the deck.

She still couldn't quite process the fact that he knew how to do this. That he wasn't just steering—he was reading the wind, adjusting the sail, working the lines like it was second nature. All this time she assumed Jake would naturally know how to sail and that Phillip was, well, what Jake said he was, a brooding city boy.

"You're really not faking this, huh?" she called over the breeze.

Phillip shot her a humorous look as he tightened a cleat. "No, Casey. I am not faking the ability to operate a sailboat."

She huffed, leaning against the railing. "I don't know. You've already proven to be alarmingly competent at too many things."

He gave her a look. "Do you want me to be incompetent?"

"I'd like you to be average at something," she shot back.

Phillip let out a low chuckle. "Sorry to disappoint."

He moved back to the helm, guiding them smoothly through the shallows until the water beneath them shifted from bright turquoise to a deep, endless blue. They were out past the reef now, far from the boat traffic.

Phillip finally cut the engine, letting the sails catch the wind, and the boat eased into a steady, quiet glide before settling in the water.

He dropped the anchor and then reached for a dry bag near the helm. He pulled out a set of fins and a dive mask, tossing them onto the bench beside her.

Casey eyed them warily. "I'm really doing this, huh?"

Phillip sat on the edge of the bench, resting his forearms on his knees. "You're not going to die, if that's what you're worried about."

"Not helping."

He shrugged. "You can always stay on the boat."

That made her bristle. "And let you be all graceful and skilled by yourself? Absolutely not."

"That's the spirit. There's a wetsuit that belongs to Terry's girlfriend in the cabin; that will fit you. I'll grab that and her gear and come help you get suited up."

Phillip disappeared below deck, leaving Casey alone with the sound of the water licking gently against the hull. The boat swayed with the breeze, and Casey held the rail, gazing out over the horizon. It was blindingly blue in every direction—sky and sea indistinguishable in places, stitched together only by the occasional dart of a gull overhead.

She took a deep breath, letting the salt air fill her lungs. There was something about being out here, far from land, far from the drama, that made her feel small in the best possible way.

Phillip returned, a wetsuit draped over one shoulder and other gear in his hands. He tossed it next to her, then dropped the bag of gear beside the bench. "Terry's girlfriend is taller than you, so it'll probably be a little long in the legs, but it should fit."

Casey picked up the wetsuit and held it out in front of her like it might bite. "This looks...very form-fitting."

"Welcome to the sport."

She shot him a glare. "You enjoying this?"

Phillip smirked. "A little."

She began changing, struggling into the neoprene with more grunts than she'd admit, tugging the zipper up her back. Phillip was already in his wetsuit, securing tanks at the stern.

Casey stepped out, pulling her hair into a rough ponytail. "You're lucky I didn't die trying to get this thing on."

He didn't turn around, just said, "Would've been a real shame to have to tell Betty and Marley."

"Would've been your fault for making it sound like this would be easy."

He finally turned, and when he saw her, he paused for a beat longer than necessary. "You look good."

She arched a brow. "In this?" She motioned at the clinging black suit like it was a betrayal.

"Especially in that."

Casey watched Phillip prep the last of the dive gear with the same calm precision he used when sketching—every motion sure and deliberate, no wasted effort. He clipped her BCD vest to the tank and then turned to her with a crooked grin that made her stomach dip, and not from the waves.

"Alright, rookie," he said, lifting the gear. "Time to suit you up."

She raised an eyebrow. "Is this where you make some cheesy comment about strapping me in?"

"I was going to say something very professional," he replied, deadpan, stepping behind her. "But now I'm tempted."

Casey smirked as he helped her into the vest, his hands guiding the straps over her shoulders. His touch was gentle, firm in all the right ways, and it was suddenly very hard to think about anything except how close he was standing.

"You're going to feel a little snug," he murmured, reaching around her to fasten the front clasps. His breath brushed her ear. "But that's how you know it's safe."

She swallowed. "Good to know. I'll be sure to apply that logic to all my future life decisions."

He chuckled, his fingers brushing against her collarbone as he tightened the last strap. "Okay, that should be good. Give me a turn."

She pivoted, and he crouched to check the weight belt.

"Look at you," she said, hands on hips, teasing to cover the heat rising to her cheeks. "You're kind of hot when you're in dive instructor mode."

He glanced up from her waist, lips tilting into a slow smile. "Only when I'm in dive instructor mode?"

She stepped closer, brushing her fingers through the curls at his temple. "Let's call it an especially attractive subset of your skills."

He straightened, and for a moment they just stood there, inches apart, the boat rocking gently beneath them.

"I wasn't lying before," he said, voice quiet. "You really do look good."

"In a wetsuit?" she laughed.

"In my world, you'd look good in a potato sack."

Her smile faltered, just a little. "You're gonna make it hard to get in the water if you keep talking like that."

"Good thing I'm about to show you how," he said, stepping back just enough to break the moment, though the look in his eyes lingered like a touch.

He grabbed her fins and handed them over, then slipped his on with practiced ease. "Sit on the edge of the boat. You're going to do a back roll into the water."

Casey's eyes widened. "A *what*?"

Phillip grinned. "It's easier than it sounds. Trust me. Just sit with your back to the water, hold your mask and regulator in place with one hand, and cross your fins over the edge."

"This sounds suspiciously like you're trying to throw me overboard."

"I would *never*," he said, dramatically placing a hand over his heart. "I'm just giving you the full experience."

She sighed, sat down, and mimicked his instructions. "You're lucky I'm into you. Otherwise I'd be reconsidering every decision that led to this moment."

He crouched beside her, his mask already in place. "That's the good thing about being underwater. You can't talk yourself out of it once you're in."

"Phillip—" she started, nervous laughter catching in her throat.

But he kissed her before she could finish. Just a quick brush of lips, warm and sure.

"For luck," he said, then flipped backward into the sea.

Casey sat blinking for half a second, heart pounding— then held her mask, took a breath, and followed him in.

The world shifted the second Casey hit the water. For a moment, there was nothing but cold, the rush of bubbles, the weight of her gear pressing against her as she sank just beneath the surface. Then—buoyancy.

She bobbed back up, breaking through the waterline with a sharp inhale, her mask securely in place, regulator clenched between her teeth. The boat floated a few feet away, rocking gently. The sky stretched wide above her, cloudless and infinite.

And in front of her—Phillip, effortlessly hovering in the water with a clear sense of comfort and familiarity.

"Not bad," he said, his voice slightly muffled as he adjusted his own regulator.

Casey exhaled, blinking against the water dripping from her lashes.

"That was terrible."

"And yet, here you are."

She scowled, trying to get her bearings. The weight of the tank felt wrong, too heavy against her back, the vest stiff around her torso.

Phillip must have noticed her discomfort because he reached over, tapping her inflator hose.

"Here," he said, pressing the button for just a second. The vest filled slightly, adjusting her buoyancy, and suddenly, she wasn't fighting to stay upright—she was floating effortlessly.

She blinked at him. "That's… better."

"Magic, right?"

She rolled her eyes, but the tension in her shoulders eased.

"Alright," Phillip said, his voice steady and calm. "We're going to go slow. Just remember what I told you—breathe steady, don't fight the water, and equalize your ears as we descend."

Casey swallowed hard.

The surface felt safe. The deep blue stretching below them? Not so much.

He lifted his hand, palm up, fingers relaxed.

A silent offer.

Casey hesitated for only half a second before gripping his hand.

He gave a small squeeze before releasing her. Then, without hesitation, he tipped forward and began to descend. Casey inhaled slowly, forcing herself to follow.

Everything became quieter, the sounds of the surface fading away, replaced by the steady, rhythmic whoosh of her own breath through the regulator.

For a few seconds, panic threatened—the instinct to kick, to fight against the unnatural weightlessness, to rush back up where the air wasn't bottled in a tank strapped to her back.

But then—Phillip turned toward her, his eyes sharp through the mask, waiting.

Not pulling her. Not rushing her.

Just watching.

She exhaled, slow and deliberate.

And with that, the fear loosened its grip.

Her ears popped as she equalized, and suddenly—she wasn't sinking anymore.

She was floating.

Suspended in a world unlike anything she had ever known. The ocean stretched endlessly around them, an expanse of sapphire fading into deeper shades of blue. Phillip drifted closer, giving her a small nod.

You're okay.

And, to her surprise—she was.

Phillip gestured ahead to where the reef sloped downward, teeming with movement—an explosion of color and life that shifted with the slow rhythm of the current. Fish darted between coral structures, flashes of yellow and electric blue. A school of silvery barracuda glided just above them, moving as one. In the distance, a sea turtle drifted lazily, its flippers cutting through the water like wings.

Everything was slow. Weightless.

Casey followed Phillip, her breaths steady, watching as he moved through the water smooth, unhurried, completely at ease. Phillip turned back toward her, gesturing with one hand.

Casey nodded. And—just for a second—he smiled behind his regulator, a quick flash before he turned and motioned for her to follow. They drifted lower, where the reef sloped gently into the remnants of an old shipwreck, its skeletal frame covered in coral and swaying sea fans.

Casey's heart kicked up.

She pointed at it, eyes wide.

Phillip nodded and gestured for her to follow.

He led her closer, guiding them toward the open hull where fish darted in and out of the rusted remains. The ship had been here for years—decades, maybe—claimed by the ocean, and transformed into something new.

Casey hovered at the entrance, watching the way the light filtered through broken beams, scattering in long, golden streaks. For some reason, it made her ache. Phillip reached out, brushing his fingers against hers, a quick, grounding touch. She exhaled, shaking herself free from how profound the sight was and followed him inside. It was different inside—cooler and quieter, the water darker where the sunlight couldn't quite reach. Phillip moved ahead, his fingers grazing along the barnacle-covered walls, careful not to disturb anything.

Casey trailed after him, her eyes tracing the shadows of what once was—a rusted anchor chain snaking along the floor, a broken wheel half-buried in sand. She reached out, barely touching the curve of a metal railing, now softened by time.

What had this ship been before? Before it sank, before it was forgotten? Before the ocean decided to make it something else?

She let her fingers drift away, exhaling a slow breath through the regulator. Phillip turned toward her then, head tilting slightly, like he wanted to ask her something.

Since they couldn't speak, he just watched her, his expression unreadable behind his mask. Then he reached out slowly and deliberately. And together, they let the current carry them forward.

CHAPTER 23
LAST MAN STANDING

By the time Casey and Phillip made it back to land, her legs still felt weightless from the dive, the lingering sensation of the ocean wrapping around her like a second skin. She hadn't expected to love it. She hadn't expected to feel calm beneath the surface, like she belonged there as much as Phillip did. And she definitely hadn't expected to be this hungry.

So now, they were at a waterfront seafood shack tucked along the edge of the quiet marina back on the main island. Phillip wanted Casey to try the Hogfish Bar and Grill on Stock Island, but they said they'd come another day—Casey would need to get back home to check on Marley. She knew Betty would take care of him, but she felt guilty for leaving him for so long. She sent Betty a quick text, and Betty encouraged her to stay out as long as she'd like, so Phillip convinced Casey to have lunch near the marina on Key West. They sat at a shaded patio table, the afternoon sun warm but not unbearable, a slow breeze rolling in from the water.

Casey leaned back in her chair and stretched out her legs still drying off from the dive. "So how many people have you convinced to try diving just so you could look cool?"

Phillip took a comically long time considering. "Hard to say. The list is long."

"Oh, of course it is."

"But," he continued, "you're my favorite so far."

Her stomach fluttered.

The server arrived, a woman with sunglasses propped on her head and a pen tucked behind her ear. She dropped off two glasses of water.

"What can I get you two?"

Phillip barely glanced at the menu. "Shrimp tacos, extra lime. And a beer."

Casey hesitated before closing her own menu. "Fish sandwich. And fries."

"And a beer?"

Casey nodded. "Definitely a beer."

The server jotted down the order and disappeared back inside, leaving them alone with the lull of waves slapping gently against the dock and the occasional cry of a gull overhead. Phillip took a sip from his water, eyes skimming the horizon. "You really surprised me today."

Casey cocked her head. "Because I didn't drown?"

"Because you didn't panic," he said. "Not when

we tipped backward into the water, not when the reef dropped off beneath us. You were just... there. Present."

Casey looked down at her napkin, folding and unfolding the edge of it. "I'm glad it looked like I didn't panic. I did at first. But then it was nice. Everything was quiet down there, you know? No texts, no drama, no voices in my head telling me I'm fucking everything up."

Phillip watched her, silent for a beat. "You're not fucking everything up."

She didn't answer right away. Instead, she picked up her glass of water, took a slow sip, then set it down carefully. "You don't know that."

"I know more than you think," he said softly.

Casey looked up, brow furrowed. "Like what?"

Phillip ran a hand through his damp hair, pausing as if debating whether to say it. "Like where the spare key is hidden to Betty's bungalow that you're living in."

Her eyes narrowed. "What?"

He leaned forward, resting his forearms on the table. "That night. During the storm. I didn't break in to get you home, Casey. I let myself in. I knew where the key was because I lived there once."

Casey stared, dumbfounded. "Wait—you lived in my bungalow?"

"Years ago," he nodded. "When I first moved to Key West. Before I had anything figured out, before Southernmost Tattoo, before... well, everything."

She blinked. "I never knew that."

"You never asked," he said gently, echoing her words from earlier that morning.

She rolled her eyes at herself, then shook her head. "Okay, fine. Fair. But still—why didn't you say anything before?"

Phillip tilted his head, considering. "Maybe I liked seeing how you made the place yours. It was never really mine, not like it is for you now. I think Betty knew it too. That's why she offered it to you. She saw something in you she thought needed it."

Casey folded her arms. "So... you just followed me that night, found me passed out, let yourself in and then tucked me in like a stormy-night babysitter?"

"You were soaking wet. Your ankle was bruised. You were barely coherent. So yeah," he said, lips twitching, "I put you to bed and made sure you were safe."

She looked at him, really looked, and the full weight of everything that had passed between them settled like a tide receding. "Why didn't you tell me it was you sooner?"

Phillip's expression sobered. "I texted and asked how you were, but you never answered."

Casey winced. "That's... not untrue."

Their server reappeared with their beers and food, setting glasses and plates down in front of them and breaking the moment. They both murmured their thanks and fell into a quiet rhythm of adding condiments and squeezing lime.

It wasn't until Casey had taken a bite of her fish sandwich and chased it with a gulp of beer that she leaned forward again.

"So... what else don't I know about you?" she asked, half-teasing, half-earnest.

Phillip smiled, a slow grin that made the corners of his eyes crinkle. "I guess you'll have to stick around to find out."

Casey nodded, her voice soft. "Yeah. I think I just might."

Their eyes locked and Phillip raised his beer.

"We were so hungry we forgot to cheers." He raised his beer. "To learning to dive beneath the surface."

Casey raised her beer and clinked it to his. It was a small, intimate moment, and Casey was starting to realize it had been him all along. Everything she was looking for in Jake, it was actually in Phillip.

Her thoughts were interrupted by a loud, unsteady voice cutting through the quiet of the marina.

"Oh, you have GOT to be kidding me."

Casey's entire body tensed, recognizing the voice. Up the road, stumbling out of a bar, was Jake.

And he was drunk.

The stumble in Jake's step, the too-loud voice, the way his eyes locked onto her and Phillip like a heat-seeking missile—it was all bad.

Casey exhaled slowly, pressing her fingertips against the cool condensation of her beer. Phillip, across from her, didn't react right away. He just took a slow sip of his beer, completely unfazed.

"I think he had a bit too much tequila," Casey sighed.

"Or not quite enough." Phillip said, voice dry as ever.

Up the road, Jake wobbled forward, squinting against the bright afternoon sun like it personally offended him. His shirt was unbuttoned, his hair messier than usual. Even from a distance, Casey could see that this wasn't just Jake being his usual cocky self—this was him spiraling.

And now he had an audience.

A few tables glanced over, conversations dipping into hushed curiosity as Jake stalked closer. Phillip set his beer down, finally looking at him.

Casey rubbed her temples.

"Just once," she muttered, "I'd like to eat a meal without unnecessary drama."

"You sure you came to the right island for that?"

Before she could answer, Jake reached their table, gripping the back of an empty chair like he needed it to stay upright.

"So this is it, huh?" he slurred, waving his tequila bottle between them. "You just—what? Move right on? Not even a hesitation?"

Casey sat back in her chair, expression neutral. "Jake, you're drunk."

Jake laughed sharply, his head tilting back. "No shit, sweetheart."

Phillip exhaled through his nose, maintaining his composure. "Jake, go home."

Jake's eyes snapped to him with an ugly glare.

"Oh, you'd love that, wouldn't you?" He took a step

closer, his knuckles turning white against the chair back. "Just sit there all smug and let her come to you? That's your whole thing, huh?"

Phillip didn't react.

Which only made Jake angrier.

"You don't even have to try, do you?" Jake's voice rose. "Just sit there, acting like nothing touches you, like you're above it all."

Phillip's expression didn't change. "You done?"

Jake let out a humorless laugh, shaking his head.

Then—before Casey could stop him— Jake grabbed the edge of the table and pulled.

Casey's drink spilled, french fries jumped from their basket.

The patio went dead silent.

Phillip finally moved—just a shift, just a glance down at the mess, then back up at Jake.

"Feel better?" he asked, tone flat.

Jake's chest heaved, his face twisting into something Casey had never seen from him before.

For a second, Casey thought he might actually swing at Phillip—again. But Phillip just sat there, completely un-affected, and that—more than anything else—seemed to rattle Jake the most. Jake's fists clenched and unclenched. Then, his shoulders sagged, something flickering in his eyes—something like realization. He stepped back. And let out a quiet, bitter laugh.

"Yeah," he muttered. "That's about right."

Then, without another word, he turned and stumbled away, disappearing back up the road. He left nothing behind but the scent of tequila and the weight of everything unsaid.

Casey sat in the thick silence, watching the last of Jake's shaky retreat.

Phillip leaned back in his chair, calm as ever, and reached for his beer.

"So," he said casually, "am I supposed to pretend that didn't just make you want me more?"

Casey turned to him, incredulous.

"Oh my God," she muttered. "I hate you."

"No," he said, lifting his beer. "You don't."

And despite everything, Casey laughed. She let out a slow breath and reached for a napkin, absently wiping up the spilled food and drink while Phillip took another sip of his beer, completely unbothered.

A server hurried over, her eyes flicking between them and the wet tabletop.

"You guys okay?" she asked, cautiously.

"We're fine," Casey muttered, pressing the napkin down over the ice.

Phillip just nodded toward the mess. "Could we grab another beer? And maybe a towel?"

The server hesitated, like she wanted to ask what the hell just happened, but ultimately just nodded and hurried off.

Casey let out another slow breath, shaking her head. "Well. That was spectacular."

Phillip tilted his head, watching her. "You good?"

She met his gaze, chewing the inside of her cheek. "I don't know," she admitted. "That felt… different."

Phillip set his beer down, stretching one arm over the back of his chair. "How so?"

Casey sighed, tossing the soaked napkin onto her plate. "He's always been a little reckless, a little impulsive, but this?" She gestured vaguely toward the direction Jake had stumbled off in. "This was worse."

Phillip nodded slowly, watching her. "And how much of that do you think is about you?"

Casey frowned, the question hitting harder than she expected.

She didn't answer right away, and Phillip didn't push.

A moment later, the server returned with a towel and another beer, her gaze flicking toward the road like she half-expected Jake to come back.

"On the house," she said, setting the glass down.

Casey forced a smile. "Thanks."

As the server walked off, Casey took a sip, the cool hoppy taste doing very little to settle the unease twisting in her gut.

Phillip watched her, his fingers idly tapping against his beer bottle. "You know this isn't your fault, right?"

Casey let out a slow breath, her fingers tracing the condensation on her glass. "Yeah," she said finally. "I know."

But she wasn't sure if she believed it.

"Really, Casey," Phillip continued. "He lied to you. About something really big.

She sighed, pressing her fingers against her temple. "I don't know what to do with this."

Phillip studied her, his gaze sharp but not unkind. "Well," he said, "you could keep sitting here thinking about him."

Casey's eyes snapped to his, her glare instantaneous.

"Or," Phillip continued, as he leaned back again, "you could let it go and enjoy lunch with a charming and incredibly good-looking man instead."

Casey let her face give in to a smile.

Phillip shrugged. "I'm just saying. Your call."

She exhaled, then—despite herself—picked up a fry and threw it at him. He caught it and ate it in one motion.

They sat in comfortable silence for a moment, the sounds of the marina filling in the gaps—waves lapping against the docks, the occasional burst of laughter from another table, the distant hum of a boat engine starting up.

It should have felt awkward after what had just happened. But it didn't.

And maybe that was the part that threw her the most. She wasn't used to silence being easy with someone. Finally, she sighed, stretching her arms over her head before dropping them into her lap.

"Well, at least the food was good."

Phillip nodded, finishing off the last of his shrimp tacos. "And the entertainment was free."

Casey shot him a look. "You're impossible."

Phillip's eyes glinted with amusement.

She opened her mouth for a comeback—something sharp, something to wipe that look off his face—but she didn't have one. Because he was right. So instead, she just exhaled, shaking her head with a reluctant smile. Phillip chuckled, leaning back, entirely too pleased with himself. And just like that, Jake was forgotten—if only for the moment.

After lunch, Casey and Phillip walked back toward his motorcycle. Casey tugged her sunglasses down over her eyes and adjusted the strap of her bag over her shoulder.

"Back to the bungalow?" Phillip questioned.

Casey nodded, and they were off.

CHAPTER 24
LOVE AND OTHER ISLAND GHOST STORIES

Casey leaned her cheek against Phillip's back, her arms loose around his waist, the wind tangling her hair. Her skin was sun-warmed, her limbs still buzzing from the dive, and her mind strangely quiet.

When they turned off the main road and pulled onto the crushed-shell drive, her breath caught in her throat. The little bungalow—her bungalow now, somehow—stood tucked behind Betty's house like a secret. The porch was bathed in late afternoon light, and there, on Betty's front steps, sat Betty herself, one leg slung over the other, a sweating glass in her hand. Marley flopped across the porch beside her, tail thumping lazily at the sound of the bike.

"Well," Betty said, raising her glass. "Look who decided to come home."

Casey laughed and swung off the bike, immediately crouching to greet Marley, who bounded down the steps with a bark that was equal parts joyful and scolding.

"I know, I know," she murmured into his fur. "I'm the worst. I owe you, buddy."

Phillip parked the bike. Betty's eyes sparkled as she took them both in.

"You kids have a nice day?" she asked, her tone innocent but her smirk betraying her.

"Quiet," Phillip said, deadpan.

"Deep," Casey added, and Betty let out a laugh that startled a pigeon from the porch railing.

"Come on up," Betty said. "I'll pour two more glasses."

They joined her on the porch, settling into mismatched chairs that had clearly weathered years of Florida sun and salt air. The drinks were some kind of fresh fruit juice—bright pink, icy, and deceptively smooth.

Marley stretched out at Casey's feet, and Phillip leaned back in his chair, gaze drifting toward the horizon.

"I saw your text earlier," Betty said, sipping her drink. "Told you not to worry about him. He's been a perfect angel. Except for the part where he stole my sandwich."

Casey winced. "He does that."

"I do too," Betty replied with a wink. "He's in good company."

The porch fell into an easy rhythm—the occasional creak of the rocking chair, the soft rustle of palm fronds, the distant hum of a neighbor's lawn mower somewhere down the block.

Casey stared out at the backyard, eyes tracking the shadows stretching long across the grass.

"I didn't know Phillip lived in my bungalow before me," she said softly.

Betty didn't look surprised. "He needed it, once."

Casey turned to her. "So did I."

Betty nodded. "That place has always had a way of catching people right before they fall."

Phillip glanced sideways at Casey, a small smile tugging at the corner of his mouth.

"I didn't expect it to feel like home," Casey said. "Not really. I thought I was just hiding out until I figured out what came next."

"And now?" Betty asked.

Casey looked down at Marley, at the glass sweating in her hand, at the porch that smelled faintly of salt and lemon oil and distant music.

"Now I'm not in such a hurry."

Betty raised her glass. "That's the trick, sweetheart. Let the ghosts keep walking. You just have to sit still long enough for the rest to find you."

Casey met her gaze and clinked her glass gently to Betty's.

"Then I think I'm staying."

From beside her, Phillip reached out, his fingers brushing hers where they rested on the arm of the chair. She didn't move. Neither did he. And on the little porch behind the little house on the quiet island, the world kept turning—slowly, sweetly, just as it should.

Casey wasn't sure how Betty always knew things first—just that she did. A few days had passed since her dive date with Phillip, and things were, well, easy. Phillip had been staying the night because it was much closer to work and, frankly, the new couple couldn't keep their hands off each other.

One morning after Phllip had left for work, Betty joined Casey on the bungalow's porch.

"You heard about Jake?"

Casey sighed, leaning back into the wicker seat. "What about him?"

Betty nodded, stepping closer. "He's leaving."

Casey frowned. "For where?"

"Cruise ship gig." Betty gave a small, wry smile. "Guess he figured if he was gonna run, he might as well get paid for it."

Casey huffed a quiet laugh, shaking her head. "That tracks."

A gig on a cruise line. A floating, nowhere kind of life. Not tied down. Not stuck. Always moving.

Betty watched her carefully. "You gonna say goodbye?"

Casey ran her thumb over the condensation on her water bottle, pausing a little too long before answering.

"No," she said finally. "I don't think I need to."

Betty nodded, like she'd already expected that answer. "Good."

Casey let out a slow breath, watching the sun sink lower on the horizon. "Some people aren't meant to be part of your life forever," she murmured.

Betty hummed. "Doesn't mean they weren't important in some way, though."

Casey swallowed, her throat tight in a way she hadn't expected. She wasn't sure if it was sadness or relief. Maybe both.

Betty nudged her arm, voice softer now. "You did the right thing, you know. Not fixing him."

Casey shook her head. "I don't think he wanted to be fixed."

Betty snorted. "Oh, honey. None of 'em do."

That made Casey laugh—really laugh—and suddenly, the weight pressing against her ribs didn't feel so heavy anymore. She straightened, rolling her shoulders back, shaking off whatever this was. Then, without thinking too much about it, she turned to Betty.

"You wanna get a drink?"

"Now you're talking."

Betty didn't hesitate. She simply turned on her heel and started walking, like the invitation had been her idea all along. Casey fell into step beside her, the two of them strolling along the docks, Marley trotting ahead sniffing at discarded fishing nets and wagging his tail at passing tourists.

The evening air was thick with salt, the heat of the day finally giving way to the cooler breeze rolling off the water. The island was coming alive again, just as it always did at sundown—the bars filling, the music starting, the promise of long, wild nights stretching ahead for those who wanted them.

Casey didn't. Not tonight. She just wanted a quiet drink and maybe a little wisdom from someone who had seen it all before.

Betty led them to a small, tucked-away bar just off the main drag—one Casey had never been to before. It was the kind of place that didn't advertise, didn't need to. No neon signs, no frozen drinks, no tourist traps—just a handful of locals, a long wooden bar worn smooth from years of use, and the sound of ice clinking in glasses.

They took seats at the bar, Marley curling up under Casey's stool. The bartender, an older man with wrinkled hands and a white beard that made him look more like an ex-pirate than anything else, nodded in greeting.

"The usual, Betty?"

Betty drummed her fingers against the wood. "Make it two."

Casey raised an eyebrow. "You don't even know what I drink."

"Yeah, but I know what you need."

A minute later, two glasses of dark rum, neat, were set in front of them.

Casey lifted hers, swirling the amber liquid, watching the way the dim light caught in the glass.

"So," Betty said, propping her chin in her hand. "You're officially over the whole Jake thing?"

Casey exhaled. "Yeah."

Betty didn't look surprised. Just pleased. "Good," she said simply, taking a slow sip of her drink.

Casey stared at her for a beat. "That's it? No lecture? No deep insight?"

Betty shrugged. "What else is there to say? You already figured it out."

Casey let out a dry laugh, shaking her head. "I don't feel like I figured out anything. It just seemed to work itself out."

Betty turned toward her, watching her carefully. "That's how the island works, honey. You're still here, aren't you?"

Casey hesitated. Because—yeah. She was. Somehow, through all of it, through Jake, through Phillip, through the push and pull of wanting to leave and wanting to stay—she was still here. And it didn't feel like she was just passing through anymore. Betty looked Casey over, like she could see the realization settling

"There it is," she said, tipping her glass in Casey's direction.

Casey smiled, picking up her own drink, tasting the warmth of the rum as it slid down her throat. She glanced around the room—at the old fishermen nursing beers, at the bartender who probably knew every secret this island had to offer, at Betty who had watched Casey stumble her way through this whole mess fand still somehow looked proud of her.

And she realized something else.

She wasn't alone here.

Not anymore.

Not really.

Betty clinked her glass against Casey's again. "To whatever comes next."

Casey exhaled as she lifted her drink. "To not over-thinking it."

And with that, she let the last of the weight go, down-ing her rum along with it.

"I should probably head back. I start back at Moon-Dog tomorrow and I don't want to be too exhausted for my first shift back. Thank you for the drink."

"Anytime," Betty said. "You know, you can take Duval most of the way back toward home if you want.

"Betty, I've lived here for over two months; I know how to get home," Casey chuckled.

"No doubt, honey, but you spent a month of that on a sailboat to Antigua," Betty winked. "Anways, I was tell-ing you because I happened to see a certain tattoo artist working when I passed Southernmost on my way down to the water."

Casey's face flushed.

"I'm just saying; I can bring Marley home if you want to…stop in and say hello," Betty winked. Without waiting for a response, Betty took Marley's leash out of Casey's hands. "Go on, girl."

Casey exhaled, running a hand through her hair, feel-ing the warmth of the rum sitting low in her stomach. She smiled at Betty and left the bar.

Her gaze flicked up toward Duval Street, where neon

signs flickered to life and couples spilled onto sidewalks while laughter and music spilled into the night air.

And just up the road—Southernmost Tattoo.

Phillip.

Still working.

She could pretend she wasn't thinking about him. But that would be a lie.

So, instead of overthinking it, Casey turned and walked toward the shop.

The hum of the street outside faded as the door swung shut behind her. She glanced around. Empty. Phillip was alone.

"We're closed," he said in a loud but measured voice, without ever looking up from his notebook. The tone was flat, automatic, the kind of thing he'd said a thousand times to wandering tourists looking for a last-minute tattoo.

"Oh, I guess I'll just go home then," Casey said.

Phillip's hand stilled. Slowly, he looked up. His gaze flicked over her—barefoot, still sun-warmed from the day, her hair slightly windblown from the walk. The smile was almost immediate.

"Well, now," he murmured, setting his pencil down. "That's different."

Casey stepped forward, taking her time, trailing her fingers along the cool glass of the counter.

"Betty said you were working late," she said.

Phillip exhaled through his nose, shaking his head. "Of course she did."

She stopped a few feet away, watching him. He wasn't in his usual work mode—no gloves, no tattoo machine humming, just a sketchpad filled with ideas that hadn't yet become permanent.

"You drawing something for a client?" she asked.

Phillip leaned back in his chair, stretching his arms above his head before letting them drop lazily into his lap.

"No."

Casey raised an eyebrow. "Then what?"

Phillip tilted his head, watching her like she was missing something obvious.

Instead of answering, he stepped back slightly and turned the sketchpad toward her. Casey's breath caught in her throat. She had expected some generic design, maybe something abstract.

It was the same concept as before—the waves, the horizon, the open sky—but now, it had evolved. The waves were more detailed, the crests breaking with a natural flow, each curve giving the illusion of constant motion, a rhythm that never stopped. The horizon line wasn't just a line anymore. It had depth now, subtle shading that gave it weight—like it wasn't just the end of something, but the start of something else. It was designed in a circular frame, as if it were a window to a brand new world—the world Casey stepped into just more than a month ago.

She exhaled, shaking her head with a small, breathy laugh. "You really don't do anything halfway, do you?"

Phillip's lips curled at the corner. "Not my style."

The air between them shifted—heavy, charged. Phillip set the sketchpad down, stepping forward, slow and deliberate.

"So?" he murmured, eyes never leaving hers. "You gonna let me tattoo it?"

Casey's breath hitched as he closed the space between them.

One of his hands found her hip, fingertips barely pressing into the fabric of her shirt. The other lifted, brushing a stray strand of hair from her face.

Casey tilted her chin up, pulse hammering. "Maybe."

Phillip looked deeply into her eyes, his thumb ghosting over the curve of her jaw. "Not tonight?"

Her fingers curled into his shirt, pulling just slightly. "Not tonight."

His lips hovered just above hers, waiting.

And then, finally, she closed the space between them.

EPILOGUE

Casey walked through the heartbeat of the island, her sandals dangling from one hand, the warm pavement beneath her bare feet. The air smelled thick with salt and rum, the distant notes of a steel drum band weaving through the humid night. Duval Street was alive, pulsing with the familiar rhythm of Key West—a place where time didn't quite exist the way it did everywhere else.

She moved through it all, through the waves of people and music, past the open doors of bars humming with conversation, past glimpses of stories unfolding all around her.

She saw them everywhere. New flirtations—couples pressed against bar counters, whispering between drinks, hands already too familiar for strangers. Longtime lovers—walking hand in hand, their steps easy, their silences comfortable. The messy, complicated, half-in-half-out couples—stumbling out of bars, tangled in passion and disaster alike, fighting or making up, sometimes both at once.

Love and lust was everywhere here.

Wild. Fleeting. Permanent. Intoxicating.

Some of it lasted. Some of it didn't. But it all belonged to the island.

And her?

Maybe she was in it.

Maybe she wasn't.

But it didn't matter.

She turned onto a quieter street, the sounds of Duval fading behind her, the scent of night-blooming jasmine catching on the breeze. She breathed it all in—the life, the movement, the electric energy of this place she had once thought was a temporary escape before finding a long-term plan.

She smiled to herself, feeling the night settle around her.

Then she kept walking—toward whatever came next.

ACKNOWLEDGEMENTS

Writing a book may be a solitary endeavor, but bringing it into the world is anything but. I'm endlessly grateful to the people who supported me throughout the journey of *Fins and Flames*.

To my partner, Bryan—thank you for being my anchor. Your unwavering support, thoughtful reads, and willingness to listen to me talk through every plot twist made this book possible. I'm lucky to be in your corner.

To my mom, who instilled in me a love for Jimmy Buffett from an early age—thank you for filling my childhood with music, sunshine, and a belief in the magic of laid-back living. This book, born of that spirit, owes so much to you.

To the people and places of Key West—you are the soul of this story. Every quirky character, tropical breeze, and salty sunset I've experienced on the island finds its way into these pages. Thank you for the inspiration, the laughter, and the stories I carry with me.

To Jimmy Buffett—thank you for writing "Fins," the song that sparked this novel. Your music has always been a lighthouse guiding dreamers to their next adventure. This book is a tribute to your storytelling, your heart, and your ability to remind us all that it's five o'clock somewhere.

And to my editor, Jena Groshek—your insight, guidance, and keen editorial eye made this story stronger in every way. Thank you for your patience, encouragement, and the care you took with every word. I truly couldn't have done this without you.

ABOUT THE AUTHOR

H.R. Gordon is a writer, publisher, and lifelong beach bum at heart. The founder of Gordon Publishing and the imprint Beach Bum Books, Hannah brings to life stories soaked in sunshine, sea breeze, and second chances. With a career spanning more than a decade in publishing—as a copywriter, editor, marketer, and acquisitions manager—she knows her way around a good story and how to bring it into the world.

When she's not writing novels set in salty, sun-drenched places, Hannah is likely listening to Jimmy Buffett with a tropical drink in hand, dreaming up her next island escape. Her deep love for Key West—its music, magic, and motley cast of characters—inspires every page she writes.

Hannah lives in Buffalo, New York, with her librarian partner and three dogs, but her heart is always somewhere south of the mainland. Whether she's working on the next Beach Bum Book manuscript or diving into one of her many creative projects, she's here to prove that paradise is more than a place—it's a state of mind.

ABOUT THE SERIES

The Beach Bum Books romance and mystery series are sister series' set in the same sun-drenched universe—where dive bars, boat docks, and buried secrets collide. Each book can be read on its own, but keep an eye out for familiar faces and favorite hangouts popping up across stories.

Fall in love with a Key West romance one day, then dive into a tropical whodunit the next. If you find yourself missing a character, don't worry—they might just wander into the next Beach Bum book, cocktail in hand. You never quite know who you'll run into on the island.

ABOUT THE PUBLISHER

BEACH BUM BOOKS is your ultimate destination for sun-soaked stories and tropical tales. We're all about the laid-back, beach bum lifestyle, bringing you captivating reads that whisk you away to sandy shores and sunny skies.

Whether you're lounging by the ocean, dreaming of your next seaside escape, or simply looking for a moment of paradise in your day, we've got you covered. Plus, a portion of proceeds from all Beach Bum Books sales supports Save the Manatee, Mr. Jimmy Buffett's nonprofit organization.

So, grab your favorite beach chair, sip a tropical drink, and get ready to escape with Beach Bum Books—where every page is a step closer to paradise.